# ADIRONDACK DETECTIVE

## John H. Briant

Chalet Publishing
P.O. Box 1154
Old Forge, New York

# Adirondack Detective

Library of Congress Catalog Card Number 99-96188


*Graphics and book Design*
*by*
*John D. Mahaffy*


ISBN 0-9648327-2-0


Published in The United States by
Chalet Publishing
PO Box 1154
Old Forge, New York 13420-1154

# DEDICATION

To my wife Margaret and in memory of my parents, John D. and Marjorie A. Briant.

June 14, 2008

To Paul,

Hope you enjoy
The Adirondack Story!
The Very Best To you
in all your pursuits
in life —

Best Wishes,
John H. Briant

III

# ACKNOWLEDGMENTS

I wish to extend thanks to John D. Mahaffy for "steering the canoe" and Rapid Rick Carman for "paddling it."

And of course my wife, Margaret for her untiring patience, understanding, insight and opinion and for keeping the oil lamp lit.

# FORWARD

I consider it a privilege to reside inside the Blue Line of the Adirondack Park, therefore I felt it necessary to write a story about ordinary people facing trials and tribulations along a common path known to us as, life's journey.

My career with the State police was spent out on the streets and roadways with the People of the State of New York. I learned many things in those twenty-eight years. The interaction and exchange of the bits and pieces was in itself a learning experience. There were smiles and tears and hours of dedication.

It is my honor to introduce to you, one, JASON BLACK, also known as ADIRONDACK DETECTIVE.

*Other books by the Author*
One Cop's Story: A Life Remembered 1995
Adirondack Detective 2000
Adirondack Detective Returns 2002
Adirondack Detective III 2004
Adirondack Detective Goes West 2005

# CHAPTER ONE

My name is Jason Black. I'm a private investigator, licensed by the State of New York. I'm forty-eight years old, twice divorced, no kids. I know many people from all walks of life. After I retired from the State Police, I settled in the Adirondack Park of northern New York State. There isn't a big demand for private-investigation work throughout the region, but I'm able to put gas in my Ford Bronco, and bread on the table. I chose the mountains for the fresh air and the beautiful landscape. Like any other person I have my favorite places. I invested in a small piece of property on the outskirts of Old Forge. Centered in the middle of the two-acre plot of land is my home, a modest one-and-one-half-story log cabin with two bedrooms, a kitchen, living-room, bath and den. It is situated in the woods, close to Bald Mountain, one of summer tourists' favorite places for climbing. The home is furnished with good used colonial furniture.

I chase bad checks for some of the businesses throughout the park. In addition, some of the lawyers hire me to do background-checks and gather information relative to divorce cases pending on the court calendar. During the heavy tourist season the check cases build up. Some of the difficult ones I turn over to the police. Interesting credit-card cases pop up. Many of these cases end up in the hands of the police, especially if they happen to be forgeries. Basically, my job as an investigator boils down to the gathering of information and the writing of reports. A lot of reports. In addition, I work on white-collar-crime cases and missing persons. Once in a while I even get

1

a call to get a cat out of a tree. The soles on my shoes are worn.

In the world of private-eye work any investigator worth his salt has contacts with people in the business all over the country and sometimes the world. One such person I hear from is an old service buddy, who spent twenty years with the Phoenix, Arizona, Police Department. He has his own business in Phoenix, called Flynn Investigations, located on 99th Avenue. Jack Flynn is also forty-eight years old and served with me in the U.S. Marine Corps. He has a buddy, Lieutenant Jay Silverstein, in charge of one hundred homicide detectives. Jack, the Lieutenant, and Jack's secretary, Ruby Olkowski, pooled their savings and purchased a run-down shopping center on 99th Avenue. They rent out store space to fourteen tenants. The fourteen businesses are varied. In the small plaza there is a shoe cobbler, a bakery, an insurance office, an art supply shop, a pizza shop, a car rental office and several others. Jack has told me that all the monies taken in for rent are placed in a business account as a part of their retirement package for the future. Jack begged me to join him in Phoenix several times. He tempted me with a straight salary of one thousand dollars a week, plus fifteen percent on every check I collected. I thought it over carefully. I decided that one-hundred-and-twenty-degree days in Phoenix were not for me. I told him over the phone, "Jack, you're more than generous, but you remember when we were in the South Pacific how the intense heat bothered me."

"Jason, we have an air-conditioned office and I have an air-conditioned car you can use."

"I appreciate the offer, Jack, but the Adirondacks is where I want to be."

"Ok, but can I count on you to work leads for me, if the occasion ever arises?"

"You mean in the Adirondacks?"

"Yeah, that's what I mean."

"Sure, I'll be glad to, Jack."

Sometimes I think about the carrot that Jack offered me, but with my love for the region, I could not accept his offer. You have heard the phrase, *location, location, location.* Well, this is where I want to be. You can't hear the call of the loon in downtown Phoenix where 2,700,000 people exist. And in Arizona just about everybody carries a gun in their car or has it strapped to their left or right hip. Road rage is common in Maricopa County, and the drivers ride about two inches off your rear bumper. No, the Adirondack Mountains in New York State seems to be much tamer.

Although my love for the Troopers is everlasting, I can't help forget the time, about two weeks after my retirement, five years ago, I had to call the barracks that I used to command, and after I told him who I was, the Trooper asked,

"How do you spell your name?"

"I must have the wrong number," I responded.

I hung the phone up, shaking my head in disbelief. You are soon forgotten. I remember an old partner I had in the Troopers. I can hear his voice now.

"Who cares?" he would say.

"Those are true words," I said to myself.

Old Forge is a hamlet, with a general population of fifteen hundred. The tourist season, hunting season, and snowmobile season increase the population, as it does most of the villages throughout the park. During the peak season many people pass through town heading to other locations. The roads are generally two-lane macadam, and many times there are long lines of traffic. The business people in the area work hard, and I find them friendly.

I think back to my young-childhood days when I spent time riding with my father in his log truck. Dad was called Jack by all his friends. He did pulping in the Barnes Corner area, which is west of Lowville, New York. He would take his pulpwood to Lyons Falls and add it to the huge mountains of pulpwood which would become paper and other products. Sometimes he would drive through Old Forge. I could barely see over the bottom edge of the truck's side window. We would stop at John's Diner in Old Forge for a donut. Dad would have coffee, while I sipped on a mug of hot chocolate.

One time I took Dad's keys out of the ignition and dropped them in the woods. I can still feel the sting on my hinder. Dad had a large hand. He was a man of few words. If he did speak, it was smart to listen to what he had to say. Of course, he's gone, and Mother, too. I miss them both, but we all know life has to go on. In those years families were very close.

I stop by the Old Forge Post Office every day, except Sunday, unless I drop a few letters in the outside mailbox. I rent a large box. Sometimes it is full of bad checks from various business places throughout the park. I always look forward to my magazines and other publications. I subscribe to the *New York Times,* and the *Wall Street Journal.* I can still hear the voice of my former BCI (Bureau of Criminal Investigation) Captain: "Read all the papers that you can." He spoke sharply.

"Yes sir," I would say.

The Captain, Frank Temple, was an avid reader and he wanted his people to be abreast of current events. We used to donate all those stacks of papers to the Boy Scouts for their paper drives. I'm certain that wherever Frank is today, he is reading some newspaper from somewhere. I believe it kept our minds active and alert. Oh well! That's history now.

I returned to my log home one rainy afternoon, after chatting with some of the locals at John's Diner. My loyal German shepherd, Ruben, who weighs about one hundred pounds, greeted me at the side door with a low growl.

"Settle down, Ruben," I said.

The flashing light on my answering machine was pulsating. I pressed the play bar. The voice said, "This is Tom Huston from Breakshire Lodge in Lake Placid. Could you give me a call, please?"

I continued to listen to my other calls. There were six, all related to bounced checks. They indicated that they were having the checks protested and would send them to my post office box. This was standard procedure. I would then attempt to contact the writer of the check and diplomatically inform them of the situation. Nine times out of ten they would say, "I'll take care of it."

In a few days I would check with the business places to see if the checks were paid. As a rule they were reimbursed and the matter was closed. Some of the checks that remained outstanding would be turned over to our efficient police department for possible criminal action.

I placed a call to the Breakshire Lodge and asked for Tom Huston.

"Hello, this is Tom Huston. Can I help you?"

"This is Jason Black. You called me."

"Oh yes, Mr. Black. I was wondering if you could drop by my office the next time you come to Lake Placid?"

" What is this in reference to, Mr. Huston?"

"I'd rather not discuss this on the phone, if you don't mind." He spoke in a low voice.

" No. I don't mind. I'll drop by tomorrow. I have a couple of matters that I have to take care of in that area. No problem, Mr. Huston. I will see you tomorrow."

"Thank you. I'll see you tomorrow, Mr. Black."

I wondered to myself what that was all about. I had visited the Breakshire Lodge and had stayed there a few times. I had never met Mr. Huston; however, I did know that he was the owner and had moved to Lake Placid several years ago from Long Island. The rumor was that Huston was from old money and in some circles was considered very wealthy. I pondered some more. *I wonder what he wants to see me for.*

Ruben nuzzled his big head against my knee as I entered the phone calls in my telephone log. I noted that I had made a great many phone calls. I always noted my calls to the telephone bills each month. Most of the time they would check out right to the call, but once in a while I had to call the phone company and have them look up their records.

"Come on, Ruben, let's go for a walk." I snapped his chain to his collar and he thanked me by running his wet tongue against my hand. Ruben was ready for the trail.

We left by the side door just off my combination den and office. Already, Ruben was pulling hard on the chain. I always wear gloves, as Ruben is powerful and pulls hard. I've had some good bruises on my hand in the past.

The squirrels and chipmunks are plentiful around my log home. They dart back and forth across the front porch. Ruben goes berserk and takes off after them, but they are faster and dart into a crevice in one of the many trees.

I was worn out when we returned from climbing Bald Mountain. Ruben was panting hard by the time we reached the door, and so was I. In the summer you meet many people on the trail. Most of them say hello and remark, "That's a great dog you have." Ruben seems to know when people are making over him. His ears go up and his tail starts to wag. He loves his dog food and drinks water, with much splashing out of his dish. I often think he would look better at seventy-five pounds instead of a hundred. It must be the mountain air that makes him hungry. Just like most late afternoons, I chopped wood for about an hour, while Ruben chewed on his hard rubber bone. Once in a while he'll leap up and chase a chipmunk into a brush pile. In the fall when the nights are cooler we sit on the porch looking up at the tree-tops. Oh, what solace I have here in the woods! I know Ruben would agree if he could talk. He loves to lie on the porch with his head between his front paws.

Between the climbing of Bald Mountain and chopping wood I was tired and went to bed about 10:30 p.m. I started to read and dozed off. I had set the alarm for 6:00 a.m., and when it sounded I must have been dreaming for I heard the clang of a bell off in the distance. I was startled to find the light on. The alarm clock wound down. Ruben was at my bedside wagging that strong tail of his; it rapped against the footboard. I could hear a crow cawing off in the distance. After a close shave and a hot shower I felt like a new person.

The Ford Bronco started on the first turn of the switch. I looked toward Ruben, who jumped up on his wire fence and let out two sharp barks. I rolled the window down and said, "Settle down, Ruben. I'll see you later."

Ruben had plenty of food and water. I had put up a wire fence runway for him and he had plenty of room to run and play with his hard rubber bone. I have several signs displayed, "WATCH OUT FOR THE DOG." I knew that everything would be secure with Ruben on duty. He had been a K-9 dog with the Troopers, and was retired. We had that in common. I knew if any uninvited guests came around and tried to enter the log home or his runway area, they would get quite a welcome.

There wasn't any traffic on Route 28 toward Blue Mountain Lake. As I stopped at the stop sign for Route 30 a large log truck was slowly moving northbound, headed for Tupper Lake. When the highway widened in front of the Blue Mountain Museum, I made my move and was able to pass the truck, which was loaded down with hardwood logs. The chains were snug, I saw as I glanced to the right. I tooted and the log truck driver gave me a blast on his air horn.

I stopped at the Long Lake Diner for a cup of coffee and one of Gertie's delicious sweet rolls chuck full of raisins. Gertie and her husband, Bob Walker, had run the diner for several years. They both worked hard. Two of their children had gone off to college, one at Potsdam and the other at Paul Smith. Gertie always wore a big smile, even if she had an off day. Everybody for miles around knew Gertie and loved her. Both she and her husband Bob would give the shirts off their backs to help a person. Bob, however, didn't like bad check passers and had stopped accepting checks from anyone. He had been stuck more than once. In this country you cannot make a profit if you have bad checks in the bottom of your cash drawer. Bob's new policy was cash or a good Mastercard. As I finished my coffee, Gertie approached the counter with a steaming full pot.

"Jason, would you like a refill?" Gertie asked with the coffee pot in her hand.

"Sure would," I replied.

"How have you been? Are you doing any fishing lately?"

"Gertie, everything has been good. No, I haven't had much of a chance to fish; you see, I've been trying to get my firewood all cut up for next winter. The checks are keeping me busy and I've got some marital cases I'm working on. I can't say too much about those things--sort of private, you know!"

"Yeah, I know." Her face flushed. "Do you see many of your ol' Trooper friends?"

"Gertie, you know, once you leave and go on to other things it's difficult to go back. Things change. The older guys retire and the younger ones, well, they are busy with their work, so you really don't have much time to meet the new men and women of the ranks."

"Yeah, you're right."

"I had a great career, and if I could do it all over again, I would. I enjoyed serving the People of New York State. There seems to be a lot of unrest in certain parts of our society. My heart aches for these kids that get involved in violent conduct. It has to be difficult to raise children nowadays."

"Yes, you're right," she threw her hands up in the air.

"Well, Gertie, I've got to be on my way. Say hello to Bob for me."

"I will, Jason. It was nice that you stopped in. Take care."

"Best to you both. I'll be seeing you."

I arrived at the Breakshire Lodge at about eleven-thirty a.m. and was greeted by Huston. He appeared to be in his early sixties, slender, with graying hair. A very distinguished-looking gentleman. He was wearing a blue blazer, white shirt and a plain blue tie and gray trousers. His black wing tips were shined.

"Good morning Mr. Black," he spoke softly. "Thank you for coming by."

"Good morning, Mr. Huston," speaking distinctly. "May I be of service to you?"

"Let's go to my office where we can talk in private, Mr. Black."

The office was located on the second floor. It was large and done completely in cherry. The desk was oak and there were several stuffed chairs in the room. The wall was covered with framed pictures, including one of a handsome young man in a U.S. Naval uniform.

"That is a picture of my son, Gerald." Mr. Huston commented proudly.

"Gerald recently received a promotion to Captain and he is assigned to the Pentagon."

"I bet you are very proud of him, sir."

"Yes, I am. His mother would have been, too, but she has recently passed away."

"I'm sorry to hear that, Mr. Huston."

"Yes, cancer is a terrible thing. She went quickly."

I noticed tears forming in his eyes. I could tell that Mr. Huston was suffering the loss of his wife.

"How can I help you?" I asked.

"Jason--you don't mind if I call you by your first name, do you?"

"No, not at all, Tom.

"Jason, I've made an observation concerning one of our guests. I do not want to call the police. Would you be able to check this fellow out, confidentially?"

"What observations have you made?"

"The name he goes by is Truman Hickman. Age, about forty. He arrived here about three weeks ago, driving a 1988 Lincoln Town Car, bearing Arizona registration T H – 2. He claims he is from the Sedona, Arizona, area. He seems to stay in his room most of the time. He is quiet. I have noticed that he buys a *New York Times* every morning. Our cleaning people inform me that when they go in to clean his room, he will leave until they have completed their housekeeping duties."

"What would you like me to do?"

"Jason, if you could check him out for me, I'd appreciate it. He doesn't cause anyone trouble, but he acts suspicious."

"I do have some contacts in Arizona. Possibly, I could have them inquire about him."

"That would be appreciated. He may be all right, but I don't understand why he stays in his room all the time. You'd think that a tourist would be out looking at the beauty we have here, or playing golf or tennis. He doesn't seem to fit the profile of an out-of-town tourist visiting the East."

"I see your point."

"As I said, I do not want to call the police at this time. Jason, what is your fee for something like this?"

"I usually get twenty-five dollars an hour, plus seventy-five dollars a day for expenses."

"That's reasonable. When can you start?"

"Right now."

I could tell that Tom Huston was a gentleman, and that he didn't want to cause anyone trouble. I left his office feeling good. Now, I had some work to do. I told Tom that I would contact him as soon as anything developed. Naturally, I was thinking of Private Investigator Jack Flynn in Phoenix, Arizona. Although Sedona is north of Phoenix, I was certain that Jack could help me out. Probably there was nothing to this. Maybe a distraught husband looking for a few weeks away from his wife or just a lonely person wanting to be left alone.

I left by the front door of Breakshire Lodge. It had been called the Jefferson Inn, but since Huston purchased it, the stately structure had a new name and a new paint job. It was an old New England type building and was nestled in among a hundred tall pine trees. The Lodge had a hundred rooms and the former owner had had a tree planted for each room. The dining room was done in cherry wood with no knots.

Graceful hanging wagon-wheel lamps adorned the ceilings, and white linen cloths covered the cherry wood tables.   It was elegant.  The prices were high.   All the waitresses wore colonial-style dresses which were always immaculate.

I went down the long descending stone steps and took a stroll through the garden.  I noted some bees buzzing around the white trellises covered with beautiful red roses.  I picked up my step a little as I didn't do bee stings very well.  I ducked into the large one-story parking garage, which had the appearance of the old style carriage buildings of the early 20$^{th}$ century.  The only cars in the garage were two cars that Huston owned, a Cadillac and a Ford Station Wagon.  At the far end of the building was the white Lincoln Town Car, bearing Arizona plates T H-2.  The car was dirty, but underneath the grime you could tell that it was heavily waxed.  On the rear back window was a sticker which displayed the words *Sedona Chamber of Commerce Member*.  I could see where some pigeons had been using the car for target practice.  The wheels in my inquisitive mind started to grind.

I said to myself, "What is this guy doing here from the southwest hiding out in a room of the Breakshire Lodge?  Well, Mr. Hickman, I'm going to find out who you are and what you are doing here in the Adirondacks."  The circumstances  certainly deserved a discreet inquiry.

I could understand the concern that Mr. Huston was fostering.  He was probably worried whether the fellow was despondent or just a strange person.  If the cleaning staff seemed concerned enough to notify their boss,  probably other customers were aware of it, too.

The Bronco was hot inside.  The engine started on the first turn of the ignition switch.  I looked at my Timex and noted that it was three o'clock p.m.  I was soon on Route Three heading toward Tupper Lake.  I went by the Red Fox Restaurant on the outskirts of Saranac Lake.  I couldn't help but think of the 1980 Olympics and the two weeks I had spent there with other Troopers.  It had been one of the highlights of my career.  Meeting the athletes from all over the world.  Observing the thousands of people who attended dressed in warm clothing with scarfs wrapped around their necks and faces, to combat the chilling cold of the winter season.  I was assigned to the skating rink for a couple of days, then to the big Blue Bird busses that transported the athletes to the different venues. I remembered that the bus service at the beginning of the Olympics had problems bringing the spectators to the area. It took one State Trooper to correct the situation and soon the busses were rolling into the area filled with excited fans.

I can recall one morning at the Olympics I boarded my assigned bus driven by an Irishman from Pittsburgh, Pennsylvania. Eddie O'Hara was about fifty-five years old with graying hair. He was a jolly soul. Well, on the bus were two huge KGB agents from Russia, who gave me a grunt when I said good morning to them. They were wearing heavy fur coats and large fur hats. The KGB's were being housed at an old farmhouse outside of Lake Placid. When Eddie stopped the bus to let them off, they grunted again when Eddie said, " So long, fellas."

After Eddie closed the door he looked at me and said, "Jason, those two KGB fellas were talking better English than both of us can, just before you got on the bus."

"Is that right, Eddie?"

"Yep," Eddie replied.

The big night of the hockey game when the U.S.A. beat the Russians, we were watching a large screen in one of the dormitory rooms. There were about a hundred of us, all off-duty. When the winning puck entered the goal area and the win was achieved, everyone jumped up and down with excitement. I can remember the floor shaking. Nobody could sleep that night.

It was five-fifteen p.m. when I pulled the Bronco into my narrow driveway. I had just exited the vehicle when I heard Ruben's loud bark. His tail was going like a propeller on a Piper Cub airplane. I checked his water. His food dish was still half full.

"Good, Ruben. Did you miss me, boy?"

Ruben pushed against my pant leg, licking my shoes.

I turned on the news. After watching it on television for ten minutes I turned off the switch.

Ruben was again at my pant leg. I could tell he'd missed his master. I warmed up some goulash and made myself a leafy lettuce salad. Whipped up some of my own dressing with salad dressing and ketchup. Cut two slices of Italian bread and sat down for a light supper. I was tired and didn't feel like going to any diner tonight.

I was rowing a canoe down the Moose River, approaching some rapids, when I found myself wide awake. Ruben was growling and I heard a scratching noise on the porch. The tinkle of the chimes sounded. Ruben was getting restless; his growl was deep and threatening. I fumbled for my yard light switch and turned it on. I have four floodlights affixed to a twenty-five-foot pole, which is located in front of the porch. I quickly looked out through my venetian blinds, and what I saw was frightening. The two black bears had been startled by the four floods illuminating the yard. The large one must have weighed six hundred pounds on its hind legs it stood over six-foot in height. The smaller bear, about three hundred pounds, was at my bird feeder. Ruben barked loudly. I unbolted the front door.

"Get the hell out of here!" I hollered.

The bears hesitated for a few seconds, then slowly walked into the woods. "No more birdseed for you fellas," I said to myself. Ruben went back to his favorite corner and lay down on his flat bed pad. He looked up at me and placed his nose between his two front paws. I climbed back into my bed, hit the pillow with my hand, and went back to dream land. I thought about the canoe and the rapids, and dozed off.

# CHAPTER TWO

The sun's rays came through the blinds and Ruben was tugging on the bedspread. It was time for him to take his quick run into the forest. I climbed out of bed and unbolted the door, and Ruben almost pushed me aside as he raced for the woods. I filled the teakettle with water and turned on the gas stove. I needed a cup of decaf.

Soon, Ruben was back on the porch. I took a moment and led him to his fenced runway. He raced to his food dish.

I could hear the air horns blasting as Charlie Perkins passed by down on the highway. Charlie would blow those horns five days a week, whether I was home or not. He had a big rig. He loved his Peterbilt. What he didn't like was the monthly payment of fifteen hundred dollars. Charlie was self-employed. He sought out land-owners who had large wood lots. Charlie would approach the land-owners and propose a contract to cut and haul the saleable timber to the sawmills. Sometimes Charlie would be hauling large logs and other times he'd be hauling four-foot pulpwood to Lyon Falls. I liked Charlie. He was good people. He and his wife had six children. I had met him years ago at a roadblock the Troopers were holding near Boonville. His load of logs was about six inches over the legal height limit. He removed the top logs and continued on his way. Charlie came back later that afternoon and reloaded the eight logs involved. He never forgot that kind gesture shown him by the Troopers.

I waited till noon before I called Private Investigator Jack Flynn. The telephone rang four times before I heard the voice.

13

"Flynn Investigations. May I help you?"

It was Ruby Wolkowski, Jack's secretary, confidante and partner.

"Good morning, Ruby. How have you been? Jason Black, here."

"Jason, is this really you? We haven't heard from you in ages."

"Ruby, I've been fine, just busy. Is Jack in?"

"Yes, I'll buzz him for you. Gee! Jason, it is so good to hear from you."

Ruby hit the buzzer and Jack answered.

"Jason, we thought you had flown the coop. Haven't heard from you in ages."

"Jack, I think of you folks all the time. It's just that I've been busy working on check cases and trying to keep ahead of the bill collectors. I don't have the lucrative cases that you have."

"Jason, you know I offered you a great position with my firm and you declined. Do you remember, my buddy?"

"I know you did, Jack, but you know I can't stand those high temperatures and I love the Adirondacks."

"Yes, I'm very much aware of your love for the woods. You know, we have woods, too. The Flagstaff area has plenty of forests. You come out here and we'll split the state. You can work all the cases north of Phoenix and I'll take the southern region. There are a lot of divorce cases here, missing persons, white-collar crime, background checks for attorneys. You name it, we've got it."

"Jack, I appreciate your offer and concern. Now, I'm calling you for a favor. Could you check a person out for me?"

"Yes, what's the name?"

I told Jack what I had. I told him about the Lodge and the concern of its owner.

"His name is Truman Hickman. He apparently resides in Sedona. He has a 1988 Lincoln Town Car, color white, bearing Arizona Registration Plate T H-2. On the rear window is a Sedona Chamber of Commerce Member sticker. The car is filthy, but is highly waxed and apparently has had good care."

"Jason, I've got enough information. I'll be glad to check it out for you. When I get the facts, I'll call you.

"Thanks, Jack. Take care and say good-bye to Ruby for me."

"Will do, buddy. Take care."

I looked at my Timex, and noted that it was time for lunch. I checked to see if Ruben had enough water. He did.

John's Diner was packed. My favorite table was occupied. I always sat by the window to watch the people pass by. The Old Forge Hardware was across the street. The large store attracted many tourists. If you couldn't find it there, you couldn't find it anyplace. People were streaming into the store.

"Hey, Sherlock. What can I do for you today?"

It was Patty Olson, the waitress. She stood about five feet in height, with blonde curly hair, and I noted that it was pulled back behind her petite ears. She is thirty-six years old, divorced with no children.

"Patty! What did I tell you about calling me Sherlock?" I asked sternly. "I could be tailing a person; you could put me on the spot. Please call me Jason."

"I'm so sorry, Jason. I was just funning you a little." She smiled sheepishly.

"You're forgiven, sweetheart. Now for the important things, I would like a grilled cheese sandwich and a bowl of Lila's wonderful tomato soup. Give me some oyster crackers, a large glass of iced water and a cup of hot green tea." I spoke softly.

"We have your favorite rice pudding today. Want some?"

"You bet I do, after I finish my main course," I replied ardently.

"Okay!"

Patty has a wonderful personality. She was happily married for five years. Her husband started drinking more than he should have. One night when he came home intoxicated, Patty asked him where he had been. Kenneth Olson struck Patty. It was all over. The blow had been so powerful that it broke her nose. The next day Kenneth got on his knees and apologized, but Patty held her ground. The marriage ended. Kenneth moved to South Carolina very hastily after the divorce. I believe it was because Patty's five big brothers were going to go after him for what he did to their sister.

"Here you go. The soup is hot, Jason. You'd better sip it until it cools down a little."

"Thanks, Patty. Boy, am I hungry."

As I sipped my soup my mind drifted over the counter to where

Patty was wiping the coffee urns. Since my second divorce I had decided that the commitment of marriage wasn't for me. I had seen so much in my police career: broken homes, children in crisis, distraught mothers and fathers. But there was something about Patty that got my attention.

"Jason, here is your rice pudding. Lila gave you a little extra whipped cream and two maraschino cherries."

"Thanks, Patty, and thank Lila for me, too."

My check came to five dollars and sixty-four cents. I left Patty a two-dollar tip.

"So long, Patty, see ya later," I said as I turned to leave.

"Have a good afternoon, Jason." Patty smiled and looked into my eyes.

Wilt Chambers, a burly log-truck driver nodded at me as I left John's Diner. Wilt took almost two stools at the counter because he was such a large man. I raised my hand as I passed. One night in a terrible snowstorm I had become stuck in a ditch. It was Wilt who came by, and hooked a log chain on my vehicle, and yanked me out of the three-foot drift.

I never forgot that gesture. And Wilt didn't either. We had become good friends. Over the years Wilt and I would attend the Boonville Woodsman Field Days. Wilt was an expert with a chainsaw and was known for his bears that he would cut out of logs with different-sized blades. It took a steady hand and a lot of skill. There, too, I would run into many people I had met over the years. It was Wilt who started me collecting the old two-man saws that the lumberjacks used before the chainsaws arrived. I always felt that I had derived my love for the woods and the entire Adirondack region from my father, Jack. It was dad who actually used the two-man saws in the 1930's. This memory stimulated my desire to start a collection of them.

I stopped at the Post Office. When I unlocked my box a couple letters slid out onto the floor. As I bent over to pick them up, my ballpoint pen fell to the floor. I picked up my pen and left for my log home and Ruben. His tail was wagging when I got out of the Bronco.

"Good boy, Ruben."

I threw the mail on my desk and immediately called the Breakshire Lodge. Mr. Huston was pleased to hear from me. I informed him about what had transpired.

"I should be hearing from my Arizona contact soon, sir," I said.

"Jason, I appreciate this very much. This particular guest is making my whole staff a little nervous."

"Mr. Huston, is there anything you'd like to tell me about the fellow?"

"No, he seems to leave for a few minutes when the housecleaning people are in his room."

"I'll call you the minute I hear from Arizona."

"Good, Jason. I'll let you know if anything should develop here." He wanted to help.

"Thank you, Mr. Huston. Good-bye." I appreciated his cooperation.

"Good-bye, Jason."

I went to my desk. There had been no calls on my answering machine. I thumbed through my mail. There were some bills and several bad checks from several business places that I serviced. I couldn't help thinking about Patty.

"Her husband, Kenneth, was certainly a jerk."

I grabbed Ruben's chain, went to his runway, snapped the chain on the big dog's collar, and took him for a walk in the woods. Ruben pulled hard on the chain and I had to almost run behind him to keep up. When we returned I was tired and Ruben gulped his water down. We had had a fast walk.

Three days passed before I heard from Jack Flynn.

I had just returned from the Post Office, and was entering my home, when the telephone rang. I picked up the receiver.

"Jason Black here." I was anxious.

"Hello, Jason." It was Ruby Wolkowski.

"Hello, Ruby. How are you?" I was happy to hear her voice.

"Great. Just a second, Jason." She sounded excited.

"Hello, Jason. This is Jack."

"Hello, buddy. What's up? Have you found something out already?" I asked.

"Are you sitting down? I checked out Truman Hickman in Sedona. The guy in Lake Placid at the Breakshire Lodge is not Hickman."

"He's not?" I exclaimed in shock.

"No, he isn't. When I went to Sedona, I dropped by the Police Station and saw a friend of mine, Detective Jim Ferguson. I asked him to go with me to Hickman's residence. When we got there everything looked normal, until we went to the back of the house. Apparently, Hickman was well off. Anyway, when we went to the back of the house, we found a window broken and it was up. Detective Ferguson entered and opened the rear patio door. When we entered a den-type room on the second story we found Truman Hickman on the floor. He was dead, Jason. There was a bullet hole in his forehead."

"Holy God! Are you serious, Jack?"

"Very serious, my good friend. The Sedona Police Department have begun an investigation. Ferguson has got the case. Their evidence people have gone over the house with a fine-tooth comb. The grounds have been searched. They didn't come up with anything. Hickman owned two cars. The Lincoln, and a small Austin-Healy. He lived alone. He was retired and had been an engineer with ACE Electronics, in Flagstaff, Arizona. Hickman had a son that was killed in Vietnam, during the war. No other relatives. He was seventy-one years old. No weapons were found in the home."

"I will contact the Troopers right away and have them check this guy out in Lake Placid."

"One thing. It is believed that Hickman's wallet was stolen. It wasn't in the house."

"I appreciate everything you have done. I'll make the contact with the Troopers and they will be in touch with Detective Ferguson. It is going to be interesting to see who this subject is that is staying at the lodge. By the way, if there is any charge, bill me at my Old Forge address."

"No charge. You and I have been through too much together. You can return the favor sometime. Ok?"

"Will do. Good-bye."

"Good-bye. I'll talk with you later and keep you posted," I said as I hung up the phone.

Rather than phone Lieutenant Garrison, I decided to drive to Troop S Headquarters at Raybrook. I arrived two hours later. I hadn't realized how fast the Bronco could go. This was important. I went directly to the Troop Headquarters. My old friend, Lieutenant Roy Garrison, was in his office.

"Hello, Jason." He was surprised to see me.

"Hi, Roy. I think I have something you might be interested in."

"What's that?" he asked, leaning forward, curiously.

I told Roy the whole story. As I spoke, his eyes started to get bigger and his curiosity blossomed.

"Can I use your telephone, Roy? I want to check with Mr. Huston."

"Sure," he said pushing the phone toward me.

I called Mr. Huston at the Breakshire Lodge and told him what had developed. Huston confirmed that the subject posing as Hickman was still at the Lodge. The owner requested that the Troopers should come to the Lodge in plain cars without sirens blaring. I explained that the matter would be handled by the Troopers and that I would not be present. He was worried that the man in the room could be a killer.

"Send me your bill, Jason, and I will forward you a check."

"I'll do that, Mr. Huston. Thank you."

"When you are up here again, stop in and we'll have some tea and a chat."

"I will, sir." I hung up the phone and turned to Roy.

"Roy, thank you. When you have time, let me know what happened. The name of the Sedona, Arizona, Detective working the case on that end is Jim Ferguson."

"Jason, we appreciate you sharing this information with us and we'll head up to the Lodge just as soon as I can get some men together."

"Roy, as I told you, there were no weapons found at the scene in Arizona. This guy may be armed and dangerous. I didn't get a chance to see him, but Mr. Huston indicated that he was acting very strange."

"Don't worry, Jason. We'll find out what this fellow is doing here."

"Take care, Roy. It's great seeing you again."

On my way out of the building, several ladies working at Troop Headquarters said hello to me. I nodded and left. When I reached the Bronco, I noticed some antifreeze on the concrete pavement. I lifted the hood to find that one of the radiator hose clamps had come loose. I went to my glove compartment and took out a screwdriver. The hose clamp was tightened. I wished that I could have joined Lieutenant Garrison and his men at the Breakshire. I hoped that no one would get hurt.

Over the years I had been on many canoe trips throughout the region. As I drove back through Tupper Lake and into Long Lake, my memories captured those moments of paddling against strong currents and camping at Skip-Jack's campsite in Long Lake. I remembered the fourteen-foot aluminum boat I had used on the lake and the fish I caught. I could taste the filet of perch cooked over an outside wood-fire, and those baked potatoes topped with sweet butter.

The local kids in Long Lake loved to play softball. They could be seen about four nights a week hitting the well trounced ball over the fence.

I was wondering how Lieutenant Garrison was making out at the Breakshire Lodge. I had served well in the Troopers and now that I was retired and doing private investigation work, I respected that professional line between private investigation and the police. I had a good relationship with all the police departments throughout the region. The exchange of information was on a need-to-know basis. I was well aware of the splendid job the police were doing. They would investigate accidents of all types, and search for lost hunters, along with the State DEC Rangers and Foresters. The cooperation was there and that was important.

The Bronco seemed to know where the parking lot of the Long Lake Diner was located, or at least I thought it did.

Gertie and Bob were both busy behind the counter. Several people were having a mid-afternoon snack. Gertie spoke up.

"What can I do for you, Jason? Coffee?"

"Yes, coffee and an order of toast with jelly."

"How's that big mutt of yours?" Bob asked. I knew he would love to own my dog.

"Ruben is doing okay. I should bring him with me oftener, but he loves that runway I built for him. He thinks he owns it."

"Well, he's a beautiful dog, Jason." He spoke loudly.

"That he is, thank you."

"Bob, do you ever see Zing Zing around?" I missed talking with him.

"Oh, yes, Zing stops in quite often."

"I can remember many good conversations with him years ago. I believe he lived and worked in New York City before he came here to live."

"That's right, Jason."

"He always wore that green Ducks Back shirt and his slouch hat. We'd talk for hours about the region and different folks that passed through here. He had some great stories about the hunting trips he'd been on and the big-racked bucks that were taken in the hunts. He loved to sip a cold beer, and the stories would get better, especially on the third one. Guess they were all true stories."

"Yep, Zing Zing is quite a gentleman and, ya know, Jason, the world would be better off if we had a lot of Zing Zings. He's a very kind and thoughtful person."

"I do agree with you on that, Bob."

"Jason, would you like a fill-up on your coffee?" Gertie asked.

"Just a half a cup. That's great coffee."

"The best," Bob commented, "Jason, I remember you told me once that you liked to sketch."

"Yes, Bob, I do. I enjoy taking a drawing pad to sketch mountains and old cabins. My grandmother was an artist and she did landscapes. She did some here in the Adirondacks and in Gloucester, Massachusetts, by the ocean. Possibly some of that talent was passed down to me, but gramma's was really professional. Mine are very elementary, but I love to sketch. All it costs you is for the pad and pencils, and a little creativity." I wondered if she was sketching in heaven. "Well, I'd better get down the road, folks."

"Take care, Jason."

"Yep, so long. I'll see you my next trip through."

I left Gertie a dollar tip.

# CHAPTER THREE

The trip to Bald Mountain was longer than I expected. The rain came down in sheets. My mind raced back to the very early days of the Adirondacks when the Indians hunted the region. History indicated that they hunted in the lower sections. The game was plentiful. I wondered what it must have been like before the park was settled by white people.

As I passed through Blue Mountain on Route 30 onto Route 28 toward Inlet, I thought about my first days of deer hunting in the late 1940's, when my father had brought me to the Indian Lake region with a large group of hunters. I remembered there were forty people in the hunt, which took place between Blue Mountain and Indian Lake north of the Indian River. Twenty would be placed on watch and twenty would do the driving, shouting and making noise to move the deer toward the watchers. I remembered that the first drive bagged six bucks. Their racks ranged from four points to twelve points. It was my first experience of hunting in the park. My father had shot a six-point buck on the first drive.

When I pulled in front of my log home, Ruben began barking loudly. He was glad to see his master. The rain had stopped and the air was much cooler. I gave him a bear hug. I then took some kindling and started a fire in the woodstove. Ruben ran off among the trees for a couple of minutes and then back to me while I waited by the back door. He lay down in his favorite spot and placed his head between his paws. He didn't stir or otherwise apparently realize that a large doe had come into the yard. It isn't uncommon for any of the Adirondack animals to make a visit in the yards of the inhabitants. They live in the woods, too, and their ancestors were there long before humankind came to the area.

These days I have very little interest in hunting. If it was a matter of life or death, I'd probably take a deer or rabbit, but I love the animals of the forest and take a much different view than I had when I was young. I owned a couple of rifles, but only took them out a couple times a year for target practice. Over the years I've had several revolvers and pistols and other long arms, but I decided to sell them. The U.S. Marine Corps had trained me well. I was an expert with both rifles and pistols. Jack Flynn and I had taken top honors at a shoot while competing against members of the U.S. Army Pistol Team. Both Jack and I were tough in competition when it came to shooting contests.

After a supper of baked haddock and mashed potatoes, I washed the dishes and read the paper. Ruben lay on the floor by my feet. I fell asleep and woke up only when Ruben wanted to go outside. The lights went out at midnight.

A week went by before I heard from Lieutenant Garrison. One afternoon, while I was writing reports on some check cases, the phone rang.

"Jason, this is Roy at the Barracks. Have you read the papers?"

"Not yet, Roy."

"Jason, we here at Barracks want you to know how much we appreciated your cooperation on this case. We have arrested the nervous visitor of Breakshire Lodge. After you left my office, six Investigators and myself took one of our unmarked vans and went to Breakshire. We talked to Mr. Huston and he filled us in on the man's behavior at the lodge."

"Wonderful," I said. I was happy for Roy and his detail.

"We then went to his room and I knocked on the door. He asked who it was. We had one of the cleaning ladies call out, 'towels, extra towels'. The fellow came to the door. We grabbed him. He struggled, but we had the power in our corner. He is an escapee from a Washington State Prison. He was serving time for Murder lst Degree. He escaped in a laundry truck and made his way into Arizona. He has so many aliases that we are not giving out his name. There is a possibility that he may have been involved in more than one homicide as he made his way across the country."

"Sounds like a complex case."

"Yes, it is. He will be turned over to the FBI. The Lincoln is being impounded. We found a Smith & Wesson 9 mm wrapped in an oily cloth behind the spare tire in the car. This guy's fingerprints were all over it. The pistol belonged to the Arizona victim." He sounded excited. "Like I said, we appreciate you contacting us."

"Roy, thank you. I've known you for many years. And if it was the other way around, I know you'd call me, too."

"You bet I would. We'll give you a call if anything else should develop."

It was just past 8:30 a.m. when Ruben started barking with rapidity. A Dodge pick-up had pulled into the yard. I had a mug of coffee in my hand and went out to greet my visitor. It was Wilt Chambers.

"Good morning, Wilt. Kind of early for you to be visiting."

"Jason, I'm sorry to bother you, but come here and see what I have in the back of my pickup." He had a big smile.

I was glad to see my good friend Wilt, no matter what time of the day or night. I sauntered over to his truck.

"I went to an auction the other day over to Boonville. Ninety-year-old Jeremiah Lewis is going to the nursing home, and his son, Steve, sold some of his father's property. These four two-man saws are for you, Jason. I picked them up for twenty-eight dollars. Remember you told me to keep my eye open in the event I came across any saws of this description. Do ya want them?"

"Yes, Wilt, that was thoughtful of you. This will make a total of thirty saws for my collection. Here's thirty-five dollars. The extra is for your time and gas." I was so happy to get these saws.

"You don't have to do that, Jason. Twenty-eight is what I paid for them."

"I know, but that's fine. I appreciate it."

"Thanks, Jason. I knew you'd like to have them. They are in good shape, and sharp, too. Jeremiah must have sharpened them every day. They're like a razor's edge."

"How about some coffee?"

"Sure! Just black will do." Wilt pulled his ear. "By the way, Jason, Patty was asking if I've seen you lately. I think that gal likes you, Jason."

"She did ask, huh?"

"Yep, I told her that I thought you were up in Tupper or Long Lake area, working on some bad-check cases. Oh, something I had to tell ya! Did ya see the paper? They caught a killer up in Lake Placid. He was staying at one of the Lodges."

"Is that right? No, I haven't seen the paper."

I didn't mention anything about the case to Wilt. Even though he is a good friend, I like to keep my work along these lines somewhat confidential. The main thing, was that an alleged serial killer was off the street. And that was important to me and the entire society.

"Well, Jason, I must be running along. I've got a timber job to estimate and there is some mighty fine white oak in this particular woodlot."

"Can you imagine what it was like to cut the timber with these two-man saws?"

"It was hard work, and your father knew all about that. Pulling those logs out of the woods wasn't an easy task. Today with the skidders, the chainsaws, and all the other equipment, I guess they call it progress. There were some great stories back there in those old logging camps. My pappy was there for years bringing that timber down. God! He told me about some of the fights they'd have back in the boondocks. My dad weighed two hundred and fifty pounds and he could handle three men in a fist fight, if he had to. He was a tough bird. If you did that today, they'd lock you up."

"That's right. It is a much different society today. You know hard work didn't hurt anyone. A lot of folks today are soft. I know they have all kinds of health centers, fruit juice bars, marathons. If they spent some time in the backcountry doing what our fathers did, they'd sleep soundly at night."

"That's for sure." He laughed. "Well, Jason, gotta be going."

"Take it easy," I said as he climbed into his truck.

"Yep. See ya later."

The Dodge pick-up backed around and Wilt was gone. Ruben sat in his run watching a chippy darting around him. I went back to my desk and filled my coffee cup on the way.

Just before supper, Ruben and I went for our walk into the forest. Like always, Ruben was pulling hard on the chain and I was jogging to keep up with him. A large doe and a small fawn ran from behind some downed tree branches. I looked around for the buck that was usually with them, but I couldn't see him. I knew that many of the deer would die in the wintertime and, with the deer herd growing each year, the hunters would thin out the herd a little more. I thought about some of the hunters, too. Generally they were good sportsmen, but once in a while, a hunter might abuse the ethics of good sportsmanship.

We returned to the log home after about forty-five minutes. I decided that I would change the menu for supper and prepare some flapjacks with crisp bacon and more hot coffee. I had purchased a gallon of class A maple syrup and wanted to try it.

Ruben was given a treat, too. There was one large flapjack left, so I fixed a special dish for my K-9 buddy. It was downed in two bites. I gathered up the dishes and washed them. Ruben wasn't far away. His nose was between his two paws and his eyes were staring up at me.

I let Ruben out for a quick run to the woods. It was about 10:30 p.m. Soon he returned and headed for his favorite sleeping spot. I checked the doors, locked them, and went to bed. I read for awhile until my eyes couldn't stay open any longer. I thought about all the check cases that were still pending. *Why do people write checks knowing at the time there are not sufficient funds in their accounts to cover them? I thought, too, about the hard-working people within the Blue Line that struggle to pay their bills.* It wasn't an easy task for them. I said my nightly prayers and fell off into slumber-land. My last thoughts were about Patty and the hardships she had endured with her assaultive husband.

The alarm clock radio went off and I could hear the voice of Clint Black coming over 101.3 FM. He was singing a cowboy song. I threw the covers back. Ruben was down at the foot of the bed pulling on the spread. I had a patchwork quilt my granny had given me just before she passed on. My mother had kept the patchwork quilt in a cedar chest and she told me to always treasure it. It was old and beautiful I never placed it on my bed, though. With Ruben, you never know when he's going to tug on a blanket or towel. I had always thought that K-9's had discipline, but not Ruben. He had his own mind.

After my shower I got dressed. I thought this would be a good morning to visit John's Diner for breakfast. I let Ruben out and he made a bee-line to the woods. In a couple of minutes his one hundred pounds came charging down the trail. He waited at his run gate for me. I gave the mutt a big ole bear hug and let him into the runway area. His water and food dishes were full. I looked over at the bird feeders and spotted a hummingbird targeting the sweet sugar solution in the special feeder I had placed above the runway on a twelve-foot post. The hummingbird was there, then it wasn't. I checked the door.

The Ford Bronco sputtered a little after it started, but soon straightened out after it warmed up a little. I thought that it probably needed a tune-up, but decided it would have to wait until I had a day to leave it off at the garage. Don, my mechanic, was good, but getting an appointment was difficult.

John's Diner was busy as usual. There was a small table in the far corner. Several locals nodded at me as I went to sit down. Patty Olson, with two coffee pots in her hands, was busy pouring decaf into Tom Dawson's coffee mug. She gave me a smile.

"I'll be right with you, Jason."

"Take your time." I looked at her understandingly.

I knew the menu by heart. Lila was in the kitchen baking her prize-winning pies for the day. She usually baked pies three or four times a week. Her favorite was apple. She added the right spices, and the pies were a little on the tart side. Everybody loved Lila and her pies. She turned out some excellent creams, including banana, chocolate and lemon. People from miles around would stop by for a piece of her pie and a cup of coffee. With the apple she served some extra sharp cheese that pleased many of the customers. It was my favorite cheese.

Today Patty had on a light blue blouse with red roses detailed on the short sleeves. It looked immaculate on her. She wore a fancy dark blue short skirt with large white buttons on the left side. A medium blue ribbon held her blond hair in a tight bun. She wore southwestern jewelry and a silver-banded lady's watch. Her eyes sparkled. The smile she gave me was warm and alluring.

"Sorry I took so long, Jason, but as you can see we're busy."

"Patty, I'm in no hurry this morning. I'd like a large orange juice and a western omelet with some home fries and whole wheat toast. Tell the cook to braise off the onions and green peppers."

I looked into Patty's eyes and my heart started to beat a little faster.

"This shouldn't take too long, Jason," she spoke as she rushed off to the kitchen with my order.

"Like I said, I'm in no hurry."

She had brought me the paper. I couldn't concentrate, so I folded it and laid it on my table. My eyes were focused on Patty. She had suffered so much in her young adult life.

She came toward me with my breakfast. I was hungry. Her smile really got to me this morning. Was it because of what Wilt had said when he delivered my saws? I knew one thing: I wanted to get to know Patty.

"Jason, would you like some grape jelly for your toast?" She asked as she set my plate down.

"I'd love some."

Patty's hand rested on my shoulder for a second.

"Patty, I don't mean to be out of order, but would you like to have a home-cooked dinner sometime at my place?"

I looked up at her and she smiled down at me, and then the smile disappeared. I waited for her reply. It seemed that it was taking forever.

"Jason, yes, I would love to," she answered, smiling broadly, without hesitation.

"Do you like pot roast with vegetables?

"One of my favorites," she said.

"Good. I'll call you during the week and let you know which night," I said, pleased with her quick response.

"Okay. Thank you, Jason." She was wearing that smile again.

My omelet had cooled a little, but my heart was racing. It had been a long time since I had prepared a dinner for anyone except Ruben and me. I finished my breakfast. Patty dropped the check off at the table and refreshed my coffee. The hot liquid burned my mouth. I paid my check and left.

The Post Office lot was filled with cars. I was able to park in the Postmaster's area. I checked my box and found several bad checks along with their attached certificates of protest. There was a letter from Tom Huston. I then remembered that I had not sent him a bill for my services. There were some other letters from the west coast.

As I was leaving the Post Office I almost got stuck in the door when I met head on with Wilt Chambers. Wilt backed out of the door to let me through. I talked with him.

"Wilt, I love those saws you dropped off."

"I had to pick them up for you, Jason. They're in very good condition."

"Yes, they are. Sharp, too." Wilt was always thoughtful.

"I'm looking forward to the next Woodsman Field Days."

"We'll go, Wilt. I'm looking forward to it myself."

"I probably shouldn't be asking you this, Jason, but did you happen to see Patty?"

"Yes, this morning. In fact, I asked her to join me for dinner at my place, soon."

"I'm glad." His smile was genuine.

"Yes, Wilt, maybe Patty and I can talk a little."

"Jason, you take care. See ya later."

"Take it easy, Wilt."

I went to my Bronco and headed home. Ruben was glad to see me. I gave him a big hug and decided to take him for a walk. His water dish was getting low and the food dish was empty. The chain pulled tight as Ruben leapt forward. I had to run to keep up with this retired K-9.

"Settle down, boy," I said.

We walked for about an hour. I wondered where Ruben got all his energy from. It must be that dog food I feed him. On our walk we had seen a large red fox. I could tell that Ruben wanted to chase him, but I had him on a short chain. That was the first fox I'd seen in a long time. The birds in our area were plentiful and we always had plenty of chipmunks and squirrels. I put him back in his run and filled his water and food dishes.

Working for yourself has its advantages. Unless I was working a dedicated case, I could do just about anything I wanted to. I went to the bathroom and let the water run. The strong well pump worked up to about forty pounds of pressure. The water I held in my hands felt good as I splashed it against my face. I looked in the mirror and could see that youthful face I once possessed had left. But I had managed to stay in pretty good shape over the years. I could still split wood with the best of them. A little slower, but respectable. I had more split firewood piled in cords than I would ever use, but this was a ritual with me. And darn good therapy, too.

I went to my desk and opened my mail, especially interested in Tom Huston's letter. I was surprised to see that he had enclosed a check made payable to me. It was for an excessive amount. I couldn't believe that Tom would send me a check when I hadn't billed him yet. The check was for four hundred dollars. The letter thanked me for my services relative to the nervous man he had staying at his Lodge. He went on to thank me for driving to Lake Placid the next day after he had called me.

I phoned Tom Huston and told him that the check was excessive. I informed him that I was sending him back his check. My time spent on the matter came to two hundred and ten dollars. Tom understood. I sent the four-hundred-dollar check to him, and in a few days I received one with the corrected amount. Tom had put a note in the envelope. The note indicated that he was going to contact me in the future if they had any problems that would fit into my occupational area. Tom advised me that he had sent a letter to Division Headquarters of the Troopers praising the work of Lieutenant Roy Garrison and his men.

I went outside to check on Ruben. I was just about to enter my side door when I heard the air horns. It was Charlie Perkins going by with his last load of logs for the day. Two large crows, startled by Charlie's horns, took off from the top of a tree.

"Caw, caw, caw."

Charlie put in many hours to support his family. He was a good man. I liked Charlie.

I found myself thinking about Patty. I was glad that she had agreed to come to supper. I didn't give her the day that this would take place, but for certain it would be soon.

The next morning the telephone woke me. I tried to get my eyes open. The hands on my Big Ben alarm clock indicated that it was 8:30 a.m.

I grabbed for the phone and it fell on the floor. I finally retrieved it.

"Hello."

"Jason, Dale Rush here!"

"What's up, Dale?" I asked curiously.

"I have finally finished checking out the Lycoming engine on the Stinson and thought I'd fly up to Lake Placid for breakfast. Would you like to join me?"

"Let's see… I just woke up." I shook my head sleepily.

"Can you be ready in a half an hour?"

"Yeah." Still drowsy.

"Good. I'll be along in a few minutes to pick you up. Keep Ruben in the run; there's some reason your dog doesn't like me."

"Okay, no problem."

"See ya, Jason."

I threw the covers back and jumped out of bed. Took a fast shower and had a quick cup of coffee. Dale, who stood about five-feet-nine inches tall, was a college man who had served in the U.S. Marine Corps during the Korean War. He had been a pilot assigned to a squadron of Douglas A-1 Skyraiders. The AD's were used to attack installations deep in North Korea. He had been assigned to the carrier Valley Forge and later flew VA-216's off the carrier USS Boxer. He came out of the service as an Ace, with seven MiG-17 fighters downed to his credit. He had an old 1947 Stinson gull-winged-reliant with floats. The plane was immaculate, bright red with white floats.

I heard Ruben growling, and looked out. Dale had just pulled into the yard. I noticed that he didn't get out of the car. I couldn't understand why Ruben was growling.

I locked the door. Ruben's food and water dishes were full. The run had good shade from the mighty oaks in the yard and there was always a breeze. When I had built the run I had placed it under the trees for that reason. I can't stand to see a dog in the hot rays of the sun. Many times I've seen dogs left in cars in the heat of the day.

I went to the passenger side of Dale's car, opened the door, and got in.

"Good morning, Dale. How are you?"

"Great, Jason. I'll feel better when we're in the air. These wonderful drivers on our two-lane roads scare me, if ya know what I mean."

"Yep, I agree with you. Thanks for inviting me along." I was looking forward to the plane ride. Dale put the car in gear and proceeded to Route 28.

"Jason, how's the detective business?"

"Just the check cases alone keep me busy at the typewriter."

"I suppose there's a lot to it."

"Not much. The ones that I can't recover for the business places, I turn over to the police department in whatever jurisdiction the check was passed in."

"Oh! I see."

Dale pulled into Kirby's Boat Marina and found a parking spot right away. The red Stinson was tied to Kirby's small dock. Dale and I were wearing jackets. We both knew it would be cool up above. Dale nodded at Paul Kirby. I nodded, but with an icy stare. Kirby and I had had an argument one time when he removed a workable part from my Glaspar boat to use on another customer's boat.

Dale gave his pride and joy a cursory check before opening the door. I had flown with Dale only a few times. He was in charge of the meat department at the Big M in town. He worked hard six days a week Any spare time he had, one could find him with his Stinson. He was a stickler for maintenance.

"Okay, Jason, climb aboard."

I placed my foot on the two-step-ladder and climbed in. Dale's plane could hold four people including the pilot. We both fastened our seatbelts. One of Kirby's dock attendants unfastened the line and pushed us off, away from the dock. Fourth Lake was dead ahead. Dale hit the ignition and the big prop flipped over a couple of times.

"Come on, baby, let's fire up."

The plane was rigged with a hand-choke. Dale gave the ignition another try and the engine purred, first loudly, then gently. Dale gave it the throttle and we moved across the waters of Fourth Lake. We turned near Dollar Island and, after checking for any boats or people swimming, gave the plane the power. But it seemed we'd never lift off. I noticed since the last time I'd flown with Dale, the engine seemed to function better. We finally lifted and he climbed to twenty-five-hundred-feet. The view was fantastic. There wasn't a cloud in the sky and Dale seemed to be in paradise. He handed me half of a Mounds bar. He knew that I loved chocolate.

The altimeter showed that we had climbed to twenty-seven hundred feet. I looked out the side window and saw we already passed over Raquette Lake. The camps and the boats below looked liked tiny play houses, specks in and near the water. When we reached Long Lake, Dale took the Stinson down to seven hundred feet and circled over the Long Lake Lumber Company. A lumber truck turned right onto Route 30 headed toward Tupper Lake.

"Jason, I love the Adirondacks like you do. To me, there isn't another place on earth that can compare with our four seasons. Our people are hard working and the politicians seem to by-pass our needs up here in the mountains. They talk a lot, but generally there is very little realization of programs that would better our lives. Can you imagine the money that goes to New York City from the north country?"

"You may have a point there. Just look at the history of our park and the north country. My dad started pulping during the Depression in order to place the food on the table. He had been gassed at Alsace-Lorraine during World War I, but never had a government pension until a year before he passed on."

We were soon over Tupper Lake.

"Jason, I brought a couple of hunters up here by plane last fall. It was clear when I left Old Forge, but at Long Lake we were hit by strong winds and rain. I tried to fly over the storm. The downdraft was wicked. I then took it down and landed in front of the Adirondack Hotel. The two hunters were white as ghosts. We stayed overnight. The next morning we took off at 7:30 a.m. When we landed at Tupper Lake, the hunters were so relieved they wanted to give me a hundred-dollar tip. I couldn't take it. They were working fellows like ourselves."

"Dale, you're a good man. Did those guys know they were flying with a war hero?"

"You know I don't talk about that. I was lucky to get home after the war. I thank the good Lord for bringing me back. I was so nervous after that experience. I had to bail out one time, just north of the 38th Parallel. I'll tell you, it was scary. One of the U.S. Army patrols scooped me up and we nearly got caught. Their faces were blackened, and when they approached me, one of them whispered out, 'Carmel, California.' I had my 45 automatic ready to fire. There were six of them. I was lucky. They had their weapons pointed at my head. When they got real close I could see their smiles. I knew they had to be our guys. They were."

Dale brought the Stinson low over Lake Placid. His landing was smooth and I slid the window back halfway as he taxied toward the public dock. The Stinson glistened in the mid-morning sunlight. I could tell that Dale was in his glory. The right side float gently touched the dock. I climbed out and secured the plane to a tie-up ring. Dale switched the ignition off. A puff of smoke escaped from the exhaust of the powerful Lycoming engine.

"Do you have any specific restaurant in mind, Dale?"

"No, I don't care. You're here more than I am."

"How would you like to go to the Breakshire Lodge? We can walk there."

"We could use a little walk." As we were strolling toward the lodge, Dale asked, "How did you like the flight, Jason?"

"Loved it, Dale. You're a fine pilot."

"Thank you. I had good training."

"You did," I agreed.

Traffic was flying by us as we walked toward the Breakshire. I thought, *Tom Huston will be surprised to see me so soon and unexpected.*

Dale and I walked up the steps. The grounds were beautiful. The shrubs were trimmed and the birdbaths ran over with water. Dale had never been to the Breakshire before.

We went into the dining area, where several guests were just finishing their mid-morning breakfast. The three waitresses on duty wore maroon skirts with starched white blouses. They were immaculate. The hostess approached us.

"You gentlemen may sit wherever you desire. Your waitress will be with you shortly. How have you been, Mr. Black?"

I didn't think the hostess would have remembered me, but apparently she did.

"Oh, I've been fine, Ms. Shaver. I'd like you to meet my friend, Dale Rush from Old Forge."

"How do you do, Mr. Rush? Welcome to Breakshire. Is this your first visit?"

"Yes, and it is a pleasure to meet you, Ms. Shaver," Dale said to the hostess.

"Likewise," smiling.

Ms. Shaver had been hostess since Mr. Huston took over ownership of the Lodge. I had learned that bit of information on one of my previous visits to Breakshire. I noticed that Dale was busy studying the menu. Just before we landed he had told me, "Boy, am I hungry!"

The smiling waitress approached the table.

"Are you gentlemen ready to order?" she asked pleasantly.

She stood about five foot nine and--I have to admit it--was lovely.

"Dale, go ahead and order," I said.

"Waitress, I'll have a cheese omelet. I prefer Swiss cheese if it's possible, a few home fries, whole wheat toast with some orange marmalade. I'd like my coffee strong and black. Thank you," Dale said with a winning grin.

"Sir, what would you like?" asked the waitress as she turned to me.

"I'll have the flapjacks with the lumberjack slice of ham, coffee with cream, and some strawberry jam on the side. Bring us both a glass of orange juice."

While we were waiting for our order, we discussed the weather and our flight. In about fifteen minutes our waitress returned with our breakfast. We thanked her. We consumed our food with little conversation. We both agreed that everything was delicious. The lumberjack slice of ham was an inch thick and I shared some with Dale.

The waitress returned with a steaming pot of coffee and filled our cups. We told her how pleased we were with the food. Just as we finished our coffee, Tom Huston came to our table wearing a big smile.

"Good morning, gentlemen."

"Good morning, Tom," I said. "I'd like to introduce a friend of mine, Dale Rush."

"Good morning, Mr. Rush. It's a pleasure." Dale stood up and extended his hand to Tom. "Please call me Dale."

"Please be seated, Dale." Tom said. "Would you care for more coffee?"

"No thanks," we both replied in unison.

"Jason, you didn't have to return that fee I sent you." Tom said.

"Tom, that was adequate," I replied.

I told Tom that Dale had called me earlier that morning and asked me to accompany him to Lake Placid.

"What a nice gesture, Dale!" Tom commented.

We were given a tour of the lodge. I had seen it several times, but Mr. Huston thought that Dale would enjoy seeing this New England style building. Dale and Tom hit it off well together. I was glad. Before we departed, Dale told Tom that if he ever wanted to take an airplane ride he should call him. Dale gave Tom his card with the telephone number.

The hostess nodded at us as we left the lodge. The walk back to the dock was at a slower pace than when we first arrived. It must have been that lumberjack ham. I never had seen such a large portion. I wondered if the chef had slipped with the knife.

As we approached the Stinson we could see several older men looking it over.

"That's a beauty," one of the fellows said.

"Thank you," Dale responded.

Dale and I chatted with the gentlemen for a few minutes. We learned that two of them had been pilots during WW II. One had flown the B-29 Bomber and another flew C-47 transports.

Dale untied the mooring line and we climbed aboard. The Lycoming came to life when Dale turned the ignition switch. He didn't have to choke the engine. The 245-horsepower engine must have realized that the fellows on the dock were watching us as we taxied away toward the center of the lake. We waved at them. They waved back. When we were airborne, Dale gave the fellows on the dock a short power dive and turned toward Tupper Lake. It was a beautiful day. I thought about Patty and, of course, Ruben.

"Jason, I've worked hard to get this engine in good working order. Parts are expensive and some of them are hard to locate."

"I imagine they are," I responded.

The flight to Old Forge was smooth. Dale indicated that he had a slight tail wind and that he could conserve on fuel. Dale is a close friend of Michael Drew, who owns and operates Drew's Inn just north of Inlet. Dale had been flying at twenty-seven-hundred feet and brought it down to six hundred to circle the Inn. The bright red roof caught my eye.

"Mike has been working hard getting that roof in shape," Dale said.

"It looks great," I added.

I noted that the parking lot was full.

"Dale, the folks in the Adirondacks earn every cent they take in. Without hunting season and the snowmobiles, profits would be impossible. It costs plenty for electrical service, and don't forget the taxes, either."

"True," Dale muttered.

Dale, concentrating on sitting the Stinson down near the dock area, was waiting for a speedboat to move down the lake. The timing was on the money. Dale cut the engine about fifteen feet from the mooring ring on the south side of the dock. As I climbed out on the float, I saw Kirby running down to tie our line. He gave me a sneaky glance and I returned it with another icy stare. He should have been taken to task when he removed the part on my Glaspar, but I hadn't said anything at the time. He just never worked on my boat again.

Kirby returned to his Marina office and didn't even say hello to Dale.

"Dale, thank you for the ride and the breakfast. Next time I buy."

"I was honored, Jason."

I waited for Dale outside the office, where he had to go to pay his rental fee. I could see old man Kirby and him through the window. Kirby's mouth was running like a whirlybird.

Dale soon came out of the office shaking his head. I never did know what that was all about. And I never asked.

I bid farewell to Dale at the entrance to my place and told him we'd be in touch. We were good friends. I could hear Ruben barking with rapidity. I hurried up the lane and there was my German shepherd barking with his tail wagging back and forth.

"Hello, Ruben!" I shouted. "Did you miss me, boy?"

Ruben jumped up on me and licked my hand. I made sure that he still had food and water. I told him that we'd go for our walk a little later, then let him out of his run and went inside with him trailing me closely. He went to his favorite spot, and soon his big head lay between his huge front paws. His eyes were glued on his master. I looked over at the telephone and saw the red light flashing on my answering machine.

The phone calls were all from various businesses. The weekend had gone by and several checks were passed in town. Some of the checks had bounced. The business owners wanted their money, and rightly so. I told them to have the checks protested and I would endeavor to recover their funds.

I couldn't get Patty out of my mind. I decided to take Ruben for a walk in the forest. The trip to Lake Placid had just about done me in. When we got back, I could hardly keep my eyes open. I checked the doors. Ruben wanted to go outside again. I unlocked the front door and he almost pushed me through it getting out. He was back in a few minutes. I let him in. He went to his favorite corner and lay down. I brushed my teeth. I think I was asleep before my head hit the pillow.

The next morning after a hot shower and shave I went to John's Diner. Lila was in the kitchen manning the short-order grill. I took my usual table in the back far corner of the dining room. I was looking forward to seeing Patty's smiling face. She approached me with her order pad and pen.

"Good morning, Sherlock--oops, I'm sorry-- Jason. What would you like?"

"Patty, before I order, I'd like to know if you'd like to come to dinner Saturday night?" I had finally gotten the courage to ask her.

"I'd love to," she responded without hesitation.

I looked into her eyes and she smiled at me. Her lips were moist. I wondered why I'd waited so long to ask her. Wilt had told me before that Patty seemed to have some interest in going out with me. I had always been kind to her. I couldn't help but think of the mean man she

had married. He had used her for a punching bag. I couldn't forget
that it was the broken nose he gave her that prompted the divorce
action. Everyone in town had been in Patty's corner at the time.

I ordered scrambled eggs, whole-wheat toast with grape jelly,
and hot coffee with cream. While I was waiting for Patty to return
with my breakfast, I glanced through the Utica paper. When I turned
the page I looked up to see Patty by the front door of the restaurant
talking to Dale Rush. Patty wasn't smiling. They looked serious. He
turned and went out the door. I wondered to myself, *what's that all
about?* Perplexed, I went back to reading the paper.

It wasn't long before Patty returned with her smile and my
breakfast. I didn't mention what I had observed. She didn't tell me
anything either. I couldn't help but be curious. I continued to glance
at the paper as I consumed my breakfast. Possibly Dale hadn't seen
me in the corner. I let it pass. I told Patty I was looking forward to
Saturday evening.

"Patty, I'll see you about 6:00 p.m. tomorrow."

"I'll be there. Is there anything I can bring?"

"Just yourself."

She smiled as I left the diner.

I went to the grocery store to pick up some vegetables, beef,
napkins, a head of cabbage, apples, flour and fresh rolls. I was already
planning for the Saturday night feast. I added two candles to the list.

Ruben and I climbed Bald Mountain on Friday afternoon. I took
a sandwich along with a canteen of water, and stuffed some dog
biscuits into my small backpack. We were tired when we reached the
top. Both of us were gasping for our breath. We stayed on the
mountain until dusk.

When we returned home I put Ruben into his run. I had a cup
of tea and some toast. Both of us were tired. Ruben was ready to
come into the house. When I let him out of the run he ran into the
woods, returning shortly. I brought him into the house. He went to his
favorite spot to lay down. I proceeded to get ready for bed. I put on
my pajamas and got under the covers. I started to read, but fell off to
sleep.

It was about 8:30 a.m. when the telephone rang. I answered it
on the third ring. It was Lieutenant Roy Garrison of the State

Troopers.

"Jason, did I get you out of the sack?"

"No problem, Roy. I should have been up an hour ago. What's up?"

"We have identified the killer who was staying at the Breakshire Lodge. His name is Thornton Cole, age 42. He apparently was waiting to hook up with an old girlfriend, Susan Morris, age 40. Cole was doing a twenty-five-year-to-life for Murder 1st., when he escaped. Both of them are from Newport, Oregon. He has been returned to Washington State. Their investigation is still going on in Arizona. He will be charged for the murder of the Arizona man. I wanted to let you know. We have an investigator checking the area for the girlfriend."

"Thanks, Roy. I'll let you know if I hear anything."

"Take it easy."

"So long."

I could tell by the phone call that Roy appreciated the information I had furnished him.

# CHAPTER FOUR

I took the rest of the morning to clean and tidy up the house. I drove to the store to pick up some wine. I returned and continued my preparations for my guest.

The aroma of pot roast wafted throughout my log home. The table was set. The candles were in place. I had added the vegetables. I didn't follow a particular recipe. I had added some wine and half-a-can of beer to the au jus. The cabbage salad was made and I garnished the top of it with a tomato formed into a flower. The relish tray contained sweet and sour pickles, radishes, celery and black olives. The rolls were ready for warming in the oven. I was nervous. I wanted things to be just right.

I could tell that my guest was arriving, because Ruben was raising a ruckus. I looked out of the window. There she was. Patty Olson with her blond hair flowing over her shoulders, wearing a blue denim blouse and matching skirt. She had on her southwestern style jewelry. The skirt wasn't too long or too short. It was just right. The smile was eye-catching. Her pocketbook hung by a strap over her right shoulder. Her bosoms were firm and natural. Her blouse was buttoned from waist to her neckline. My heart picked up an extra beat.

I went to the door and opened it. Ruben was settling down. Patty had seen Ruben on only one occasion, when I was walking him in town and she had left John's diner after working all day. Ruben had been restless at the time.

"Hello, Ruben," she said.

Ruben was quiet now.

"Hi, Patty. I see you found us." I looked at her, beaming.

"You're not the only Sherlock in town," she offered with a laugh.

"You're right."

Patty came into my log home and warmly embraced me. I returned the greeting with a firm hug.

"Something smells good. You should have let me help you with dinner, Jason."

"Maybe next time, Patty. I hope you like it. When I was growing up, my mother would prepare a pot roast at least twice a month."

"My mom did, too, Jason."

As I stood there looking into Patty's alluring green eyes I couldn't help but wonder what the conversation was the day that she and Dale looked hard at each other. But this was no time to ask her. We were going to have a great supper, even if I did say so myself.

"Would you care for a drink?" I asked.

"Just an iced tea will do fine," she replied.

"I'll have one with you. I hope you don't mind, there is a little wine and beer in the pot roast."

"No, that's all right."

We drank our tea in the living room. She was quiet. I was nervous. My divorces had been agreeable to all parties concerned, but they had made me very sad and I had not dated for a long time. Then I had seen Patty. I didn't think that I would ever marry again, but possibly Patty and I could be friends. I wasn't looking for a long term relationship, but sometimes the loneliness was overwhelming.

I gave Patty a tour of my castle. It wasn't a large home, but it was just right for me. When we were in my combination office and den, she noticed my U.S. Marine discharge on the wall, and many other certificates that were presented to me during my career. They really didn't mean anything to anyone except me. There had been a lot of heartache in some of the cases that I had been recognized for. I never felt that I should have any type of hero status, but I must admit some were well deserved.

"Well, I guess we are ready to try that pot roast."

I picked up the matches, and Patty watched me as I brought the beige-colored candles to life. She smiled and looked into my eyes.

Before we sat down I took her in my arms and we experienced our first serious kiss. I felt her breasts pressing into my chest. My heart was pounding. We pulled apart. Her mouth was moist. Her lipstick was smeared. She blotted her mouth with a tissue from her denim skirt pocket. She smiled. I felt weak all over.

I pulled the captain chair out from my used oak table and seated her. I sat down and we gazed at each other. The steaming pot roast awaited us. We were quiet during supper. The candles flickered and her green eyes sparkled. We didn't discuss her failed marriage or mine either. I think she liked the dinner. Every time I looked at her, the smile was there. She chewed her food with elegance. I had to admit the meal was very good. I try to stay away from the word *excellent* I think someone else should offer that description. Patty had two helpings of everything. The dessert was rice pudding. I had chilled it in the refrigerator with the whipped cream. The coffee was hot and full flavored.

"Did you enjoy your meal?" I asked.

"I loved it, Jason."

"Patty, I loved having you here to share it with me."

She smiled. "And, I enjoyed being here," she said.

We did the dishes together. We had enough pot roast left over for another dinner. Patty and I went into the living room and sat together on the couch. We talked about everything. At about 9:30 p.m. she said, "Jason, thank you for the wonderful supper. I have to work in the morning and I'd better call it a night," she said reluctantly.

"I understand."

"Will you be in the diner tomorrow?"

"I may be. I'm not certain of my plans at this time," I said, not wanting to make a commitment.

I walked over to her and put my arms around her and gave her a long kiss. After, she looked into my eyes and I could tell that she wanted to know me better. I walked out to her Jeep. She had been awarded it in her divorce proceedings. It was in good shape. A local mechanic took care of it. We embraced again. Ruben gave a short bark. I don't know if he approved or disapproved, but I knew I liked it.

She climbed in and the engine started without hesitation. She smiled at me and whispered, "Thank you, Sherlock."

I watched her turn around and drive away. It was 9:45 p.m. I went over to the run and let Ruben out. He made a dash for the woods. When he returned I freshened his water and put food in the dish.

"You're a good boy." I patted him gently on the back.

All of a sudden Ruben started to bark fiercely. I looked around and I could see a huge black bear had come onto my property. The bear was now standing looking in my direction. For a moment the scene was intense! Then the bear disappeared into the woods. I was relieved.

"Quiet down, Ruben. He's gone." I told him reassuringly.

I went to bed. I couldn't sleep. I thought about Patty. I reached over, picked up the receiver, and dialed her home number. After the fourth ring the answering machine went on. Patty's voice was soft.

"You have reached Patty. Leave a message after the beep."

"It's me, Jason. You're probably sleeping. Just wanted to say good-night."

I fell off to sleep and didn't wake up until the alarm went off at 8:30 a.m. I couldn't believe that Patty hadn't called back. I assumed that she must have been sleeping soundly.

The engine was loud and it seemed to be on top of my roof. I quickly looked out and saw the red Stinson seaplane with the white floats flash by. I wondered what the hell Dale was buzzing me for. I went into the kitchen and lit the burner under the teakettle. I thought maybe some instant decaf would wake me up. I didn't feel like a big breakfast, so I put two slices of whole wheat bread into the toaster. Just then the phone rang. I walked over and lifted the receiver.

"Hello," I said sleepily, not having had my coffee yet.

"Jason, how are you? This is Lila. Have you seen Patty?"

"I saw her last night. She was here for supper. Didn't she show up for work?" I asked with concern.

"No, she didn't. I'm worried about her. She was supposed to open the diner at 6:30 a.m."

"I know. She told me. She left here at about 9:40 last night."

"Well, Wilt was in early, so I had him go by her place to check. He came right back and told me that she wasn't home. The garage door was open and her Jeep isn't there. That's not like her, Jason."

"I know, I know. I can't believe it. I'll be right over, Lila."

"I appreciate it, Jason. See ya."

I couldn't believe what I had just learned. Where was she? I almost panicked. The toast was burnt to a crisp. I hurriedly dressed, combed my hair, and splashed some shaving lotion on my face. Ran out to the run and checked Ruben's food and water. Filled the water. His food was all right.

I ran to the Bronco. It started on the first turn of the ignition. I applied the brake and let it idle while I ran to the house and locked the door. It took me about ten minutes to reach John's Diner. The church crowd hadn't arrived yet. I parked next to Wilt's new Dodge pickup. When I entered John's, Wilt was sitting on his two stools at the counter of twelve seats. He looked around. The giant of a man looked worried.

"Jason, I'm glad you're here."

Lila was in the kitchen at the short order grill scrambling five eggs for Wilt. Gracie Mulligan, a relief waitress, had been called in to work. She nodded at me. I nodded back.

"Jason, where do you think Patty is?" Wilt asked me. I could see the worry on his face.

"I don't know, Wilt." I shared his concern.

"I was in here Friday night just before she went off duty. We sat here at the counter and had a cup of coffee together. She was so happy that she was coming over to your place for dinner on Saturday night. She really cares about you, Jason."

"Wilt, I think the world of her, too."

"You don't suppose that no good ex-husband of hers has come up here to harm her, do ya?"

"I have no idea. He is such a drunk. You never know what some fool like that would do. I was wondering that, myself. Wilt, have you got a few minutes after you eat, and we'll check her house out?"

"Good idea, Jason. Be glad to go with ya."

I called the Chief of Police and told him what was going on. He indicated that they would send out a missing person notice over their computer system. The Chief indicated that he would be glad to initiate a search. He said he would call in the Troopers and possibly some D.E.C. people if the need for a wide search became evident. There was a forty-eight-hour time period before the message would be sent.

Wilt gobbled his five eggs down with four slices of Italian toast. He lived to eat. But he was very concerned about Patty. She was popular with all the locals. The customers always treated her with a lot of respect. The nicer she was to the fellows, the bigger the tips. She drew the line when it came to dating. There had been some rumors a couple of locals had dated her. However, there was nothing to substantiate the whispers of the wagging tongues. I couldn't help but wonder why I was the fortunate one.

I thought back to Saturday night. She had raved about the pot roast. There was no sign that she was troubled. I sifted everything through my mind over and over. Did I miss something? I looked at Wilt, who had his red handkerchief out of his back pocket wiping the cold egg off his chin. Wilt's eating habits were different than most people's. He had won many a pie-eating contest throughout the mountains. If Wilt got word of a pie-eating contest, he would show up. Only once did he lose. That was to a Canadian from Dewittville, Quebec. Wilt was at the Malone Fair. The Canadian, a former lumberjack, had entered the contest. He was about the same size as Wilt. The Canadian downed one more pie than Wilt. Wilt took a lot of ribbing about that contest. One thing that resulted from the loss was the fact that the Canadian and Wilt became good friends. The story was that they closed a tavern that night while trading stories about logging and pulping.

"I'm all set, Jason. Let's go."

Wilt drove his Dodge and I followed him in the Bronco south on Route 28. When we got to Patty's place, we pulled into the yard. Harriet Stone was standing on her side porch. Harriet is in her sixties and has been a widow for four years. Her husband had been a logger until he felled a tree that went the wrong way and landed on top of him. Harriet owns the small wooden house that Patty rents from her. I heard a car pull in and I looked around. It was the Chief of Police, Todd Wilson. He got out of the car, looking concerned. After asking Harriet if we could check through the house, he told Wilt to listen to his radio. Todd and I entered the house. Nothing seemed disturbed. Patty's bed was neatly made. There didn't seem to be anything amiss in the house. The Chief asked Harriet if she had heard anything during the evening.

She had not heard anything. I shared the information with the Chief about Patty coming to dinner and the fact that she left about 9:40 p.m. to return home. The Chief advised that he would have his patrols check for Patty's Jeep on the backcountry roads.

Before Chief Wilson left, Wilt told him that he would help in any search for Patty if it came to that. The Chief thanked Wilt.

"Thanks, Todd. Let me know if you develop any information or locate Patty."

"I'll be glad to, Jason."

Todd Wilson was a dedicated policeman and if there was any information to be had concerning Patty, Todd would find it. I was broken up. What had happened to her? I thanked Harriet, and Wilt and I returned to our vehicles.

"Wilt, if you hear anything, call me right away."

"I will. You can count on that, Jason."

Wilt backed his big Dodge out of the driveway and headed north toward Old Forge. I started the Bronco and checked a few of the back roads. I came up with nothing. Patty was nowhere to be seen. She had disappeared and so had her Jeep. I didn't know if she had reached her house last night or met some type of fate between my lane and her house. I was devastated. I called the local Troopers and later called my friend, Lieutenant Roy Garrison, at his headquarters. I was dumbfounded. Roy assured me that all patrols would be alerted in his region.

I returned to my log home. My heart was heavy. Ruben barked just once when I got out of the car. I checked his water and food. He hadn't eaten very much. A chipmunk darted out of his run and under my firewood pile. *Those pesky little creatures can be a pain in the neck*, I thought.

I went inside and checked my answering machine. The red light was flashing. All the calls, seven of them, concerned bounced checks from a local accounting office. I did some paperwork at my desk. I couldn't concentrate. Was she hurt? Was she involved in an accident and pinned in her Jeep? I couldn't ask myself the last question. Did her former husband have something to do with her disappearance? Is he at this moment torturing her? I knew one thing: he was a violent man. I had helped gather the evidence concerning her divorce from Ken Olson. I took pictures of her injured nose as it lay against the left side of her face. When the police arrested him for assault, he had threatened everybody present that evening. Todd, the Chief, made the actual arrest. I assisted Todd, as the club-swinging maniac came charging at us. It was a nightmare. A Trooper also there ended up having his right arm bitten by the wild man. Olson had broken away from Todd and come after me. I caught him with a right cross and he went down. I had been lucky. Olson was a tough guy and thought he was even tougher with the rot-gut whiskey steering his emotions. I remembered when Todd put the cuffs on him, he screamed out, "I'll kill you bastards!" His scream made my spine tingle at the time. Todd had put him in the local lock-up. The next day Todd arraigned him on Assault 2$^{nd}$ degree charges. It ended up reduced to Assault 3$^{rd}$ and the judge gave him a year in the Herkimer County Jail. During that year, Patty obtained her divorce. That was almost two years ago, however, I remember the incident vividly.

I called Dale. He claimed that he just got home.

"What's the idea of buzzing my house this morning? I thought you were coming through the roof. Where have you been? Have you heard about Patty?" I asked hurriedly, hoping he heard the annoyance in my voice.

There was a moment of silence.

"Yeah, I heard. Where do you think she is?"

"I don't have any idea, Dale, but I'm very upset about it."

"I heard she was at your place on Saturday evening for dinner?"

"Who told you?" I asked, annoyed.

"Oh, I heard."

"Dale, will you take me up in the Stinson tomorrow? I'll buy your fuel."

"Yeah, I'll be glad to."

"I appreciate that. Maybe we can check some of the backcountry roads and some of the lakes."

"Sure, buddy. I'll pick you up at 8:00 a.m."

"I'll be ready."

I called Todd at his office. He had nothing new to report. I told him that Dale was going to take me up in his plane and check out the area. Todd agreed. He told me that he was going to get a search party together and check the area around Patty's house, and the adjacent woodlands. He indicated that about two hundred people would be involved in the search. He told me that his telephone had been ringing off the hook with people volunteering.

It made me happy to know that people cared enough to assist law enforcement. Todd told me that he had an extra radio that I could use. He would have one of his officers drop it off to me. I appreciated the gesture. I remembered when I was on the job I had helped Todd with a difficult case concerning a child abuser. Todd never forgot how I had tracked the creep into a boggy area and found the slime hiding in an old abandoned shack under some cardboard. I turned the molester over to him, as it was his case. The parents of the child who was molested deeply appreciated the quick apprehension.

I set the alarm for 6:30 a.m. Ruben was settled for the night. I placed another dish of food in his runway along with extra water. It was difficult to sleep. I rolled and tossed all night, wondering about Patty and what had happened to her. I wasn't in love with her, but I was leaning that way. At one point I heard a scratching on the back portion of the roof. Ruben barked a couple of times. The noise ceased. It must have been a coon. The woods are full of them. I have to be careful about refuse and keep it in a double plastic bag in a large can in the shed at the rear of the home. As the night progressed, I eventually dozed off.

The alarm sounded like it was a long ways off. Finally I came to. I felt exhausted. My first thoughts were of Patty Olson. Was she alive? Was she trapped in her Jeep in a ravine? Where was she?

I threw the covers back and headed for the bathroom. The hot shower felt good. I finished my shower and dressed. I usually did my laundry once a week. My underwear and socks were getting low.

The coffee tasted good. I opened a can of Spam and made up some sandwiches--six altogether. Dale would be hungry around noon. I put two slices of bread into the toaster, and then heard the fire department siren. I knew that Police Chief Wilson was a man of his word. He was ready to form the search party for Patty. I heard several sirens of volunteers responding. The toast was crunchy. But my taste buds didn't seem to appreciate the blackberry jam this morning. I checked on Ruben. He was okay.

Dale still had his lights on when he came into the lane leading to my log home. It was 7:30 a.m. He was half an hour early. I was glad. I locked up the house. This morning I had brought my Smith & Wesson 9 mm just in case. I was an expert shooter with several weapons. None of us knew what was ahead of us. Patty could have been abducted by her crazed ex-husband. We didn't know what we were facing. I possessed a New York State pistol permit. I seldom carried the pistol. It held fourteen hollow point bullets.

"Good morning," said Dale grimly.

"Morning. I brought us some Spam sandwiches."

"I've got a two-quart thermos of hot coffee, Jason."

We pulled into Kirby's Marina. Old man Kirby was filling a five-gallon gas can for a fisherman. The bright red Stinson was still in the water at the small dock. Dale tooted at Kirby and headed for the parking space near his plane. I saw Dale notice that I was packing a sidearm. He didn't say a word. I knew that he knew that I meant business, if I was carrying heat. I couldn't help but wonder about the other day at John's Diner. What was that conversation that Dale and Patty had had by the front door? I could tell by their expressions that they weren't just bidding each other farewell. This bugged me to no end. I figured I'd keep my mouth shut about it and not ask Dale that question. His friendship meant a great deal to me, therefore, I chose not to jeopardize our relationship.

Both of us exited the vehicle. Dale was carrying a backpack, which contained the thermos of coffee. I had the sandwiches in a plastic bag. Dale always kept his plane fueled and ready for take-off. Sometimes he had to wait to get near the pump, and he didn't like the waiting part. Dale gave the Stinson a close cursory check. We climbed aboard.

The propeller responded to the engagement of the ignition switch. The 245-horsepower Lycoming engine didn't sputter on starting. Dale warmed up the engine at dockside. I could see old man Kirby talking with the fisherman. They watched us as Dale eased the plane away from the dock and into deeper water. I looked out and saw the white spray of Fourth Lake as the floats cut through the murky water. Later in the day the lake would be a brilliant blue. We were nearing the center of the lake when Dale turned the nose of the red Stinson towards Inlet. He powered the engine to a peak pitch, and the plane moved ahead, gaining speed, about three hundred feet over the steeple of the Inlet Church. Dale banked the big seaplane to the right and headed back toward Old Forge. I had been on a search with Dale one other time when a hunter became lost in the Moose River Plains region. At that time he began in a tight circle and broadened the circle to cover the search area. The search had been successful. The hunter from New York City was found at the bottom of a ravine with a broken leg.

I took the radio out of my jacket pocket and called the Town Police Chief. After three attempts I heard the voice of Todd Wilson.

"Wilson here. Go ahead with your transmission."

"Chief, you're coming in loud and clear."

"Jason, tell Dale to start at Patty's house and fly through those valleys over there."

"Dale's got the message, Chief, and will comply."

"Okay. Let me know if you fellows have any sightings of her Jeep or her. We have over two hundred volunteers. The Troopers are bringing in their bloodhounds. We were able to get some scent from one of Patty's jackets. Fire Chief Thomas is also involved with the search. Five forest rangers are in the group and will act as leaders. They know the region very well. Good luck, guys."

"We'll let you know right away, Chief, if we see anything."

Dale was a good pilot. He circled the area. We noted there were many fallen trees from past blowdowns. This timber would eventually go back to the land. It made me think of how vulnerable one can be when Mother Nature rears her head. You feel humble. We checked the area closely, and after three hours had come up with nothing. There had been a little radio traffic on the ground, but other than that it had been quiet. At about 12:30 p.m. Dale set the Stinson down on Fourth Lake and headed the plane toward Kirby's for fuel. I got my credit card out. Dale brought the plane in as close to the fuel pump as possible. He cut the engine. Kirby was standing on the main dock, with a smirk on his face. He fastened a line to the plane.

Dale and I climbed out and onto the dock. Kirby spoke first.

"Did you see anything, Dale? I just heard about that waitress down at John's Diner being missing."

"That's correct, Kirby."

"Need fuel, huh?"

"Fill it up," Dale requested.

Kirby didn't speak to me. He ignored me completely. Just looking at that miserable face made me sick. Kirby placed the nozzle in the tank. The red Stinson glistened in the sunlight. I had to admit this plane was a beauty. Dale worshiped his prized possession. As I watched Dale check the plane over, I still wondered what connection, if any, he had with my friend, Patty Olson. I couldn't bring myself to ask him, at this time and place, but I wouldn't forget the observation I had made at John's Diner.

"Jason, before we go upstairs let's break out those Spam sandwiches. I'll get the coffee," Dale suggested.

"Grab that plastic bag behind the seat, Dale. The sandwiches are in there."

I watched Dale climb into the Stinson. It took him only a minute. Kirby had a picnic table set up down by the waterfront. I walked toward the table. I could see that Kirby was watching our every move. What a son-of-a-gun he was! I sat down, and Dale, wearing his aviator sunglasses, approached the table. He put the bag and thermos down. In a few seconds we were munching down the Spam sandwiches. I remembered that in the Marine Corps, Spam was served at times to back up the chow line, when the cooks ran out of bacon. Spam was not one of my favorites, but I had it on hand and it was convenient. I was hungry and anything would taste good about now. I observed Dale. He was chewing away and looking at a map at the same time.

"Dale, we checked the region in the vicinity of Patty's residence. Do you think we should check the Moose River Road area? There's about a thirteen-mile stretch toward Port Leyden." I queried.

"Yeah, I was thinking about that. Also, the area around Stillwater should be included."

"Right."

I observed Dale closely. He seemed to be as worried as I was about Patty being missing. My mind raced back to Saturday and the wonderful time we had had at my home. Patty hadn't seemed depressed. She was lighthearted and full of fun. What happened after she left the lane from my place? She had made a right turn out of the lane and headed toward Old Forge. I'd listened to her motor until it went out of my hearing range. What happened to her? I should have followed her home. Did she meet with foul play? My heart continued to be sad.

Before we took off, I told Dale that I was going to call Chief Wilson. I walked over to Kirby's outside public telephone. I didn't know whether or not Todd would be in. The quarter clanged as it fell into the coin-box. The phone rang three times and Todd answered.

"Hello, Chief. Jason Black here."

"Jason, thanks for calling."

"Dale and I just had a couple of sandwiches here at Kirby's and we're about to take off, but I wanted to check with you on any progress you've made."

"We haven't located Patty or her Jeep. We have, as I speak, about two hundred and twenty searchers in the area. They are doing a clean sweep of everything. Some horse people have arrived and the parking lots are full of horse trailers. There will be about fifty people on horseback beating the bushes. I'm in the process of having flyers printed with a picture of Patty and her Jeep. Harriet Stone, her neighbor, offered to let us take the photos."

"Good, I'm glad to hear that. By the way, Todd, has anyone contacted the South Carolina authorities to run a check on Kenneth Olson?"

"Yes, that's been done, Jason. I haven't heard from them yet. When the flyers come out they are going to be hand-carried throughout the area to business places and any areas that the public gathers. Believe me, Jason, we're not leaving a stone unturned. The Troopers are bringing in a mobile command post, bloodhounds and extra radios. If Patty is in our region, we'll find her. Furthermore, some of the Trooper scuba divers are coming to the area as well as volunteer divers from the fire departments. The medical center has been alerted, too. I've had plenty of heat from the press, TV and radio stations. I told them that when we have something, we'll share it with them, and not till something develops."

"You're doing a great job, Todd. You must be getting tired. Oh, by the way, has anyone notified her family as yet?"

"Harriet and Lila are trying to get me her family's addresses.

Everybody is tired, but we've got to keep searching."

"You got that right. Thank you for the information. We haven't come up with anything yet. We've seen a lot of deer and spotted a couple of moose down by the river. We flew over a couple of people near the Moose River road. They weren't wearing much, Chief. Enjoying nature, I guess."

"Jason, I know what you mean. Well, good luck on your air search. I'll let you fellas know if anything substantial develops. Good-bye."

"Good-bye, Chief."

I hung up the receiver and found myself thinking about Patty. Did the evil of society meet her after she left the lane to my place? I looked to my right and saw Kirby watching me walk back to Dale and the plane. I wondered what that son-of-a-gun was thinking. *Anyone that would steal a part off from a customer's out-board motor and sell it to some one else should feel real proud.* I glared back at him.

Dale started the plane as soon as I climbed aboard. He had untied the mooring line. The lake had become a little choppy as a breeze blew in from the north. Dale put the power to it as we climbed slowly over Inlet. We spent the afternoon dipping down along the mountain lakes: Kayuta, Woodhull, Brantingham, Limekiln, the Fulton Chain, Raquette, Cedar, and Indian. We flew over several search parties that were on foot and horseback. I had the radio on and heard the command post send out instructions to roving Trooper patrols. Apparently telephone calls had come in with bits of information. From the transmissions we heard, the leads developed no useful information. Dale and I said very little to each other. My head was aching from holding the binoculars so tight against my eyes. Both of us were tired. I knew one thing: Dale was one hell of a pilot. He brought us close to the water several times. I could have reached out and touched a few tree tops, too. It was close to 5:15 p.m. when Dale set the Stinson down right in front of Kirby's. The fuel gauge was nearing empty.

"Dale, this is one powerful engine you have."

"I've put a lot of time and money into this engine, so it better work right."

We drove directly to the command post and met with Todd and some Troopers. There had been no useful information that would lead to the location of Patty or her Jeep. Everyone looked sad and tired. No information had been received from the South Carolina authorities. Before Dale dropped me off at my house, we stopped at John's Diner. Lila told us how packed the diner was during the day. Many locals had stopped by to offer their comments regarding Patty. Several of them had made sandwiches and hot coffee for the search teams. The fire department had set up a large tent near the command post, and cooks were busy preparing additional food for the volunteers in the search groups. Lila's husband John had been at the search sites delivering sandwiches and had returned to wait on customers.

"What can I do for you?" John asked.

"You look tired, John."

"I am. I was up all night," he replied.

Dale and I ordered liver and onions with mashed potatoes and green beans. We were both famished. Dale seemed restless. It wasn't like him to show any emotion. He was usually cool and collected. *Maybe he's just tired*, I thought.

Some of the customers nodded as they passed our table. They all seemed concerned. Many of them had participated in the initial search parties. My mind strained in wonderment. Where was she? Who or what would ever want to harm her? Dale must have caught a piece of liver in his throat. I jumped up and slapped him on the back. He gagged and then the blockage cleared.

"That's the first time I ever did that," Dale said shakily.

"It can happen to any of us," I replied.

"You didn't have to slap me so hard, Jason," he said, curtly.

"Sorry, but I wanted it to come loose."

"It did." He rubbed his throat.

We said our farewells and left the diner. Dale was still choking a little. I had him drop me off on Route 28 at the beginning of the lane to my cabin.

"See you tomorrow, Dale. If you hear anything, give me a call. I'm going to contact the Chief before I go to bed."

"Ok, Jason."

I exited his vehicle and watched him go down Route 28. He turned around and went back towards Old Forge, giving me a toot on the horn as he passed. Dale lived alone in an older Victorian house.

It was white in color. He painted it every other year whether it needed it or not. He was conservative with his money and politics. I knew that he had spent a great deal of money on his plane. He loved the Stinson. The war years had changed his personality. Prior to the war he had been a jovial person, cracking jokes continually. He didn't do that any more. He had a good mind and was good with his fists. He had done some boxing in the Marine Corps.

My eyes searched the shoulder of Route 28. I walked toward my cabin, which was hidden in the trees. A big six-point buck jumped across the lane. His tail flashed as he sped through the forest. I rounded a slight curve in the lane and noted that Charlie Perkins was sitting in his Chevrolet pickup. Ruben was watching Charlie's truck. He barked three times when he saw me. Charlie saw me, too, and climbed out of the driver's side.

"Jason. How are you?" he asked.

"Not the best, Charlie."

"I heard about the bad news."

"I'm really upset, Charlie, and everybody else is, too."

"I've got to tell you something. I just returned from Vermont and when I parked the rig I came right over here to see you."

"What have you got?"

"Saturday night, about 9:45 p.m., I was heading north toward Inlet with a heavy load of logs. I was going slow up that hill between town and your place. I had my lights on high beam. I saw Patty's Jeep parked just off the road on the shoulder headed toward Old Forge. There was a Suburban, a Chevy or a GMC, parked on the east shoulder with the hood up. I saw Patty near the left-hand corner of the vehicle and two fellows that looked a little seedy talking with her. They didn't even look up at me. The plate on that Suburban wasn't a New York plate. I don't know what the numbers or letters were on the plate. I wasn't concerned. It appeared she was offering to help the fellows. I didn't see anybody at the Police Department, so I thought I'd let you know. It was all over the diner that she was having supper with you that night."

"That's great to hear. Yes, she did have supper with me, but she left about 9:40 or 9:45 p.m. That would have had to be about that time. She had to leave earlier than I wanted her to, because she was supposed to open up the diner at 6:30 a.m. Sunday morning." I was adamant in my response.

"Will you let the Chief know, Jason?"

"Yes, I will. I'll tell the Chief that you'll give him a statement concerning what you saw. By the way, can you tell me what these guys looked like?"

"I really can't tell too much. They were seedy and looked kind of rough. I really didn't get a good look at their faces. Maybe they were legitimate or maybe they didn't have any car trouble at all. It could have been a scam."

"Charlie, you're probably right on the money. Do you know what color the Suburban was? It's important!"

"It was dark-colored and could have been a late 1980 model. I can't tell you anything else. If I had known they were up to no good or were endangering Patty, I would have pulled over to help her. I thought she knew them from the diner."

"I know you would, Charlie. I should have followed her home, damn it!"

"You never know who's on the road today. We've got more creeps running around this country."

"Yes, you're right." I agreed.

I thanked Charlie. He went over with me to check on Ruben. Charlie had been to my cabin before and Ruben knew him. He gave my dog a big hug and petted his nose. Ruben's ears pointed to the heavens above. Charlie got back in his pickup and slowly left the driveway. Knowing Charlie as I did, I could tell it was bothering him about not stopping to see if Patty was all right or not.

I called Todd right away with the information. He indicated that he would contact Charlie and take a formal statement from him. Todd was pleased with this new development. He assured me that he would send an added-information to APB (All Points Bulletin). The Chief informed me that he would continue the search in the immediate locality for about two or three days. He felt that the Jeep had to be somewhere in the vicinity. I felt that way, too, I couldn't help wonder who those two men were that Charlie had seen on Saturday night. I knew that Charlie would have stopped the big rig if he had thought for one second that Patty was in need of assistance or if she had been in

danger, but things looked normal--a motorist assisting another motorist-
-so he had continued on.

# CHAPTER FIVE

Everyone in Old Forge knew that Patty had been to my cabin for supper. The news travels fast in a small town. Of course, I'm certain that some people were wondering about our age difference. I didn't have marriage on my mind at all. I thought a great deal of Patty. She had had a difficult marriage with Olson. He used her as a punching bag when he was intoxicated, which was most of the time. He stole money out of her tips that she was saving for rent and other bills. Olson had even threatened Patty's attorney and me. I had gathered some good evidence against Olson and had turned it over to her lawyer.

Todd knew what Olson was like. My tires had been sliced on my Bronco, and one of the ladies in town had seen Olson commit this act of criminal mischief. She had given the Chief a statement, which allowed Todd to obtain a warrant from a local magistrate. The arrest hadn't gone smoothly. Olson had come at Todd with a machete sword, swinging it wildly. Todd had ducked and given Olson a hard rap in the kidneys with his night stick. The sword had fallen out of Olson's hand and skidded across the kitchen floor. Olson had lain on the floor moaning, like a baby. The Chief had had to hold him in the lock-up until he sobered up.

The next day at Olson's arraignment, he had screamed out, "There is no justice in this country." He had lurched toward the Judge. Having received his plea of guilty before the outburst, the Judge had calmly stated, "I'm sentencing you to ten months in the Herkimer County Jail." Todd and a court attendant had had to restrain Olson.

The defendant, while en route to the county jail, had kicked the side window out of the police car.

I couldn't help but wonder if Olson had returned to Old Forge and these peaceful mountains to again raise havoc in our community. I knew one thing for certain: our Chief of Police would not put up with that reckless attitude and behavior again.

I called the command post and was fortunate to catch the Chief before he left for the evening. He informed me that the Troopers would maintain the post for a few more days. In addition, Troopers would double their patrols and efforts to see if they could develop more leads regarding Patty and the Jeep and information about two men in a dark-colored Suburban.

I thanked Todd for his untiring efforts relative to Patty. I knew that he hadn't been able to sleep for seventy-two hours.

"Jason, I called the South Carolina authorities just ten minutes ago. I talked with a Sergeant Melvin Crast. He informed me Kenneth Olson is confined to the Morey County Jail and has been for two months."

My heart sank. If Olson didn't have Patty, who did? "Chief, that eliminates him then."

"Yes, it does."

I checked on Ruben and turned him loose. He ran into the woods and soon returned. I hadn't been able to give him much attention lately. I filled his food and water dishes, then sat down at the kitchen table. Ruben pushed his big head against my knee. His long ears were not pointing up to the heavens. He was relaxed and loved to be near his master. I toyed with the idea of taking him to the Eagle Bay Dog Kennel for a week or so. At least there he would be taken for walks. The telephone rang. It was Todd.

"Jason, I know it's late, but I just got off the telephone with Dale Rush. He asked me if he should keep searching with his plane. I told him to try one more day. He'll stop by and pick you up in the morning if you're free. Also, I informed Dale that the Troopers will have a helicopter in the region tomorrow sometime."

"Glad you called, Chief. I have nothing going on but this. Patty is either dead or in terrible trouble. She's apparently been abducted by those two men."

"It would appear that she has been, Jason. All the information has been entered into the national computer system. Her description, Jeep, registration and vehicle identification numbers and the information concerning two males operating a dark-colored Suburban, possibly a Chevy or a GMC. In addition I have talked with the Feds and they have alerted their field offices throughout the country. U.S. Customs have been notified, too. If they move across our borders we'll get a hit on it. In the meantime we'll just have to play the waiting game. I know it is rough on everybody. Patty doesn't have any relatives that we know of living in the Old Forge area."

I listened intently to what the Chief had to say, becoming increasingly frustrated.

I told him, "During her divorce I worked very close with her attorney, Nelson Marsh, and he informed me that Patty's parents, Thomas and Helen James, were killed ten years ago, when their Volkswagon was run over by a cement truck in Kentucky. The estate was very small. They were renters. Patty received about fifteen hundred dollars after the funeral expenses were paid. Patty has five brothers. They live all over the country. This information is confidential and I'd appreciate if it would stay that way."

"Certainly. Jason, if the three of them are together, if she is alive, they could be anyplace. We've got to see if we can come up with the Jeep. I don't think they'll be driving two vehicles. It would be too conspicuous."

"You're right. You've got a point there. Well, Chief, I'd better get some shut-eye. The morning will be here before you know it."

"Good luck tomorrow, and tell Dale that maybe we can help out with some of the fuel expense. Good-night."

"Good-night, Chief."

# CHAPTER SIX

*In an old abandoned cabin in the deep woods near Santa Clara, New York, are two desperate men. They are Jewell Norris and Ted Clovis. Both are hardened criminals, who recently escaped from a maximum-security prison in Ohio. They are sitting at a table, playing cards. Both are drinking warm beer they have stolen from a small grocery store in western New York. On the table are a hunting knife and a .45 caliber automatic pistol.*

*The cabin is old and the roof has holes in it. Its one door is hanging from one hinge. The only light is from an oil lamp that has a dirty shade. Shadows move in strange motions on the walls as the men deal each other their cards, taking time out to suck on the cans of warm beer. Both are in their forties and stand about six feet tall. Their arms are covered with tattoos of sea serpents and words of love and hate. Their trousers are loose-fitting, they belonged to a much heavier person. Paint stains the material. They are wearing T-shirts that are dirty and smell of perspiration. These men have been serving twenty-five years to life for murder.*

*In a dark corner of the cabin, lying on a cot, is Patty Olson. Her hands are bound with heavy twine. A man's leather belt is wrapped around her ankles. She looks frightened. Her dirty face shows traces where tears have flowed down her cheeks. She is still and hungry. Afraid to agitate the escaped convicts, she remains mute. Her eyes constantly move, seeking a means to escape from their control. It appears to be hopeless. Her mind goes back in time to Old Forge and John's Diner, and how she was supposed to open at 6:30 a.m. on that Sunday morning. Most of all she longs for her newly found friend, Jason Black, a private detective, who runs down check passers and missing children and helps cats out of trees. She remembers the flavor of that well-seasoned pot roast on that Saturday evening. She ponders and asks herself why she stopped to assist two men standing by a dark-colored Suburban with the hood up.*

*She thinks about the misery of her former marriage and how her ex-husband used to beat her when he staggered in from a drinking binge. Now here she is in a situation that has her frightened and worried. She overheard the men talking while she was tied up in the rear of the Suburban, traveling through the night. One of them had written an ex-convict about an old cabin near Santa Clara that he used to own. The ex-convict had written back and had described how to locate the cabin in the woods. They did not mention what the ex-convict's name was. The Suburban, she thinks, is a 1982 GMC, the escapees stole it near Salem, Ohio. She wonders if these men hurt anyone during the theft. The men have not hurt her physically, but Jewell has told her in uncertain words, "Girly, if you make a move to escape, you're all done. Do ya understand what I mean by 'done', do ya?"*

*Patty remembers shaking her head up and down in an understanding gesture. She couldn't speak because she was gagged at the time. Patty was frightened. Jewell had aimed the .45 at her head and counted to ten and pulled the trigger. The gun clicked. Jewell laughed and sucked on his warm beer. His eyes were wild. While Jewell was tormenting Patty, Clovis looked on with an evil grin and his eyes glared from their sockets. Patty knows these are dangerous men.*

# CHAPTER SEVEN

Dale tooted his horn in front of my log home at 8:15 a.m. sharp. Ruben let out his two distinct barks. His tail was wagging like a pendulum on a grandfather's clock. I filled his water dish and poured some dog food into his red dish. I could see that Ruben had begun salivating as his powerful jaw prepared for action. He always sticks his nose deep into the dish before the first bite. I petted his back.

"Good boy, Ruben."

I closed the fence gate to his runway and double-checked the side door, which I had locked.

"Morning, Jason." He looked grim and tired.

"Good morning, Dale.

We rode in silence to Kirby's Marina. My mind was with Patty, wherever she was. I had looked in the mirror when I got up this morning. The strain was beginning to tell on my face and the bags under my eyes could be used for spare change. I hadn't slept a truly deep sleep since Patty had disappeared.

A raccoon ran from behind some storm fencing as we entered the long driveway to the marina. Dale lay on the horn.

"Darn those coons, Jason," he said.

"A lot of them are around," I responded.

The red Stinson, Dale's first love, was moving gently in the water at dockside. The red and white stood out. I had to admit it was an eye-catching seaplane, one of several that flew around the Fulton Chain, but the only one with gull-wings. Dale checked the plane very closely before boarding. I had brought my small backpack containing the binoculars. Dale had his two-quart thermos filled with iced tea.

I noticed that Kirby wasn't around this morning. Dale hit the ignition switch and the propeller turned over, slowly at first and then winding to a high pitch. The lake seemed choppy. A breeze was coming from the north. Dale had had radio contact with the roving patrols still assigned to the search detail. He notified a car to relay a message to the Chief. This was to be our last day of searching by air. I was beginning to get a little depressed. The leads that were coming into the police had not developed any useful information, with the exception of the sighting of Patty and the two men by the logger on that Saturday evening.

"Make sure your belt is tight, Jason. It's a little rough," Dale advised.

"Will do," I said, checking my seat belt.

Searching by air is tiring. Your eyes are continually darting from place to place looking for two men and a woman in a backcountry area. The strain is continuous. When you come up with nothing, depression can set in. Is she still alive? Everybody in town who knew her wondered the same thing.

Dale didn't have much to say. He flew low over the tiny lakes and valleys of the area. Nature's beauty lay out below us. You could see for miles today. We spotted a bull moose and his cow in the Indian Lake region. We flew low over them. Dale concentrated on his search on old abandoned camps. We spotted a dark old station wagon behind one camp. We circled three or four times. The wheels had been removed from it. It appeared to be of the early 1950's vintage, possibly a Chrysler product.

The State helicopters were searching in other areas of the Adirondacks. There was no information that would lead one to believe that the captors and their victim were actually in the park or outside the park. I thought, *Who are these two men with an out of state plate on their vehicle? Are they drifters? Could they be criminals?* I feared the worst and so did everyone else. I would call Todd tonight and get an update on the search.

"Jason, do you have any objection if we set down at Long Lake for a bit of lunch?" Dale asked.

"Good idea," I responded. "We can use a good hot lunch."

We had just finished checking out Blue Mountain Lake. In the recesses of my mind I couldn't help but wonder about the period of the 1920's when the area was visited heavily by the well-to-do people of our society. I wondered what it would have been like to talk with people like William Durant and other people of those times. Many beautiful Adirondack Camps were built in that era. Dale circled once over the Blue Mountain Museum.

"Someday my plane will be displayed there," he said.

"Dale, that would be something, wouldn't it?"

"Jason, when I'm too old to fly anymore. That's what I intend to do with it. Put it on display for all the people to see and wonder about what we were like."

"Sounds good to me, Dale." A movement caught my eye. "Look at that hawk over there!"

"He's after something, Jason."

"That's for sure."

Dale set the Stinson down on Long Lake. The floats cut through the water, spraying diamonds into the air. He cut the engine about ten feet from the dock. The plane gently touched the rubber bumpers. Dale exited the plane and fastened a mooring line. Gertie's was directly across the street. We were both famished.

# CHAPTER EIGHT

*Pictures of Patty Olsen were posted throughout the eastern section of the United States. You couldn't go into any business establishment or town hall without seeing her face. The police agencies had been alerted on a large scale. Television stations had shown her face to a large audience across the region. Attempts had been made to locate her five brothers. Trooper patrols both on the land and in the air were watching for her and the two men in a dark-colored Suburban.*

*One such person had listened to the media announcements. Like many in the area around Old Forge, Jack Falsey knew Patty well. Jack was in his mid-fifties and frequented John's Diner. Patty liked Jack, too, she referred to him as Uncle Jack. Falsey's Plumbing was a well known service company throughout the southern Adirondacks. Falsey was a good friend of Jason Black. It was two in the afternoon when Jack pulled his bright red truck into the driveway of a remote camp off Rondaxe Road. Jack was there for the purpose of turning off the waterworks for Timothy Burr, a retired airlines pilot from Kentucky, who was a five-year summer resident in the area. The camp was a large one. It had five bathrooms. Jack knew the camp well. He had replaced each bathroom with new fixtures, sinks, tubs and toilets. Tim Burr wouldn't have anyone else do his work.*

*Jack noticed that something was amiss. The door of the three-car garage appeared to be ajar. Jack had dropped some plumbing fixtures off and knew that he had closed the garage door. The delivery had been made three weeks ago. Jack verified that when he quickly checked his order book. Before Jack got out of his truck, he looked around. Nothing else seemed out of order. Like many business people who work in the remote areas of the Adirondacks, Jack carries an H & R.22 Caliber pistol. He has a carry permit. One time Jack was almost bitten by a rabid coon and from that day on he hasn't been without an instrument of self-protection.*

*He exited his truck and made his way carefully to the weather-beaten garage door. Jack didn't know what to expect. He knew that with the closing of the landfills, bears had been on the prowl looking for food. Jack's mind raced. He thought, The wind didn't do this. The door was heavy. It had been closed when he had visited the Burr property three weeks previous. Jack flicked on his seven-cell flashlight and entered the darkened garage. He was startled.*

*"Oh! My God!" he muttered sharply.*

*Jack's stomach started to get butterflies. He felt a chill go up his back. Flight and fright almost set in. The red Jeep belonging to Patty Olson was no longer missing. Here it was in front of Jack inside Tim Burr's garage. Jack didn't look any further. He ran back to his truck, grabbed his cell phone, and called Chief of Police Todd Wilson.*

*"Chief, Patty Olson's Jeep is in Tim Burr's garage on Rondaxe Road."*

*"I'll be there in ten minutes, Jack. Be careful!" Todd said.*

*"I'll wait in my truck for you," Jack responded excitedly.*

# CHAPTER NINE

Dale and I had finished our lunch at Gertie's and had just taken off from Long Lake. We had climbed to 2800 feet and were over Blue Mountain deciding whether to search the Indian Lake region for a third time. Dale was just about to make a turn to the southeast when his radio crackled.

"Dale Rush, Stinson November 1286 Delta Romeo. If you can hear me, meet me at Kirby's as soon as possible. This is Chief Wilson."

"This is Stinson 1286 Delta Romeo. I read you loud and clear, Chief," responded Dale.

"What can this be about? It must be important or he would have told us over the radio," Dale said turning to Jason.

"It must be," Jason answered. My mind started racing with anticipation.

Dale gave his Stinson more throttle, and soon Fourth Lake was below us. The floats on the Stinson cut through the water like a chainsaw ripping a six-by-ten piece of lumber. The Lycoming engine never missed a beat. Dale cut the engine and our mooring line was soon secured. Todd was waiting for us.

"I've got some good news for you fellas. The Jeep has been located."

"Where?" I flashed back.

"It's at the Burr place on Rondaxe Road. I don't know if Patty's in the Jeep or not. Jack Falsey checked a slightly open garage door on the property and found it. He called me over his cell phone. He's waiting for us at the scene."

"Dale, did you hear that?"

"Yes, I did. Great!"

Dale secured the door on the plane and joined us at the car. Kirby was standing in the doorway of his office straining to hear our every word. The three of us climbed into Todd's patrol car. As the car lurched ahead, some loose gravel hit the patrol car's frame. We drove onto Route 28, and Todd didn't waste any time reaching our destination. Jack Falsey was waiting for us in his truck.

"Hi, Chief, Jason and Dale. About time you got here, Chief. I've got many calls today," he said loudly, sounding perturbed.

"Sorry, Jack, but I wanted Jason and Dale to be in on this. As you probably know, they have been searching high and low for the Jeep and Patty."

"Chief, I didn't go near the Jeep. As soon as I spotted it I called you. I've got another appointment on Rondaxe Road. Will you need me?"

"You go ahead and take care of your work, Jack. I'll have to get a sworn statement from you later about the observations you made. I'll contact you in a day or so."

"Thanks, Chief."

"Jack, thanks for all your help on this," I said. "You know it's important."

"Yes, Jason," Jack responded.

"Take care, Jack," added Dale.

"Fellas, I called for an evidence team and they should be here any minute."

I was getting anxious, but I knew the Chief was following the correct procedure. We didn't know whether Patty was in the Jeep or not. We'd soon find out. The evidence team pulled into the yard, and the first thing they did was to put up lines designating the area as a crime scene. When this was done, Chief Wilson and the evidence team entered the garage and carefully approached the Jeep, looking for any type of evidence that might be present.

Dale and I soon learned that Patty was not in the Jeep, nor was she in the area. The Chief had contacted several searchers still on the detail, and they swept the entire area without gathering any further information that would lead to her whereabouts.

Chief Wilson did confide in me. He indicated that the evidence technician found two different latent prints on the door handle of the Jeep. The interior was clean except for three strands of hair. Two were blond and the third was black. The evidence technicians secured the hair and the latent prints. In addition, under the driver's seat, a small southwestern-style ring was found, turquoise in color and a size 8. This ring was placed in a plastic container and secured by the technician.

I meditated to myself: *Whoever abducted Patty must have decided the Jeep should be hidden from any potential law enforcement agency.* I looked at Dale and said, "I think Patty is still alive. Maybe they plan on using her as a hostage. I've got a hunch they are bad people, Dale."

"They're bastards, Jason. I'd like to get my hands on them for a few minutes."

"So would I," I shot back.

It took several hours to process the Jeep. When the job was completed, Chief Wilson had it impounded and secured it in a safe place at his station. I noticed that Todd looked tired, like all of us. Just about everybody in the search party knew Patty and thought of her as part of their family.

Dale and I watched the two evidence technicians. Both were in their mid-thirties. I couldn't help but think back to the time I was thirty-five. In those days I felt that I could take on the world. Boy! How things change. The evidence people packed up their kits and waved goodbye to us.

"Jason, I'll drop you and Dale off at Kirby's," the Chief said.

"That will be good, Chief," I replied.

On the way to Kirby's marina no one said anything. All three of us were wondering about Patty and her safety. Where was she? Who had abducted her? The Chief dropped us off at the entrance to Kirby's and sped off toward Old Forge. I hoped that Ruben was all right and had enough food and water. Dale and I walked to the plane. I had left the borrowed binoculars behind the seat. Dale picked up his thermos.

"It's getting late, Jason. Do you want to go to John's for a little supper?" Dale asked.

"No, just drop me off at home. I'm tired. We had a long day. Dale, where in the hell is Patty and who are those two guys that abducted her?"

"I wish I knew, Jason, I wish I knew."

Dale let me off at the entrance to my log home. I could hear Ruben barking. He knew his master was home. A chipmunk darted out under a downed tree and went into a brush pile. *Those little pests*, I thought. Ruben was jumping up against his fenced runway. There was little food in his dish and the water was a third full. I opened the runway door. Ruben was all over me. What a strong dog I've got!

"Settle down, Ruben." I spoke sharply to him.

I entered my log home and went directly to my combination den and office. The answering machine was flashing. I went back to the kitchen and turned the stove on under the teakettle. The aroma of coffee soon filled my nostrils. With a mug of hot coffee, I returned to my desk and started listening to calls. The majority were regarding checks that had been returned to the business people, marked "insufficient funds." The messages indicated that the checks were being mailed to me for either collection or appropriate criminal action.

The call I made was to Chief Todd Wilson. We talked for half-an-hour. Todd brought me up to date. The main search had ended in the Old Forge area. Patrols were still checking the remote areas for any sign of the Suburban containing the two strangers and Patty. He went on to say that photos and a description of Patty had been sent all over the country. Newspapers, radio and television included information about her alleged abduction. Telephone numbers were provided for any information that the general public might obtain. I thanked the Chief for the information. He assured me that he would notify me if anything developed.

One of the calls came from the Mountain Bank. It pertained to the Vincent estate. The property had recently been taken over by the bank. Information had been received that illegal logging operations were taking place. They asked me to conduct a check of the property to establish this fact. The bank had not called the police, as they always try to avoid taking such firm action. I put that job on my list for the next day.

I looked in the refrigerator and noticed that I needed to do some grocery shopping. I took a couple of pork chops out of the freezer, thawed them in my microwave, and peeled some potatoes, along with a couple of onions. There was just enough lettuce for a green salad. While the potatoes were cooking, I slipped out to Ruben's runway and turned him loose. He jumped on me and then sped off to the woods. In about ten minutes he returned, and not alone. He was in pursuit of a chipmunk. Ruben lost the race when the chippy ran up a tree. The dog barked sharply. I opened the gate to the runway and he entered, heading straight to his water dish.

The pork chops were nice and brown. I had made some gravy from scratch and opened a can of spicy applesauce. The cord on my mixer was frayed, so I had to mash the potatoes by hand. The onions were tender, but not overcooked. The table was set. I couldn't get Patty out of my mind. Where was she at this moment? I was hungry, but the thought of her being either dead or held captive churned my guts to a point of discomfort. I opened a bottle of Chardonnay wine that I had chilling in the refrigerator. I enjoyed my culinary efforts and finished off the wine to the last drop. I seldom ever had anything to drink, but I had to relax a little. The strain of not knowing what had happened to Patty upset me.

I was restless all night and woke up about every hour. One time I heard a racket on the rear roof. Ruben let out a series of barks. We were being visited by the coon that frequented the area. I was thinking of a hundred ways to rid our roof of those pesky, fur bearing animals. I wondered what I'd look like in a coonskin hat, or what Ruben would do with a coonskin rug for his sleeping area. I fell off to slumber-land again.

I woke up to the phone ringing. I remembered that I'd turned the answering machine off. It was Dale Rush. He said he had received a call from the Chief and that we didn't need to search anymore at this time. He indicated that two helicopters from the Troopers would be searching the region. I thanked Dale.

The hot shower gave me new life. A nick on the left side of my face stung when I applied the shaving lotion. I guessed I'd better switch to an electric shaver. The old-style straight razor had to be held with a firm grip, and I wasn't thirty anymore.

I dressed casually and looked into the mirror on the way out to the runway, where Ruben was stretching his sturdy legs. The mirror reflected what a tired forty-eight-year-old private investigator looked like, after a twenty-year career in the Troopers. I couldn't help but think about my former wives and the stress they had had to endure being married to a cop who cared about the citizens of his jurisdiction. I thought about the ten years in the elite Bureau of Criminal Investigation. They had ironed many dress shirts for me over the years and supported all that cop stuff that goes along with a career. They were the ones who should have received the commendations and awards, not me. And in their memory I placed all that stuff on the walls of my office/den.

The Bronco started on the first turn of the ignition. I let it warm up a little. It was the beginning of fall, and a chill was in the air this morning. As I sat behind the wheel, I looked over the hood, and before me at the edge of the pines was a beautiful big buck. He looked like a ten-pointer. He stood with his head held high. I eased the Bronco into drive and slowly proceeded toward the buck. He watched me getting closer, and then he was gone into the woods like a flash. I could see Ruben watching from his runway.

I had been neglecting the Post Office for a couple of days. My box was full of letters. The majority of them would be checks taken in from the anxious tourists who didn't have quite enough funds in their accounts. The business folks inside the Blue Line work hard to keep their bills paid. They don't deserve bad checks. I would do my best to recover some of the funds. Of course, the fifteen percent of the recovered amount collected helped me pay my bills. Sometimes I had to burn a tank of gas before I was able to locate the check passer. But usually a gentle to-the-point letter on my convincing stationery would do the trick.

I quickly shuffled through the stack of mail. I nodded to a couple of local people and climbed into the Bronco. I was hungry. I headed for John's Diner. Wilt Chambers and Charlie Perkins were just getting out of their pickup trucks. I pulled in beside Wilt's and caught up with them before they entered the diner. Both of them asked me if I had any new information regarding Patty. I told them that there was nothing new. They both looked concerned. We all were. Patty was the hub of our diner life and she was important to all of us.

"Wilt, do you know who is logging on the Vincent estate?" I asked.

"No, I haven't any idea, Jason."

"How about you, Charlie. Have you any idea who that might be?"

"Nope, Jason, I don't."

I told both of them about the situation. I told them I was going to check it out after breakfast. Both Wilt and Charlie indicated that if they learned anything about logging on the Vincent estate, they'd give me a call. I thanked them both. We entered the diner and they sat at the counter. I grabbed a table in the corner. I was going to look at the morning paper and see what the rest of the world was up to.

"Good morning, Jason. What are you having this morning?" Gracie Mulligan, the waitress, gave me a smile that wasn't Patty's.

"Hello, Gracie. I think I'll have a large orange juice and three scrambled eggs with whole-wheat toast. And, Gracie, a cup of tea instead of that strong coffee."

"Jason, anything new on Patty?" she asked, concerned.

"No, Gracie, nothing new," I answered, dejectedly.

Gracie Mulligan was a hard-working lady. She had put two boys through college at Colgate and she was a mighty proud mother. Her husband died ten years ago and she only had a little insurance money left after the funeral expenses. She and Patty were close friends and would fill in for each other if one had something special to do. They were both well-liked and respected in Old Forge and the surrounding area. Both of them were honest. They did well on their tips. They deserved it. They were excellent waitresses.

"Gracie, those eggs are perfect," I told her.

"I know that you love your eggs, and Lila whipped them up special for you," Gracie said with a big grin.

I finished my breakfast and a second cup of tea. I paid the check and left Gracie a tip of $1.50. *Everything tasted special this morning*, I thought. On the way out of the diner I waved at John and Lila. They were very hard-working people. This town was lucky to have folks like that. Wilt and Charlie were just leaving the parking lot. They both tooted their horns at me. I waved back.

# CHAPTER TEN

*Outside of Santa Clara, down a long winding lane deep in the woods, Jewell Norris and Ted Clovis have untied Patty Olson. Norris has made several trips to the store in St. Regis Falls for groceries. Patty has lost several pounds and looks weak. These two dangerous men watch Patty closely.*

*"Jewell, we've got to move out of this area. If we don't, we may have to deal with the cops," Clovis says.*

*"Yeah! Those freaking cops will be looking for the three of us. We've got to get rid of those Ohio plates. I haven't made up my mind yet about girly here."*

*"Maybe we should turn her loose here in the woods," comments Clovis.*

*"Yeah, that would be one less mouth to feed, but we can't do that. If we meet up with the cops, we'll use her as a hostage."*

*"I'll leave. I'll leave and I won't say anything to the police about you two. I promise!" Patty says excitedly.*

*"That ain't going to happen, girl," remarks Norris.*

*The men, savage as they are, permit Patty to bathe in the nearby creek, while Jewell Norris brandishes the .45 Caliber pistol. They let her use the outdoor toilet, but watch her closely. She is given enough food and water to sustain her mobility. For now it looks as though Patty is in a no-win situation. Deep in the recesses of her mind she is thinking about Jason and what he will do if he finds them. It is this thought that gives her courage to*

81

*go on. She wonders if these men will assault her and kill her afterwards. Inside she is fearful but does not dare show her emotions. She wonders about her friends at the diner. She has to keep her head.*

Nate Jenkins, owner of the small grocery in St. Regis Falls, waits on the man with the tattoos. He notices that this customer appears to be a little nervous. Nate also notices the dark-colored GMC Suburban with Ohio plates. Nate, being a suspicious man all his life, writes down the Ohio plate number on a piece of wrapping paper: 6C-287. Nate is used to all types of people coming into his grocery and has been for the twenty-five years that he and wife Sally have operated the store. There was something about this stranger that Nate doesn't like.

Frank Temple is busy at his desk at the Trooper Headquarters, when he is buzzed over the intercom.

"Captain, line two please. Nate Jenkins on the line," the in house receptionist says.

The Captain pushes his wire-rimmed glasses up off his nose and reaches for the telephone.

"Hello, Nate. What can I do for you?"

"Captain, it may be nothing, but a fellow with a lot of tattoos has been coming into my store. He's a scruffy-looking white man, about 40 to 45 years old. He has brown hair and is about six foot tall. He doesn't talk much. He's operating a GMC Suburban, dark in color, maybe dark blue. The plate is Ohio, 6C-287."

"Nate, was he alone?"

"Yes, he was."

"Nate, you are aware of that situation in Old Forge about the missing waitress, Patty Olson?"

"Yes, Frank, I am, and that's one reason I called."

"We appreciate you calling, Nate."

" Listen, Nate, this information about the Ohio plate may be very important. Don't say anything to anyone. We don't want to spook anybody. We'll check it out. If he comes in again, let me know."

"I will, Frank. Good-bye."

"Good-bye, Nate."

# CHAPTER ELEVEN

The sun was in my eyes when I turned into the Vincent estate. The Mountain Bank was the winner when they acquired this piece of property. It had acres of virgin timber. The chambers of my mind were constantly concerned with the whereabouts of the two men in the dark-colored Suburban and Patty. It was difficult to concentrate on anything else. It was as though they had fallen off the earth. No useful information had been developed that would shed a light on them.

My Bronco went into a deep track made by the heavy log trucks. It had rained recently in this area. I had all I could do to control the steering wheel. I went around a curve and coming toward me was an orange-colored Brockway log truck. It was loaded with hardwood logs. I blinked my lights at him and he hit his airbrakes. He climbed down from his cab and walked toward me. I didn't recognize him. He looked puzzled.

"What can I do for you, mister?" he asked.

"My name is Jason Black. I'm representing the Mountain Bank. They've just acquired this property. I believe you are trespassing. What's your name?"

"I'm Luke Lambert of Evans Mills, New York. When did the bank take possession of this property?" asked the logger.

"A month ago. I'm afraid you're going to have to turn around and unload the logs. The bank hired me to check the property before they contact law enforcement. I'd hate to see you get arrested for trespass."

"No, that's the last thing I need, Mr. Black."

"I'm sorry to have to bother you with this Luke, but the bank got wind of illegal logging going on down here. That's why they sent me. I handle cases for the bank as a private investigator. Banks do not want to call in law enforcement unless it is necessary. I can understand how you must feel about this."

"Well, I appreciate you handling it this way, Jason. I have truck payments every month and seven mouths to feed at home. I couldn't pay a fine if I had to."

"I know exactly what you mean. For the little man in this society it is a definite struggle to survive. If you should have any questions, feel free to call Jim Anderson at the Mountain Bank. In fact, Jim handles bank properties and once in a while they have to have timber cut. Maybe they might be able to help you out. This property is being sold to a company from California and any further cutting is forbidden."

"I'll unload and stop by to see Mr. Anderson. Thanks again for handling this matter the way you did."

"Take care, Luke. Remember, John Vincent has no affiliation with this property. The bank is putting a barricade at the entrance until the new owners take over. Good luck to you."

I felt bad that I had to tell Luke Lambert that he couldn't harvest the virgin timber on the Vincent estate, but life sometimes brings the bitter with the sweet; probably Lambert is unhappy about this. It's better this way, than taking a criminal trespass action against him. Lambert had enough trouble making payments on his truck and feeding his family.

On the way back home I stopped by and talked with Jim Anderson at the Mountain Bank. Jim has been a banker for twenty years and is a good man. He stands about six foot six inches tall and coaches basketball in his spare time. I told him about my encounter with Luke Lambert of Evans Mills. I shared with him the needs of Lambert. Jim promised that he would try to furnish Lambert with some logging on a couple of bank properties. He also informed me that the bank lawyers had some papers they would like me to serve on a couple of uncooperative former bank customers.

I stopped at John's Diner for a quick cup of coffee and one of

Lila's sweet-rolls filled with raisins and topped with vanilla frosting. I could have eaten a half-dozen, but two hundred and twenty pounds was enough to carry around all day. I had finished the last bite when Wilt came through the door. He had a sad expression on his face.

"Hi, Jason. Have you heard anything about Patty or that Suburban with those two fellows?" he asked with his usual concern.

"Nothing, Wilt," I responded sadly.

"You'd think that somebody would catch a glimpse of them somewhere. Do you think they have crossed into Canada?"

"I doubt it. There are a few lanes and back-country roads they could use, but I doubt that they would know where they are located."

"Jason, if I hear anything I'll let you know. I'd love to get my hands on those two bastards."

"So would I, Wilt," I said with a frown on my face.

I wished Wilt and all my friends in the diner a good day and headed home. When I pulled into the yard, Ruben was running back and forth in his runway. His sensitive ears could hear the Bronco a mile away. I opened his gate and he ran off into the woods. I cleaned up his runway and filled his dishes with food and water. He soon returned. I wrestled with the big dog for about fifteen minutes. He latched onto my ankle and squeezed hard with his powerful jaws. I knew he had missed his master. I petted him and rubbed his back. He pushed his big head against me.

"Come on, Ruben, to your dog run. Let's go, boy!"

I unlocked the door and went into my home. As I looked around I could see that I had been neglecting my weekly cleaning. Several of the local ladies who do cleaning had offered to work for me, but I had thought better of it. When I was a kid, my mother taught me to tidy up after myself, and I know that Mom, even though she's gone to heaven, would frown on her son having a cleaning person come in. I took a couple hours, and what a difference it made! I looked toward heaven for a few seconds and said, "Thank you, Mom."

The cleaning detail kept me so busy that I failed to check my answering machine. It was blinking like it always does. I listened to all the calls. Most were incoming bad check cases. The one call that brought me to full alert was Chief Todd Wilson. I called his office right away.

"Chief, this is Jason Black. What's up?"

"Jason, I just received a call from Captain Frank Temple. They received some information about an Ohio Registration Plate. Temple checked the computer and got a hit. The plate came back on a 1982 GMC Suburban, color dark blue, stolen from a parking lot in Ohio. It is believed to be occupied by two escapees from a correctional facility in that state. The operator of the Suburban and the vehicle was spotted in St. Regis Falls, but no apprehension has been made."

"Only one person in the vehicle?

"Just one, Jason."

"I don't like that, Todd."

"I don't either, but they may be hiding out in that area someplace."

"You know, Todd, Frank is a good friend of mine, and he'll send people to look for the vehicle. Hopefully something will develop."

"I know he's your friend. He asked for you."

"I was working on a case for Mountain Bank. That's why you could not find me at home."

"I won't be able to pursue the matter in that jurisdiction because I have matters to attend to here. I told the Captain that our department would cooperate in any other way except manpower. I just can't spare anyone."

"They'll have sufficient personnel in the Troop S region, so don't worry about that, Todd. I'm going to put my dog in a kennel at Eagle Bay for a few days and head up that way to do a little snooping around." I know I'll miss Ruben.

"Good idea, Jason, but for God's sake, be careful. Those convicts are killers." I knew they were capable of killing and Patty could become a victim of homicide.

"I know that. I'm certain that Captain Temple has plenty of firepower. The main thing is to find out what has happened to Patty Olson. That's my concern, Todd."

"I realize that, Jason. Just be careful."

I hung the phone up and called the Eagle Bay Kennel. They told me to drop Ruben off with a bag of his food. I grabbed a quick shower and shave, then packed a few pairs of underwear, slacks, shirts and a sweater into a medium-size suitcase.

I called Dale Rush and told him I'd be gone for a few days and to keep an eye on my place. Dale indicated that he'd be glad to fly up to the area if I needed some help. I told him that Captain Temple of the Troopers would have everything under control, and that I was just going to look around for a few days. I shared the information with Dale, as I trusted him.

"Take care, Jason, and be careful. These guys sound dangerous." Dale spoke with concern in his voice.

"I will, Dale. You know why I'm going to the Santa Clara area. I need to know if Patty is alive or dead. I know these escapees are bad, but they might be planning to hold her as a hostage. I hope and pray they haven't touched her. If I need you for anything, I'll call you."

"Okay. Take care."

"Will do."

I secured the house. I had never been bothered, but you never know about some of these divorce cases that I've worked on. I always keep all the sensitive cases locked in a safety deposit box at my bank. I put Ruben in the back of the Bronco, gave the property one more cursory check, and drove off to Eagle Bay. A big buck ran out in front of us just before we left the driveway. All the way to Eagle Bay, Ruben barked.

The attendant took Ruben and, of course, my dog got a little frisky. I told him to be good. He settled down, but had to whimper, trying to make me feel guilty about leaving him.

# CHAPTER TWELVE

*In the ramshackle camp deep in the woods near Santa Clara, Jewell Norris and Ted Clovis are preparing to leave the area with their captive. She is pale and gaunt. The two killers have not assaulted Patty, but they have instilled her with fear. Numerous times Norris has pointed his gun at her with the hammer pulled back, holding it close to her right ear. He has pulled the trigger, taunting her with threats that next time the gun may be loaded with hollow-point bullets. Then other times he treats her kindly and has protected her from Clovis, who has repeatedly threatened to rape her. During their time at the cabin, the only food has been baloney and cheese sandwiches. Norris has made coffee in an old coffee-pot that has a bullet hole in it near the top. Their clothing is dirty, although they have bathed in a nearby creek. Patty is listening carefully to everything the two men say.*

"Clovis, we need to get some money. I only have about twenty dollars left."

"Yeah, I hear you!"

"Well, you got any ideas?"

"No. You've been the one that has gone to town."

"About the only place that might have some is the grocery store. There is a gas station in town, but I have never seen any cars pull in there. We've got to be damned careful. That guy in the store looked at me suspiciously the last time I was in there."

"Yeah, we'd better be."

"I figure we'll pull into the town just at sunset. We'll look the store over close. I looked around the town the other day, and there are several roads going out of it. I wish we could get over to Canada. I'm certain there are areas that are remote, but I don't know the territory. We've got to get a pair of license plates, too. These Ohio tags stick out like a sore thumb, and we'd better try to get a map, too."

"Yeah, you're right, Jewell. We've got to change those plates."

*Patty listens intently to what the convicts have to say. She longs for Jason and wishes that she had a way to contact him. Her destiny is in the hands of these two unscrupulous men. They seldom talk to her. She wishes that she hadn't stopped that night to render aid to a fellow human. She wants to scream so the world can hear her, but instead calls on all her strength to keep herself composed.*

*Norris knows that the store stays open till ten o'clock at night. He has heard the storeowner tell some campers who inquired about picking up ice for their campsite. It is just getting dark when Norris and Clovis open the rear of the Suburban and make Patty climb in. They have tied her hands, but not her legs. Clovis threatens her with bodily harm if she makes any wrong moves.*

*Jewell Norris gets behind the wheel after he closes the door to the old camp. He drives slowly on the one-lane dirt road. High bushes and young saplings plink against the sides of the Suburban as it makes its way to the macadam road to St. Regis Falls. Santa Clara is a small community. There is a church and an old hotel. Historically, in the 1930's, a girls' school existed in the community. Logging was once a main source of income for the region.*

*Patty is watching Norris from the back seat. She notices that he is driving slowly, looking to the left and then to the right. He pulls just beyond the grocery store and parks. It has just turned dark. There are only a few scattered light-poles in the hamlet, and they have just flickered on when they were on the outskirts of the populated area. Patty listens to the two killers talking in the front seat.*

*"Clovis, when I get out, you slide behind the steering wheel."*
*Norris takes out his 45 caliber pistol and puts a clip in it.*

*"Ok, I'll watch for you. I'll keep the Suburban running."*

*Patty knows that something is going to happen in the store,*
*but doesn't dare say a word. She is frightened from the previous*
*threats made to her by the men. She knows that they will kill her*
*if she provokes them.*

*Norris gets out and places the gun in his belt under his*
*tattered jacket. His eyes are cold and calculating. He walks*
*briskly toward the store, intent on getting some money. Another*
*customer is coming out of the small country store as Norris enters.*
*She is a large woman, about forty years of age. Her hair is*
*scraggly and she wears wire-rimmed glasses. Norris avoids eye*
*contact and slips past her. The woman takes up most of the*
*doorway. It is a tight squeeze. Nate, the store owner, has just*
*closed the cash register. He is startled to see the stranger before*
*him.*

*"I'd like a pack of cigarettes and some spearmint gum,"*
*Norris demands.*

*"Certainly," Nate replies.*

*When Nate turns around from taking a pack of cigarettes*
*from the shelf, he is looking into the muzzle of a .45 caliber*
*automatic pistol.*

*"Open the cash drawer and give me all your money!"*
*Norris, looking mean, snarls at Nate.*

*Nate, surprised by the aggressive Norris, starts shaking.*
*"You're not going to get away with this, fella."*

*"Oh, yeah? I don't think you're going to stop me, old man!"*
*Norris shouts back.*

*Norris pulls the hammer back on the pistol and sticks it under*
*Nate's nose. The old man almost passes out. He opens the cash*
*drawer and takes all the currency out of it. The amount was*
*$400.00 in U.S. Currency.*

*"Is that all, old man?" Norris demands.*

*"That's all," Nate weakly replies.*

*Norris does not see the old man's left hand as it goes forward*
*to a shelf under the cash register. Nate tries to settle down. This*

*is the second robbery at his store in all the years of operating it. There have been several night time burglaries, but only two robberies.*

*Norris grabs some flashlight batteries with his free hand and puts them into his pocket. He starts to turn to leave, but hesitates as he catches the glimpse of a movement behind the counter. Nate has his .380 automatic pistol in his left hand and fires twice at Norris. The first shot goes wild and strikes a bottle of cranberry juice on the shelf by the entrance. The second bullet strikes Norris in his left side, just grazing him. Norris lets out a yell. He turns and fires five shots from his .45 caliber pistol. None strike Nate as he escapes into a storeroom, locking the door behind him. Norris, realizing that the gunfire will attract attention, runs out of the store holding his left side. On the way out, he hollers at Nate. "I'm coming back for you, old man, maybe not now, but sometime. You can count on that."*

*Norris makes a painful run to the Suburban. He climbs in. Clovis roars away as the people gather in front of the store. Patty's eyes are wide and she is terrified of her abductors. She has heard the gunfire and wonders if Norris has killed the man in the store.*

*"Did you shoot the man in the store?" she inquires.*

*"Naw, but the old bastard shot me," Norris whimpers.*

*Back at the store, Nate is on the telephone talking with Captain Frank Temple. The Captain relates that since the first contact with Nate about the stranger in town, he has assigned a plainclothes detail of officers to the area. The fleeing Suburban and its three occupants have unfortunately just lucked out in making their getaway.*

*The plainclothes officer coming into town for night duty observes the commotion in front of Nate's store and stops by. Nate has finished talking with Captain Temple and meets the investigator at the front door of the store.*

*"If you had been here ten minutes ago, you would have seen the convict come out of my store with my money." Nate was excited and upset. "I shot at him, and by the way he yelled, I must have hit him. I didn't see the vehicle he was in. I'm assuming it*

was the same dark blue Suburban that he was driving the last time he was in the store," Nate blurts out.

"Can I use your telephone right now?" Investigator Roy Timmer asks.

The investigator calls his headquarters and tells the dispatcher to have roadblocks set up immediately in the area. He informs the dispatcher that it was apparently the Suburban containing the two killers, and the abducted female could possibly be with them. They should be considered armed and dangerous. The girl is being held by these two killers against her will. Use extreme caution in any apprehension or contact.

Nate notices that the investigator is calm and precise in his requests for roadblocks and follow-up information. These men are dangerous and they have nothing to lose.

Investigator Timmer gives the store a cursory examination and makes notes of his findings. The five bullets that the robber fired were from a .45 automatic and lodged in various locations behind the counter. The cash register took a slug, as well as a hanging antique clock, in which the cuckoo won't be coo-cooing anymore. The three remaining slugs penetrated the plank wall over the cooler.

The investigator diligently secures the area and advises Nate that when he spoke with his headquarters they advised him an evidence team is en route to the scene. The local people in front of the store, figuring that the action has ended, disperse and go to their homes.

# CHAPTER THIRTEEN

At the time the robbery was taking place in St. Regis Falls, I was on the northern outskirts of Tupper Lake. My eyes squinted as I met a southbound car coming my way. I knew down deep inside that I had to get my glasses changed. I had heard over the radio about the robbery. There was very little information given out. The pit of my stomach was aching, worrying about Patty. These convicts are brazen, I thought, pulling off a robbery in that small town. Several troop cars flashed by me, probably en route to set up roadblocks at key intersections. I theorized that the evidence people would be at Nate's store. I knew Nate very well, for he had served that community when I was on the force.

I had vivid memories of my former patrol district in the northern part of the Adirondacks. I remembered the log trucks and all the people I knew in the forestry industry. They were hard-working folks. I remembered some of the good times I had when I was off-duty while on the force. There were pig roasts, skeet shooting contests, dancing, hiking the high peaks, and especially the 1980 Olympics.

When I was a rookie I had played on a couple of softball teams in the Long Lake area. I thought highly of everyone who deserved my good thoughts inside the Blue Line. I continued on toward Lake Placid and the Breakshire Lodge, where I would spend the night. Tom Huston would be surprised to see me.

It was late when I pulled into the parking lot of the Breakshire Lodge. The night clerk was yawning when I approached his counter.

He recognized me.

"Jason! Good to see you. I've been listening to the radio. They had a robbery in St. Regis Falls, and there was some gunfire at a grocery store."

"Yes, Jeff, there was some action over there. They figure it is those two escapees and the girl from Old Forge that they abducted."

"Do you know the girl?"

"Yes, Jeff, I do. Her name is Patty Olson, a waitress from our town." I thought of Patty and was concerned for her safety.

"I'm sorry to hear that, Jason. Have they hurt her?"

"I don't know the answer to that question, Jeff. Wish I did."

Jeff Thomas, the night clerk, was about thirty years old. He was a little over six feet in height, slender, with a ruddy complexion. He was working his way through Albany Law School. Tom Huston was assisting Jeff with financial aid. I could tell that he'd make a good attorney. Hopefully he would practice law with high ethical standards and treat his client base with dignity and, above all, honesty.

He assigned me room 201 on the second floor. I had stayed in many of the rooms at the lodge over the past two years. They were tastefully furnished with oak furniture. Instant coffee and tea bags were provided in each of the rooms. The drapes, as well as the towels that neatly lined the towel holder in the adjoining bathroom, were an oyster color. A small bottle of bubble bath, along with a pine scented soap, were neatly arranged in a deep soap-dish. On the oak stand near the television set was an English pitcher and bowl set. Tom Huston was proud of the sets and personally inspected the rooms daily to insure that they were always dusted. The cleaning staff of the lodge were constantly reminded that if they dropped or broke any of the sets, they could count on having their paychecks attached for the cost of the loss.

I placed my suitcase on the stand provided and hung up my jacket. I had brought a small bottle of brandy with me. I wanted to sleep soundly, as I knew the next morning would be a busy one. I broke the seal on the bottle and poured a small amount into a glass. The blackberry brandy tasted good. It was not my practice to imbibe any alcohol, but tonight I was under terrible stress and took it for medicinal purposes. I pulled the covers back on the bed, undressed, and put on my newly purchased pajamas. I put my 9mm—unloaded--under the mattress. I was asleep by the time my head hit the pillow. The last thought before I got into bed was of Patty, and my prayers were for her this night.

At 7:00 a.m. sharp the telephone rang. It was Jeff.

"Time to rise, Mr. Black," he said.

"Good…good morning, Jeff. You must be going off duty," I said sleepily.

"Yes, I am." He paused. "I didn't hear any further news overnight."

"Thank you. I appreciate your listening. Have a good sleep yourself."

"Oh! I will. After I finish a paper on search and seizure for class next week."

"Wish you well, Jeff."

"Good-bye."

I shaved and showered and put on a pair of medium-weight slacks and a green long-sleeved shirt. The temperatures were cooling this time of the year. I didn't know how long I would be here, but I was prepared to stay several days. Again I wondered where Patty and the two killers were. Had they got past the roadblocks, or were they still inside the Blue Line? Time would tell. I tidied the room and took my 9mm pistol from beneath the mattress. I was licensed to carry a concealed weapon, and this was one time that I used that privilege.

The elegant dining room of the Breakshire Lodge was full of guests this morning. The foliage of the Adirondack region brings people from all over the country. I located a small table near the large window. I didn't recognize anyone except the waitress staff. I sat down and started to read the paper that I had picked up at the entrance. I read the large print. "STORE OWNER INVOLVED IN SHOOT OUT – ROBBER ESCAPES." I frantically read the article. It said that Captain Frank Temple was in charge of the investigation and that roadblocks had been set up throughout the region.

"Good morning, Mr. Black."

It was Julia, a veteran waitress of the Breakshire Lodge. Her last name was Nelson. She was of medium build, about thirty years of age, and stood about five foot three inches tall. She wore her auburn-colored hair in a neat bun, and she complemented her beautiful face with small diamond earrings. The scent of a mild perfume could be detected. Her winning smile was warm and friendly.

"Hello, Julia." I returned the greeting.

"Would you like some coffee, Mr. Black?" she asked politely.

"I would like tea, and I believe I will have the mountain climber special this morning. I'm hungry. I would like my eggs scrambled, and please add some brown sugar to my ham."

"I'll tell the chef," she said cordially.

"Thank you, Julia."

"You are most welcome, Jason."

I continued with my reading and noticed an article about six youths who had been severely injured in a one-car accident near Jay, New York. My heart went out to their parents. I thought, *you raise a child to seventeen or eighteen, only to be disappointed when they make bad choices, a parent's worst nightmare.* I put the paper down as Julia appeared with my breakfast and hot tea.

Mr. Huston didn't seem to be around this morning. I enjoyed my breakfast. Julia presented me with the check, and I left her a sizable gratuity, and thanked her. I returned to room 201 and called Captain Frank Temple. He was glad to hear from me.

"Jason, I called Old Forge this morning. I forgot that you were staying at the Breakshire Lodge. Sorry." He added apologetically.

"No problem, sir. My room is 201. Do you have any new additional information regarding the killers and Patty Olson?"

"Not much, Jason. Our evidence team spent most of the night at Nate's store in St. Regis Falls. I know you know Nate. He is pretty shook up. That killer that went into the store fired five rounds into the walls and his antique cuckoo clock. I told him he was a fool to have it in the store. No, he's lucky he's still with us."

"How much money did they get away with?"

"Probably about four hundred dollars and some flashlight batteries."

"Have they been spotted at all?" I couldn't believe that someone hadn't seen them.

"No, Jason, but we have the area all sealed off. We have

roadblocks all over the area, and we've drawn on other Troopers from around the State. All the Troopers are seasoned and are experts with firearms. Someone told me that the girl, Patty, is a friend of yours, Jason. Rest assured we'll take every precaution, but remember these two bastards have no regard for life. The Ohio authorities advised that they are rock-hardened criminals. The story is that Norris's mother was killed in front of him when he was six years old, in a barroom. He never got over it. The other guy, Clovis, was whipped by his father continually when he was growing up. Both of them pursued a life of crime and have no regard for human life."

"Captain, my concern is the safety of Patty Olson. My worry is that those escapees will harm her, if they haven't already. She has gone through one hell of an ordeal. This is the only time that I wished I was back on the job."

"I know, I know, Jason, but you are not a member anymore. I hope you understand that. You know you were kind of a loose cannon on the job."

"Come on, Captain, with all respect, cut the bullshit. I worked myself to a frazzle on many cases and you know it." I spoke sharply and to the point.

"I know you did, but that doesn't mean you complied with what the people upstairs wanted," he said in agreement.

"True, sir, but a man has to look in the mirror, and I can look into any mirror or face without flinching. Some people can't," I retorted.

"Well, I'm not going to debate you on that, but remember you're not in the equation anymore. You are a private investigator. You know the rules, Jason."

"Yes, I do know the rules. I know you are doing your job. I don't object to that. I want you to know that I'm looking for a missing person from our town and that's what I'm going to be doing, sir."

"I'm going to tell you once more: you are not on the job, and I will recommend that your private investigator's license be revoked if you interfere with my investigation. Do we understand each other?" He spoke with conviction.

"Let's cool it, Captain. True, I'm not on the job, and if it will satisfy your ego, go ahead and have my private investigator's license pulled. I will still look for my friend. Do you understand me?" I answered in like manner.

I heard the click of the telephone. My former boss had hung up in my ear. I wasn't upset, but my memory bank started grinding to a night many years ago when I was on patrol in a different location and a speeding car went by me. I was a sworn officer and I pursued that car. I chased it for a long distance and pulled it over. I wrote the young man behind the wheel a summons for speeding fifty miles an hour in a thirty-five-mile speed zone. He had been doing seventy. The young man was a civilian. His name was Frank Temple. I did the job that I was sworn to do. Unfortunately, he eventually became my boss. Under his command, my career ended, as far as he was concerned. Talk about a Catch 22 situation. No, I didn't think that Frank Temple would fool with my private investigator's license. I don't dislike Frank. I did, however, feel that he shouldn't have held that ticket incident against me all during my career, especially when I was doing my job and making him look good.

# CHAPTER FOURTEEN

*Patty Olson is cold and hungry. She is again tied at her ankles and wrists. Her captors are both snoring loudly. She is aware that Norris has robbed the store in St. Regis Falls. She knows that Norris has been slightly wounded by a bullet fired by the store owner and that Norris has four hundred dollars from the cash register. She thinks about Jason. Frightened as she is, Patty is tough and she knows she has to be to survive the ordeal she is going through. They are in an old barn just off a dirt road in the northern part of the Adirondacks. Patty has no idea that she is within thirty miles of her friend, Jason.*

*Patty notices that Norris is awakening. He gags and coughs and coughs. He finally stands up and looks at Patty.*

*"What the hell are you looking at, girly?" he asks.*

*"Nothing," she replies.*

*Dawn is just breaking when they hear the sound of a vehicle driving up to the barn door. Norris quickly rushes over to a crack in the door and peeks out. He sees a black Ford one-half-ton pickup parked about seventy feet from the barn doors. Getting out of the truck is a man in his sixties with gray hair. He is wearing bib-overalls and has a flashlight in his hand. Norris takes his .45 Caliber pistol from his waistband and pulls the hammer back. Patty is restless and Norris says in a raised whisper, "Shut up, girly."*

*The farmer enters the barn by sliding one of the doors*

*partially open.*

*"What the--?" the farmer exclaims.*

*"Put your hands up in the air, old man," demands Norris.*

*"What are you doing in my barn, fella?" asks the farmer.*

*"None of your business. Put your hands up or I'll fill you full of lead," Norris commands.*

*"Don't shoot! Don't shoot!" the farmer cries.*

*"Ted, bring that rope over here. Lay down, old man, and give me that flashlight."*

*The farmer does as he is told. Clovis springs into action and ties the farmer's hands and ankles. Clovis removes the old man's wallet and takes the currency out of it. Clovis looks at the old man's driver's license. The license bears the name of Patrick Miller of RD #1, Jay, New York.*

*"We're trading vehicles with ya, Patrick," Norris says.*

*"Go ahead. Take anything I got, mister."*

*"Untie girly," Norris orders Clovis.*

*Clovis goes over to where Patty is lying on some hay and unties her. Norris is brandishing his gun toward the farmer. The farmer is visibly shaken. He remains mute, but looks at Patty with sadness in his face.*

*"We're not going to kill you, old man, but remember we can come back any time, so keep your mouth shut," Clovis orders.*

*The Suburban has been driven into the barn. The gas tank is almost empty. Norris removes the Ohio plates and throws them down an abandoned well near the barn. Patty has a difficult time walking because she has been tied up so long. Her face is dirty and her clothes are soiled and wrinkled, and she smells of perspiration. The two killers look just as bad. Both of them have hatred in their faces. The Ford pickup looks in good shape and the gas gauge registers full. They place Patty in the seat and Norris gets behind the wheel. Clovis is looking around to see if anyone is in the area. He climbs in and Norris backs out onto the road. They speed off, heading easterly on an unknown road. They have no idea where they are.*

*"How much money did ya get from the old man, Clovis?" Norris asked.*

*"Almost a hundred dollars."*

*"That's good."*

They hang to the back roads. They know that the main roads must be flooded with police. But the police would be looking for a Blue GMC Suburban, not a Black Ford pickup. Norris is certain that they are on their way to freedom. He is thinking of what to do with Patty. He has evil thoughts. The .45 Caliber pistol is shoved into his waistband. Patty is cold and frightened of these two madmen. So far they have not run into any police roadblocks.

The wife of Patrick Miller is in her kitchen waiting for her husband Patrick to return from the barn, which is located a mile from their home. She looks at the clock over the sink and realizes that her husband should have returned an hour ago. She is concerned that he may have had a heart attack. She puts on her jacket and goes to the nearby garage. Patrick and Judy have been married for forty-five years and have been farming for twenty-five years. She gets into their Ford station wagon and backs it out of the garage.

When she arrives at the barn, things do not look disturbed, but she notices the sliding door is partially open. She parks the car and approaches the barn. She is nearing the barn when she hears a voice.

*"Help me, help me, for God's sake, help me."*

*"Patrick? Patrick, is that you?"*

*"Hurry, honey, it's me."* His voice is weak and pleading.

She slides the large gray weathered wood door open further and immediately sees Patrick lying on the barn floor.

*"Who did this to you, Patrick?"* she asks, distraughtly.

*"I think it was those killers that the Troopers are looking for. There were two men and the young woman. The men looked mean and one of them had a pistol. They took the money out of my wallet."* The farmer was ghostly white and frightened. *"The Suburban here in the barn is the vehicle they must have stolen from Ohio. The girl must have been the missing waitress from Old Forge. She looked scared."*

*"Let me untie you, dear,"* she says and reaches down and unties her husband.

*"It is a wonder they didn't kill me. I'm glad you came, honey."  Patrick's eyes are full of tears.*

*"Let me help you up," Judy says.*

*"I shouldn't have entered the barn. The door was ajar. Whew! I'm lucky to be alive. We've got to call the Troopers right away." Patrick, assisted by his wife gets up, his legs are weak and shaky.*

*Judy and Patrick get into the station wagon and return to their home. Patrick is too nerve-wracked to call on the telephone, so he has Judy make the call to the Troopers. The dispatcher tells them that they will send Troopers to their home.*

*Fifteen minutes pass before the first two Troopers arrive. Patrick Miller describes to the officers what has taken place. Their exchange lasts for several minutes. One Trooper asks the questions and the other takes notes. Soon an evidence team arrives and Patrick accompanies the officers to the barn. Lines are put up designating the barn and the stolen--now recovered--vehicle as a crime scene. A careful cursory examination of the area is undertaken. The Troopers take more notes and measurements. The evidence people take pictures of the barn's interior and exterior, and spend a great amount of time dusting the Suburban for latent fingerprints, hair samples and contents.*

*The plainclothes detectives arrive and interview the uniform personnel. More notes and additional photos are secured. Long-distance photos are taken of the barn from one side to the other side and front and rear. News media arrive and are forbidden in the area, with the polite request that they allow the police to conduct their extensive investigation and stay a considerable distance from the barn and recovered vehicle.*

# CHAPTER FIFTEEN

I arrived at the Miller barn. I knew some of the older Troopers at the scene. I talked with some of the plainclothes personnel and evidence technicians. I tried to avoid my probative ways. The scene of the recovered Suburban reminded me of my many years in the Troopers and the hundreds of cases I worked on.

Because of my close association with Patty Olson and being a retired Investigator of the Bureau of Criminal Investigation, I am permitted to have a short conversation with Patrick Miller. I asked Mr. Miller how the girl looked who was with the two killers.

"She looked tired and sad. Her clothes were tattered. She appeared alert, but frightened." His lips quivered as he spoke, obviously still shaken from his encounter with the killers.

"Thank you, Mr. Miller. Sorry to bother you. Your ordeal was difficult."

I appreciated this information. Mr. Miller had noticed that I was wearing a shoulder holster with an automatic pistol, but he didn't ask me what it was for. I shared the fact that the hostage is a close friend of mine and I am terribly worried about her safety and welfare.

The lead detective came over and showed the photos to Mr. Miller. He asked,

"Mr. Miller, would you be kind enough to look at these photographs of eight white males who look similar?"

The detective had the photos arranged neatly in a three-ring notebook. No names were listed. Mr. Miller takes his time and looks at each photo intensely.

"Officer, these are the two men who were in my barn, without a doubt." Mr. Miller pointed to the photos of the two men.

"Mr. Miller, you have identified Jewell Norris and Ted Clovis, who are escaped convicts from a state correctional facility in the State of Ohio."

Mr. Miller gulped a little and said, "I hope this helps you with your investigation. These men are dangerous and the young lady with them is terribly frightened. I could tell that by the way she looked at me as they were tying me up."

"We are doing our best to find them, sir. We thank you for your cooperation in this matter. I don't think that they will be back, but we'll have a patrol on your highway here all night long. Just as a precautionary measure, it might be a good idea to keep your yard lights on. I see that you have a couple of good dogs."

"Thank you, detective. My wife and I will help in any way we can. I probably won't sleep all night. I'll load my shotgun. They'd better not show up here. Yes, those dogs are darn good watch dogs," Miller comments.

I walked around the area and noticed near the barn an old abandoned well. I walked over to my Bronco and took out a large flashlight. I returned to the well and pushed the tin cover off it. I took the flashlight, turned it on, and pointed it down the dark well.

"Hey! One of you Troopers, over here!" I shouted loudly!

A Trooper immediately ran over to where I was leaning over the well.

"What do you see down there, Trooper?" I pointed my extended arm down the well.

My light casts a reflection from an Ohio license plate.

Several other officers, as well as Mr. Miller, ran over to the well.

"I've got a ladder lying in the rear of the barn," Miller said.

The ladder is brought to the well, and one of the Troopers removed his hat and climbed down into the depth of the well. He came up holding two Ohio Plates bearing the numbers of 6C-287. The plates were placed in a plastic evidence bag.

I observed the plates and thought about the night Patty had left my home and turned right out of my entrance to her waiting fate of being abducted by two killers, whom she apparently thought were two people in need of assistance along a dark highway. I speculated it was too bad that Charlie Perkins hadn't stopped his log truck that night. But then I thought, *what could Charlie have done?* He probably would have been shot or abducted along with Patty. It was all in the cut of the cards. One never knows. I stared at the barn and the Troopers securing the evidence.

A large tow truck from Jay arrived and the Suburban was removed from the barn and fastened to the hook. The vehicle was officially impounded by the officers at the scene and removed to a secure location at their headquarters.

The lead detective told the detail at the scene that the description and plate number have been entered into the computer and the roadblocks would now be alerted to watch for a black Ford pickup containing two killers and a female being held against her will. The pressure was mounting. Where are the killers and what are they up to?

I returned to my Bronco and headed back to the Breakshire Lodge. On the way I checked several back roads that lead into the high peak region. I arrived at the Lodge just after dark. I felt that it would be a good idea to freshen up before a late supper. I'm hungry as I hadn't had any lunch because of the excitement of the day. Yet I have to call Captain Temple out of curiosity. I knew the habits of Frank Temple. The Captain answered his telephone and was surprised to hear my voice.

"Jason, have you settled down a little? You were a little shook up when we talked last," he asked sternly.

"You're the one who hung up on me, Frank," I responded coolly.

"What can I do for you, Jason? Let's get back on track," he said somewhat apologetically.

"Okay with me, Frank. You must know by now that the girl with those killers means a lot to me, and the folks and my friends are counting on me to help locate her."

"Yeah, I'm aware of that, but I have to let you know that you have to let us do the police work on this case. You know I have to answer to people up above, too, and I do not want to get in their cross hairs, if you know what I mean."

"I understand, Frank. I give you my word I'll let your guys do the police work."

"Okay, Jason. You're a good friend of mine and I don't want anything to happen to you. I knew that there were people gunning for you when you were on the job. Just remember, they were jealous of your accomplishments. If I had been upstairs, it would have been different. Understand?"

"Yeah, I understand." Deep in my heart, I knew he was one of the main conspirators, but right now, Patty's welfare was my top priority.

"Okay, let's get with it. You at the Breakshire?"

"Yeah," I replied.

" If you see Tom Huston, give him my regards, will you?"

"Yes, I will."

"You still in Room 201?" he asked, keeping the conversation light.

"Yep," I replied, not wanting to continue.

"Okay, I'll sign off now. And, Jason, if anything develops, I'll call you personally. You were a darn good copper and you knew the people. There are many of us that miss you, fella, and don't forget it."

"Ok, Captain. Good night." I hung up the receiver. The 'bull' was getting deep.

I threw some ice cold water onto my face, combed my graying hair, locked up my 9mm pistol, and went down to the dining room. The night waitresses were carrying trays heaped with steaks, pork chops, chicken, and salmon.

I took a seat in the corner at a small round table. I noticed how neatly the napkin and silverware are placed and how there are fresh flowers in the small vase. I already had made up my mind when Eleanor Puchett came to my table. She is French, and has worked at the Lodge for about six months. Her purple earrings and shoulder-length straight black hair caught my eye. She has waited on me several times.

"Good evening, Mr. Black," she said with a warm smile.

"Good evening, Eleanor. You look great, as usual."

"Jason, you're making me blush. Are you ready to order?" she asked.

"I'm all set. I'll have the grilled salmon, baked potato, coleslaw, and later some of that wonderful rice pudding and a cup of green tea."

She wrote the order on her pad and asked, "Have you heard anything about those killers and the girl? I was stopped at a roadblock down by the Wolf Inn when I was coming to work."

"No, Eleanor, I haven't heard anything. Make certain you lock your car doors when you leave tonight and it is a good idea not to help strangers on the side of the road," I said adamantly.

"You can be certain I will lock my doors. This world is nuts, Jason."

"Yeah, you've got a point there," I agreed.

"Be back shortly with your order."

While waiting for my dinner, I began to meditate about the past few days.

I was sipping my ice water and thinking about Patty. I heard a loud voice by the cashier's table. I looked up and saw a short squatty man wearing a red sweater and horned-rimmed glasses perched on the end of his nose. I heard the cashier pleading with the man to turn his hearing aid up. There seemed to be an aura of confusion about the paying of his bill.

Eleanor appeared at my table wearing a big smile. The salmon was huge and my taste buds started to tingle. The chef had performed his culinary artistry to the height of perfection. I enjoyed my supper. I wished that Patty was here with me.

# CHAPTER SIXTEEN

*The fear of being discovered by the Troopers forces Jewell Norris to select just the backcountry roads. He is clever. He knows that the police will be relentless in their search for the three of them.*

*"Clovis, keep a close watch for the police. We should have taken that old farmer along with us. By now the cops will know that we switched vehicles."*

*"Yeah, you're right."*

*"We're just about out of food. We didn't have room for the old man anyway." Norris says, with a look of hatred on his face.*

*"I'm starving" responds Clovis.*

*Patty doesn't say anything. It appears she has fallen asleep.*

*"There was a custard stand about a mile back," Clovis offers.*

*"Yeah, let's see if they have anything."*

*Norris pulls into a church parking lot and turns around. He strips the gears as he shifts into second. He slows down when he reaches the custard stand. It is getting late. Norris pulls into the far end of the parking lot in a dark corner not illuminated by the floodlights. He hands Clovis a ten-dollar bill.*

*"Order anything they have ready. We don't wanna be here too long."*

*"Okay."*

*Clovis, ragged and dirty, strolls to the custard stand and,* *after reading the outside posted menu, orders six burgers, a triple order of French fries, and three chocolate milkshakes. The two people in the custard stand hurry around the small cooking area. The six burgers are already wrapped and the fries are taken from a container under a heating lamp. The workers put the order in three paper bags. The bill comes to $9.50. Clovis hands the clerk the ten-dollar bill and tells her to keep the change. Clovis returns to the Ford with the order.*

*The three occupants in the black Ford gulp the food down. The burgers are cold, the fries greasy, and the shakes thin.*

*"Clovis, this food is terrible."*

*"Yeah, tastes like the food we had in the joint."*

*"You can say that again."*

*"Hey, girly, aren't you talking?"*

*"I appreciated the food," Patty comments in a weak response.*

*The three people in the pickup don't see the two Trooper cars enter the parking area of the custard-stand with their lights out. Unbeknownst to Norris and Clovis, one of the custard-stand workers had called the local barracks.*

*The four Troopers, each with a loaded 12 gauge shotgun, approach the parked stolen black Ford pickup which contains two killers and a helpless young waitress from Old Forge. The parking lot in that particular location is pitch black. The Troopers split into pairs. Their plan is for a complete surprise.*

*As the Troopers approach from the rear, Clovis happens to look in the right-side mirror of the pickup and for an instance sees a Trooper's Stetson.*

*"Let's get the hell out of here!" Clovis screams.*

*Norris starts the Ford and lunges ahead, striking a refuse-can, and spins the tires on the grass. At that moment two loud blasts are heard.*

*"The cop's are shooting at us!" Norris barks.*

*Norris pushes the gas pedal to the floor, and the pickup fishtails onto the pavement of Route 30 just east of Indian Lake Village.*

*"One of our tires has been hit!" Clovis adds, in a loud voice.*

*Norris is on the shoulder and then back on the pavement.*

*The truck seems out of control. Patty is horrified, but doesn't utter a word. Norris gives Clovis his pistol. The flashing lights of the cops are bearing down on them. Norris struggles with the steering wheel and goes onto the shoulder again.*

*"Shoot at their lights," Norris orders.*

*Clovis turns in the seat, and opens the window, and with his left hand pulls the trigger repeatedly, firing the .45 caliber automatic pistol. The barking of the weapon is deafening to the ears of the three occupants. Norris continues to try controlling the swerving truck. He pulls the wheel sharply to the left, causing the truck to diagonally cross Route 30, strike three guardposts, and careen down a steep bank. Patty screams loudly. It is a tree near the raging river that stops the truck. Clovis is catapulted through the windshield into the air, slamming against the big oak. Patty's head strikes the dashboard and she is knocked unconscious. Norris is dazed, but able to retrieve his pistol. Unable to open the driver's door, he is finally able to squeeze through the window. He can tell that Clovis has met his maker and leaves Patty for dead.*

*Norris looks up the steep bank and sees the police cars with their flashing red lights. He can see the shadows of the Troopers readying themselves to descend down the steep incline. He knows that he has to get away in a hurry. He feels the pain in his left leg as he began crossing the river. He grits his teeth as the cold water reaches his crotch.*

# CHAPTER SEVENTEEN

I returned to room 201 and prepared to go to bed. My last thoughts before dozing off are of Patty Olson. I realized that, against my better wishes, I hold a special feeling toward her. It is hard for me to use the word <u>love</u>, but my emotions seem to be approaching that juncture in our short relationship.

Somewhere in the vastness of space, a bell is ringing. I turn over. The bell doesn't fade away. I finally force my eyes open. It is five minutes past four in the morning. I reach out for the telephone on the bed-stand.

"Hel--hello," I said, sleepily.

"Jason, wake up! This is Captain Temple. Wake up!"

"I'm awake. What's up?" I'm afraid it's bad news about Patty.

"Our Troopers at Indian Lake met up with Norris, Clovis and Patty Olson!"

"What the hell are you saying?" I asked excitedly.

"Just that. The three of them were parked in behind the custard stand over there and, as the Troopers were about to grab them, the Ford pickup sped out of the parking lot. One of the Troopers fired at the pickup and blew a tire apart. The pickup continued on Route 30 at a high rate of speed. Norris apparently was driving and went off the road near that curve and down a steep embankment."

"Wow! Are you serious? How's Patty? Is she Ok?"

"A copter took her to the Saranac Hospital. Jason, she's in a coma. It looks bad for her, but to early to tell. Clovis is dead. They

115

found him up in a tree sprawled over a limb about fifteen feet off the ground. Norris was able to escape and apparently crossed the river. They've got the bloodhounds out of headquarters and there's about fifty Troopers and Conservation Officers beating the bushes for the son-of-a-bitch. We figure he's got that .45 Caliber automatic pistol with him. No idea how much ammunition he might have."

"Can I help in any way?" I asked, alarmed!

"You can feel free to go to the hospital and wait around there to see if Patty comes out of the coma. The doctors didn't think it was a deep one. They have movement in her arms and legs. She also had some facial lacerations. The doctor I talked with indicated that she was very dirty and has lost a great deal of weight. The X-rays showed no broken bones, and her internal organs seem all right. Jason, if she comes out of the coma, she can consider herself one lucky girl."

"I'll grab a shower and head over to the hospital." I was worried about her condition.

"Jason, I can't stop you from going to the scene, but if you do, stay out of the way and let our people do their job. Do you understand?"

"Yes, I understand. I appreciate you calling me. See you later."

"Take care."

I took a fast shower and dressed. It took me about twenty minutes to get to the hospital. I identified myself. Several of the older nurses know me and take me into intensive care. I had visited Saranac Hospital more than I'd like to remember; when I was assigned to that district years ago.

I looked at Patty, so pale and gaunt. She is on her back, with her eyes closed. Tubes have been placed in her mouth and a saline solution is dripping from the hanging plastic bag through a thin tube into her arm. The nurses have bathed her, and her blond hair flows on her shoulders. It deeply disturbs me to see Patty in this condition. I grilled the doctors and nurses. They have high hopes that she will come out of her coma. The impact with the oak tree was tremendous. Patty is lucky to be alive. I prayed to myself that she would pull through this ordeal.

Moved by the events taking place I changed my mind about waiting at the hospital. No one can determine when and if Patty will survive or come out of the coma. I am adamant in my thoughts and

I know in my heart that I have to go to Indian Lake, even as an observer; but deep down in my guts, I wanted Jewell Norris and I wanted him badly for doing this to Patty. I knew the rules and I mulled over the words that Captain Temple so eloquently related to me over the telephone. I approached the night duty nurse in charge. I knew her from years ago.

"Hilda Renick, may I have a word with you?"

"You certainly can, Jason."

Hilda has been a nurse all her adult life. She has bright red hair and her beautiful face is sprinkled with tiny freckles. She has had feelings for me in the past when I wore the uniform and the big hat, but adopted me as an honorary brother.

"Hilda, it is nice seeing you again, but not under these circumstances. I was planning to wait around here, but I have to leave. If Frank Temple calls for me, tell him I've gone to Indian Lake."

"I will, Jason. Don't worry; we'll take good care of Patty. I'm working a double shift. I'll watch over her closely. I understand she is from Old Forge."

"Yes. She is loved by everyone in town." I added. "Hilda, she had a miserable marriage. I think a great deal of her."

"Oh, I can tell that you do, Jason. Don't worry, we'll watch over her."

"Thank you. I'll check back with you later in the day."

"Okay. Take care."

"You, too."

I was torn between staying by Patty's side at the hospital or becoming involved in the manhunt for Jewell Norris. I make up my mind to look for Norris on my own. I had planned on returning to Old Forge, but this change of events took me in a different direction. I'd stay at the Breakshire as long as necessary. The check cases and other matters pending would have to wait.

The Bronco knew the way to Indian Lake and I didn't waste any time in making the trip. It was daylight when I arrived. I had passed several roadblocks manned by Troopers and Conservation Officers. I knew some of the people but decided to continue southeast on Route 30, without stopping. I knew the search area fairly well because I had hunted the region when I was eighteen years old. I also knew that in the backcountry it was easy to get turned around, sometimes even with a compass. My first thoughts were to stop at the Indian Lake Diner for coffee and to pick up some sandwiches.

I pulled into the diner parking lot. I noticed there were several Troop cars. The Troopers were sitting in their cars drinking coffee and munching on sandwiches. Several of the fellows waved as I was about to enter the diner. I assumed that these men were another search team getting ready to enter the woods across the Indian River. I thought about the escaped killer, Jewell Norris, and wondered where he was hiding. It was the general consensus that Norris would be difficult to apprehend. The police knew that he was armed and dangerous. So did I. I thought about two remote cabins deep in the woods. Several years ago, when I was on duty in the area, some children walking through the forest became lost. It had been a Forest Ranger and me who located the kids. Fortunately one of them was a Boy Scout and he had led the group to one of the cabins. I remembered the look on their faces when we entered the cabin around midnight, many years ago.

I ordered two peanut butter and jelly sandwiches. I changed my mind about the coffee and decided on a nice big cup of hot chocolate. Outside the diner were some tables and benches. I paid my bill and found a comfortable spot in a shady area. The sandwiches tasted good and I sipped the steaming chocolate. I looked over to where the Troopers were and noticed that a couple of them had 270's. The rifles were equipped with good scopes. I thought about the old .30 .30 lever action carbines which were once considered the ideal rifle. I finished my snack and decided that I would return to Old Forge and pick up some different clothes in the event I decided to check out those remote cabins later on.

On the way down to Old Forge, I stopped at the Eagle Bay Kennel. Ruben was excited to see me. I asked the attendant to let him out of the fenced-in area. I hugged him, and he buried his big head in my arms. It was difficult to have to leave him there. He whined as the keeper put him back in the fenced yard.

"See you later, Ruben."

I paid the bill and told the person in charge that I didn't know exactly when I would be in to pick up my beloved canine.

I pulled into my yard. The grass had grown six inches. The cabin was musty. I opened a few windows and turned a couple of the fans on. My answering machine was flashing. The message that I had dictated somehow was erased. I dictated a new message. We evidently had a power outage and as a result, I lost any messages that were on the machine. The time on my clock radio was also flashing. I reset it.

I called Chief Todd Wilson to bring him up to date on the events. The Chief informed me that he had already been briefed. Todd advised me the town-folks had already started to take up a collection to help Patty with her medical expenses. Several of the local fellows had volunteered to join the search, but were told by a Trooper commander it was appreciated, but they had sufficient manpower. I thanked the Chief.

I attempted to call Dale Rush, Wilt Chambers, and Charlie Perkins, but they were all out. I left messages on each of their answering machines.

I placed my old hiking boots and heavier clothing into the rear of the Bronco. I took my Browning 12 gauge automatic shotgun out of my gun vault, with extra ammunition, and locked it in my gun box in the Bronco. I have been around guns since I was eleven years old and remember well the first gun my father bought for me. It was a .22 Caliber Ranger single shot with a plunger that had to be pulled out before you could fire it. I was an expert with several weapons, but down deep, I had acquired a dislike for all weaponry. I had seen too many people killed and injured for life. I had been an avid hunter, and still purchase my Sportsman License every year, but it lies in my top dresser drawer. I'm not against guns or fish-poles. But I prefer a camera, the target a fawn with her mother or a beaver building his dam. I figure that in this great country of America, we have choices and that's my choice, a good camera. Of course, in my profession as a private investigator, there may come a time when one would be required to act in self-defense.

My thoughts were about Patty. I called the Saranac Lake Hospital and was advised that there was no change in her condition. I was assured that if there were any change, they would contact me, as I had given them my cell phone number. My feelings for Patty were becoming stronger. She looks so very helpless in that hospital bed. She had taken a serious blow to the head when the pickup struck the tree.

I thought about stopping at John's Diner, but couldn't bring myself to do it. There would be too many questions, and I was depressed enough. I closed all the windows, shut the fan off, and secured my log home. I did manage to slip a box of 9mm shells into my jacket pocket. I said to myself, "The Troopers are looking for you, Jewell Norris, and so am I, you bastard." I remembered the words of Captain Frank Temple and did not intend to violate his orders. I was just going to take a look at those two cabins that were located in a remote area. It may be a long shot, but at least I would attempt to assist in the manhunt in my own way. My way.

I did not return to Indian Lake. I proceeded on to Long Lake. My plan was to stay at the Long Lake Hotel for the night and get an early start the next morning. I would leave my Bronco a few miles west of Newcomb and take the trail that wound through the woods. It wasn't a steep climb, but enough to get the ticker beating.

It was getting dark when I checked in at the hotel. I'd get to sleep early after a light supper and initiate a wake-up call of 5:00 a.m.

I went to my room on the second floor. I was still paying for my room at the Breakshire, but tonight it was prudent to stay in Long Lake. I washed up a little before supper and prepared my hiking clothes for the early morning hour.

The dining room was almost empty. I didn't know the evening waitress, but found her friendly. I was polite to her. The pork chops, baked potato, and vegetable I ordered came out piping hot. The applesauce was warm and tart. The green tea was steaming.

Not being a steady drinker, I felt that this evening a shot of B and B would help me sleep. I was in for a big day tomorrow. I needed some shut-eye. I didn't go to the bar, but had the waitress bring it to me. It was smooth. I sipped it slowly. I could understand how some people could get addicted to booze.

The waitress brought the check and some mints. I presented my Visa card and she went off to the cashier's stand. She returned momentarily and lay the slip down in front of me. I looked up at her. She gave me a wink. I'm certain the wink was innocent, but I don't do winks. I left her a gratuity and left the dining room.

When I reached my room, I made a couple of telephone calls. From the one to the hospital I learned that there was still no change. Patty was still in the coma. I then called Dale Rush and shared with him my plan for the next day.

"Dale, if I don't make it back to Old Forge, I want you to take care of things for me. Probably everything will work out, but I just wanted to let you know. The spare key to the log home is under the red rock by the side door. It is in a small metal box. You'll have to dig down about two inches and you'll find it. Okay? And, make certain that Ruben has a good home."

"Don't worry, Jason; you'll be back. I know you, and if anyone is a survivor, you are, my friend. I know you want to take precautions. That's the way you are. I'll be glad to come up and give you an assist in the morning."

"This is something I have to take care of myself. I may not even come across this bastard, but if by some chance I do, and if I can, I'm going to teach him a lesson that he will remember. It's all based on that two-letter word, <u>if</u>."

"Probably the Troops will grab him first. Those bloodhounds don't quit."

"Yeah, I know what you're saying, but you know how I feel about this. You're the only one that knows how I feel unless this damned telephone is bugged."

"I know what you are saying."

"Dale, I think I'm falling in love with Patty. At least I feel that I am. I promised myself, after my last divorce, that I wasn't going to get serious about any lady. The circumstances of her being abducted after she stopped to help a fellow human and look what happened?"

"I hear you, but let's settle down. I know you're peeved about what they did. Creeps like this are all over our land. It's the luck of the draw, Jason. You and I cannot control what's happening. You can say it's the breakdown of the family unit, or the drug culture. Many people are hard-hearted and that's it, just hard. They harm their parents sometimes. Even the professionals who look deep into human behavior can't seem to come up with the complete answers."

"True. Well, I've talked too long. Just remember I intend to return, just like that General said he would return. Remember that?"

"Sure do."

"Take it easy, Dale."

"Will do. Take care, friend."

I read for a while and my eyelids seemed like there were ten-pound weights on them. I fell into deep slumber.

The motorcycle ran off the cliff in New Hampshire. The ring was loud. The parachute had opened when the second ring awoke me. I was groggy. The dream had my heartbeat pounding in my chest. I reached for the telephone.

"Mr. Black, time to rise and shine," the night clerk said.

"Thank you," I responded.

The receiver fell to the floor. I quickly retrieved it and placed it in the holder. I rubbed my left eye. Wool blankets caused it to itch. I jumped up and went to the bathroom. The showerhead leaked as I turned on an equal amount of cold and hot water. The small bar of soap slipped out of my hand. I reached down for it and lathered up. There was nothing as refreshing as a good shower even if the showerhead did leak. The large blue bath towel was soft as I dried myself. I thought of Patty and wished that she were here. I shaved, combed my hair, and dressed.

I pulled on my medium-weight tan trousers. My beige long-sleeved shirt matched the pants. I had not put on my hiking boots in almost a year. I had ordered them through the U.S. Mail from L.L. Bean & Company in Maine. They were dark brown and went above the ankle about six inches. The rawhide laces were still in good shape. The sole of the boots had good gripping power, which was good for climbing. I had my old Marine knife that I carried in the service. I attached it to my belt. I put my shoulder holster on under my loose-fitting shirt. I placed the 9mm automatic in the holster. I didn't like to carry a gun of any kind, but this was the exception.

I thought about the fleeing Norris. I figured he was still in the woods. It was difficult to believe that he hadn't been captured, with all the Troopers and bloodhounds out there beating the bushes. I didn't underestimate him either. He probably was tiring from the pressure on him, however, the information received from the correctional facility indicated that Norris was a tough ornery convict. He had been a U.S. Army Ranger and had received a dishonorable discharge for being involved in a vicious rape during his stint in the service. He had been a guest at Leavenworth. He wasn't the type of guy you'd invite to a civilized social gathering. Information from Ohio substantiated that he was a lifer and had cleverly devised the plan for the escape with Clovis.

I packed everything neatly into my suitcase and placed it in the rear of the Bronco. I knew that they served a good breakfast at the hotel, but decided to stop up the street at Gertie's.

The aroma of sizzling bacon and fresh-baked sweet rolls filtered through the screen door as I entered the busy diner. Gertie was busy at the grill. Scrambled eggs, eggs over easy, sunny-side eggs and six hot-cakes were browning nicely. A waitress with a coffee pot in each hand was making her rounds at the few small tables. The place was packed. I was lucky. There was one stool on the end of the counter that was unoccupied. Gertie turned around with a big smile.

"Jason, where have you been? We have been worried about you." She was happy to see me.

"I've been a little busy, Gertie. I've missed you folks, too."

Gertie flipped the pancakes, then rushed toward me with the coffee pot. She turned the big mug over and filled it, leaving room for a dash of cream. In a whisper she said, "They haven't caught that killer yet. Everyone is locking their doors and loading their shotguns and rifles."

"Smart idea. I personally don't think he is here in town. That guy's in the woods. He's no fool. He's a former U.S. Army Ranger," I whispered back.

"Oh, I see what you mean. How is Patty?"

"Still in a coma, Gertie," I answered with a worried look on my face.

"I'm so sorry, Jason. Keep your chin up and say a lot of prayers."

"I'm keeping my fingers crossed."

"What would you like, Jason?"

"Gertie, those hot-cakes look good. And, put a couple of over-medium eggs on top of them with that great syrup you serve." I tried to sound cheerful to cover my inner anxiety.

"You are hungry," she said, in a low voice.

I grabbed a paper and looked at the local news. I knew a few of the folks who were rushing to finish their breakfast. Some of them had to drive to Tupper Lake for work. I think there were a couple of young Troopers at the far corner table wearing hunting clothes who must have had something to do with the manhunt. They were speaking in low tones, so I couldn't hear what they were saying. I reread the headlines. "TROOPERS LOOKING FOR ESCAPED KILLER." I knew the Long Lake region well. I could imagine that many folks were carrying a weapon of some kind for protection. I was sure of one thing: Norris better not bother any of these Adirondackers, or he'd pay the price.

"Here's your breakfast, Jason."

I looked up, folded the paper, and placed it back on the shelf. I could see that Gertie hadn't forgotten. She had placed a spoonful of soft sweet butter in the center of the top hotcake next to the two eggs. She set the small pitcher of homemade syrup next to my plate, then trotted away for a second and returned with fresh coffee.

"Thank you, Gertie. Everything looks wonderful. You're a great cook, Gertie."

I chewed my food slowly, enjoying the combination of maple syrup, egg, hotcake and cured ham. I continued to worry internally. How is Patty doing? I decided to call the hospital before I hit the woods. I wasn't going to call Frank Temple. I knew that he would frown on the idea of me going for a hike in the Newcomb area, especially when there was a major manhunt taking place within a twenty-two-mile region. I chuckled to myself. I wasn't really upset about organizational politics, but it was great to be able to look in the mirror every day of my life. I had looked forward to being in charge of a group of investigators, but it never came my way. Frank never forgot that speeding ticket.

I finished eating and said good-bye to Gertie. Her husband had gone to Tupper Lake for groceries and other supplies. She came over to the door when I was on my way out.

"Jason, be careful." She handed me a bag of sandwiches and a gallon of water. The water was ice cold.

I looked down at her and smiled, thanking her for the sandwiches and water. I placed a five-dollar bill in her right hand. She didn't want to accept it, but I insisted.

"I'll be careful."

I checked the Bronco over. The gas tank was half full. The telephone booth outside the Adirondack Hotel wasn't busy. I pulled over and stopped. I took some change out of the ashtray that I never used: just enough change to call the Saranac Hospital. I was saddened to learn that there had been no change in Patty; she was still in the coma.

I admit I did have reservations about going into the woods. I really had no business there. But the motivation was building. I thought of my close friend, Jack Flynn, in Arizona. I knew that if Jack had been involved in a similar situation in the desert country he would do the same as I. We had had some difficult times in the Marine Corps. I guess it was the right-and-wrong equation that drove us both, our feeling of what's right and what's wrong with any given set of circumstances. It was their fault that she lay in a coma in the Saranac Hospital. I wished that Jack were here.

I put the water that Gertie had given me into my large canteen and tucked the sandwiches into my small pack that contained a poncho. I reached into my pocket and brought out my old Boy Scout compass that I have had since I was twelve years old. I took about fifteen feet of strong rope and coiled it and placed it in the one pocket of the pack. There were a few treats, too. The candy bars in the pack were near the top, easy to get to. I had my cell phone with me. In the bottom of my pack was a first-aid kit. I tried to compose my thoughts and relax a little.

The road to Newcomb is a good two-lane macadam highway. I found a small parking area near the head of the Hudson River. From that point toward Indian Lake Village must be a distance of about twenty-five miles as the crow flies. Somewhere in that area was a killer fleeing for his life. He may have in his possession a .45 Caliber automatic pistol and an unknown amount of ammunition.

I had the advantage of knowing the territory--not all of it, but the area where I hunted as a much younger man. My plan was to attempt to locate the two cabins that I had visited long ago. I didn't know if they were still standing or had been torn down. I was going to find out. I estimated the distance to the cabins as five to six miles. It was cloudy and the temperature was around sixty-six degrees. I palmed my compass and took a reading. I would be going south-southwest. I would follow the west side of the river for a ways and then bear to the west slightly. This wasn't going to be an enjoyable hike. It very well could be a life-and-death situation. I would have to be on my toes at all times. I knew that the Rangers are well trained and can improvise many things for any given situation. I had to be very careful. I wanted to be sure that if he didn't shoot me in the back I would have a good chance to take him down. Not with a gun. I wanted to hurt this bastard for what he did to the girl I was falling in love with.

I double-checked the Bronco and locked everything up. I put a note on a piece of paper under the windshield wiper: "I am bird watching. I may be here for a while as I'm looking for a night owl." I didn't go into detail. The statement was partially correct, I was seeking a "jailbird."

There was a footpath that made the hiking easier. I was loaded down pretty good. My Browning 12 Gauge wasn't light, but the sling helped a lot. The canteen bounced around against my pack. The hiking boots felt good. They gave me excellent ankle support. I was in reasonably good health. My memory raced back to those long marches we went on at Camp Pendleton many years ago. God! I remember it well, young we were also rugged when we finished our training. That's where I had met Jack Flynn. He was born in Brooklyn, and at the time I met him he was eighteen years old, like myself. We had had some great times together, forming a mutual bond that has continued over the years.

I walked past an area where some fishermen had placed two or three crotched sticks into the earth to rest their fish-poles on. Some of the bushes were shoulder-high. I looked carefully ahead of me. I had quite a ways to go. Could those cabins still be standing? I flinched when a partridge took off about four feet from me. He would have been tasty if prepared properly. The trees were still a distance from me. From my deep right pocket I took out some spearmint gum. It tasted good. I had visited the Wrigley Mansion in Phoenix, Arizona, several years ago. I bet they had to sell a lot of gum to purchase that. What a beautiful place it was.

I thought about Patty and the coma. A big part of me wanted to be sitting next to her, but I had to be here. The killers had taken advantage of her. That was wrong. I had to think positively. I had to do my part to make it right. With God's help, that was what I planned to do. I was convinced that this was the place for me at the moment. I gritted my teeth in determination to find Norris. My hunches had always served me well in the past. My gut feelings spurred me on.

The trail was narrow in certain locations. I made my way slowly, paying particular attention not to walk on any sticks in the trail that might create noise. I had covered a distance of about three miles. At one point, I had heard a helicopter off in the distance, but didn't know if it were Police or Conservation Officers. It had faded out of my hearing range. I figured that I wasn't too far from the first cabin I was going to check. The brush was getting thicker in this area as I slowly walked along. My breathing was letting me know I was no longer in the best shape for walking any great distances, especially loaded down with heavier clothes than usual and carrying a backpack, binoculars, shotgun, flashlight, cell phone, and ammunition. I was getting tired, but I was still determined to locate those cabins.

I spotted a boulder off to my right, just off the trail, and decided to rest.

I stood the Browning 12 gauge next to the boulder, removed my pack, and took out one of my sandwiches. The ham and cheese that Gertie had packed for me tasted good. I opened my canteen and quenched my thirst. I had just sat back to relax when I heard a crackling noise approaching some distance away. Quietly, I laid my pack and equipment on the ground and hunkered down behind a small pine tree. Whatever was approaching was moving slow. In a couple of minutes I observed the top of a green cap. It sat on the head of an elderly man, hunched over, walking slowly on the trail. He was carrying a fishing pole and a small backpack. He had the largest ears I had ever seen, and a snow-white beard. My binoculars brought his face very close. His wire-rimmed glasses appeared to be perched on the end of his large red nose. His red hunting shirt was hanging off his rounded shoulders. I didn't want to scare him. I started to whistle a tune, "You are my sunshine." He stopped on the trail and looked around slowly.

"Who's there?" he said in a hoarse voice.

"Just a hiker," I replied.

"I can't see you," he uttered.

I approached the old man slowly. He appeared to be harmless. I told him my name.

"Well, Jason, I'm Bradley Waters. Just been doing a little fishing in a stream back there about two miles. They're not biting today."

"It seems quiet today. Did you happen to see anyone down the trail?"

"No, I didn't," Waters replied.

"Are you familiar with a couple of old cabins in the area?"

"Hmm! There used to be two, but now there's only one. The smaller one was burned down a few years back."

"I used to hunt this area when I was a seventeen-year old boy."

"Is that right?" he queried.

"Where do you live, Bradley?"

"Newcomb. I was a banker in New York City and retired a few years ago. I wouldn't live anyplace else. I even purchased my burial lot here. This is the country I love," he stated proudly.

"I can understand that. I love this territory, too."

"Is there something going on? I saw one of those helicopters flying over this way."

I didn't want to scare Bradley Waters, but felt I should tell him about the manhunt.

"I know it is unusual, but there is an escaped killer somewhere between here and Indian Lake. Those probably are police helicopters trying to locate him."

"That so?" replied Waters.

"Sorry we had to meet under these circumstances, but be careful on your way home. Just be aware, I'm certain the radio and television will be carrying the details of the search. Take care of yourself." I cautioned him as he continued on.

"Nice meeting you, and you watch your step."

Bradley Waters, banker, I thought, must be a tough old bird. I didn't ask him how old he was, but if I were going to guess, I'd say at least ninety. You have to give that fellow a lot of credit, out here fishing in the woods, all alone and at that late age in life. I hoped that when I reached his age, that I, too, would be able to enjoy the outdoors and my mountain retreat. I gathered up my things, and slowly headed down the trail. I could rule out one of the cabins. And I knew where the other one was, still about four miles away toward Indian Lake by the way the crow flies. The trail with its continual winding would add another two miles, making it a grueling six-mile hike.

I thought for a minute about Bradley Waters. I could well imagine him sitting in a big boardroom of a bank in New York City hammering out policy to the upper management. Probably he was once an icon of the banking industry, responsible for the hiring and firing of personnel, and the opening and closing of branch banks. Today I met the banking giant of yesterday, now a bent-over old man with his favorite fish-pole--and perhaps, a safety deposit box full of gold. An interesting person on a trail in the mighty Adirondacks.

I moved slowly down the trail. In about an hour I passed the remains of an old burned-out cabin that had once been the pride and joy of its builder, undoubtedly a person who loved the backcountry, who used it for hunting or fishing or just a place to find solace, a long way from the hustle and bustle of urban life with all its complexities. *If this old foundation could speak we probably would hear the voices and laughter of a card game in progress or the aroma of a venison dinner being served.* How quickly life passes. Yesterday, you're a fearless young man or woman, and tomorrow you are, if you're lucky to live that long, a Bradley Waters, walking a trail carrying a fish-pole or a pack basket.

I could just barely remember the cabin that had burned to the ground. It had been a one-room log structure with three windows. I was searching for a plank floor. There had been an outdoor toilet. The well was non-existent and water had to be carried into camp. I remembered that it had belonged to a group of hunters from Colonie, outside of Albany. Many years ago, I had observed several large bucks hanging from nearby tree limbs. I wondered if an oil lamp had been tipped over by some drunken hunter. I continued on my journey keeping alert for any signs of the hunted killer.

Jewell Norris had to be one tough individual. Nate, in St. Regis Falls, was one lucky guy to survive the robbery of his grocery store. I was certain Norris wouldn't have batted an eye in delivering Nate to his heavenly estate. I had to be very careful from now on. He could be anywhere. I was more determined than ever to find the second cabin. According to Bradley Waters, it was still standing.

By mid-afternoon I had accomplished my goal. The cabin was just off the trail. I carefully approached it and noticed there was a sign I couldn't read from where I was standing on the front wooden door. I stayed behind some hardwoods for about fifteen minutes and just observed the L-shaped structure built from logs. It looked the same as I had remembered it many years ago. Whoever owned it had stained the logs, as they seemed to be glossy and much cleaner. After I felt that it was uninhabited, I slowly approached the front door. I read the sign: "Anyone may use this cabin. It is unlocked. The only requirement is to pick up and clean up any mess you have made." On the bottom of the sign was the name of W. Wicks & Sons.

The cabin had four windows and just one door. When I opened the door and entered, I was amazed to see how neat it was. There were a few chairs, a round table, an old icebox, several kerosene lamps and five bunk beds. I looked in the icebox. To my surprise, there were four gallons of water. The cupboard contained a canister set of sugar, flour, coffee and cornmeal. There didn't seem to be any signs of mice in the camp, which appeared airtight. A woodstove was situated in the middle of the main room. An old metal container was full of kindling. I decided to spend the night.

After stacking my gear on an old sofa that was placed against the log wall, I loaded my Browning shotgun with some slugs and double-0 buckshot. I also checked my 9mm pistol. They were both ready for action in the event it became necessary to use deadly force. I wasn't going to take any chances with a killer on the prowl.

The kindling was dry. According to the thermometer on the wall, it was about 47 degrees in the cabin. I struck a match to some paper I had placed in the stove with the wood. In a few minutes the fire was going. I added some larger pieces of maple, which I found in the woodbox. Soon the dampness disappeared and the two-room log cabin became cozy. I lit the two-burner kerosene stove to make some coffee. I wanted to remove my hiking boots, but changed my mind. If Norris came around I had to be ready for him.

I attempted to call the Saranac Hospital to check on Patty's condition, but was unable to make a connection. I began to think about my other investigative work that must be piling up. I knew there were unattended check cases. The letters that I send out to the makers of the checks that are returned for insufficient funds had stopped until this matter was closed. With Norris and Clovis coming into New York State, much havoc had affected many people throughout the region. The locals were afraid in their homes, searchers and their own families were thrown off schedule. It was turmoil for all concerned.

I continued to have mixed emotions about being here in the woods hoping and waiting for an escaped killer and abductor. I was here because he had deeply wronged a friend of mine. She had seen and felt enough brutality for a lifetime in her marriage to Kenneth Olson, without this added torment.

I missed Ruben. He was probably wondering where his master was. We seldom were apart for any lengths of time. He was a great companion. He would certainly offer me protection if he were here tonight. I looked at my watch it read 8:30 p.m. I lit one kerosene lamp. It was quiet in the woods. I looked around the cabin and observed some of the photos tacked to the log wall. One was of a man and a woman. Under it were the names of William and Martha Wicks – 1947. They were a handsome couple. There were several old photos of deer hanging from the limbs of big trees with small groups of hunters kneeling for the photographer.

*Nimrods of the forest*, I thought. Some of the photos were dated, some as far back as 1932. I noticed there were two two-man saws, a bucksaw and an old ice-cutting saw. I found a small radio on a table made from small limbs. It was battery operated. I turned it on. The batteries were good. The static was on the two stations that came in faintly. I clicked the radio off. I had tried my small radio in my pack, but it didn't work either. All I heard was more static; there would be no radio tonight.

# CHAPTER EIGHTEEN

*The command center of the search detail is located at Indian Lake. All efforts to locate Norris have failed. It is assumed that when he abandoned the smashed pickup, leaving both Patty and Clovis for dead, he went directly to the river. It is theorized that the escapee went into the water and stayed there for an undetermined length of time. The bloodhounds have been unsuccessful in detecting the killer's location. Roadblocks have failed to develop useful information. Two or three sightings by residents proved unfounded in relation to Norris. The escapee, a former US Army Ranger, and now a sought-after escaped killer and abductor, is roving the forest of the Adirondack Park. He may have dug a hole to hide in or climbed a tree. His military records reflect that he is an expert in survival techniques. The search continues.*

*The police and Jason Black are unaware that Jewell Norris has built himself a tree stand high above the floor of the forest in a mighty white oak tree. The fleeing killer is exhausted. He has made a bed of leaves and branches. His only food has been some bugs and bark. His arms are covered with small lacerations from going through some wild berry bushes. His .45 Caliber automatic is next to him. The tree is located approximately one mile from the cabin where Jason is spending the night.*

*Norris wants to leave the woods and find a vehicle to steal. He has been hesitant to pursue this plan because of the police presence in the region. Shrewd and cunning, he is a dangerous man on the run. He lacks compassion for his fellow humans. Smaller pine trees next to the oak give Norris good cover from anyone seeking him from the ground or in the air. His nostrils have picked up the scent of smoke coming from the cabin. Norris is afraid of being detected. The smoke, he thinks, may be coming from a fire that the police have built to keep warm. Norris doesn't know. He falls asleep from sheer exhaustion.*

# CHAPTER NINETEEN

At the cabin, I wonder why did I come here? What a waste of time! I should have stayed in Long Lake. I'd better put some more wood on the fire. I went over to the pictures on the log wall. Beneath them was a map of the area. Newcomb was about seven miles from the cabin. It was marked on the map. I made up my mind: *I'll return to Lake Placid sometime in the morning. My hunch didn't pay off. Who knows where Norris is hiding. He could even be out of the region by now.*

I was awakened by the cawing of a crow that landed on the tin roof of the cabin. The bird paced back and forth. "Caw, caw, caw." I smiled. Probably the crow was hungry. I knew I was famished, I got out of the bottom bunk, went to the icebox, took out a jug of water and put some in a washbasin. Although the fire had gone out during the night, the cabin had not cooled off. I splashed the cold water in my face. My whiskers had a two-day growth. *I'll return to the Breakshire and have a hot bath and shave those damned whiskers.*

The bunk had been comfortable. When this mess was all cleared up, I'd drop Mr. Wicks a note and thank him for his hospitality. The address under his picture was in Springfield, Ohio. I made a note of it, then brewed myself a cup of hot coffee and finished my last peanut butter and jelly sandwich.

I tidied the bunk and swept the floor. After I placed the lamp back on the shelf, the cabin was back in order. As I closed the door to leave, I couldn't help but think about the Wicks family. They certainly must be fine folks. The birds were chirping. The crow had left. I could hear that "caw, caw, caw" from another location. I still sensed that Norris wasn't too far away, but I could be wrong. He might have left the area for parts unknown. The image of Patty lying in the hospital bed returned to my thoughts, and I quickened my pace. I was being torn between staying here in the woods or returning to Lake Placid. I decided to leave.

I unloaded my shotgun, but kept the 9mm automatic pistol loaded. I don't care for guns. They can be dangerous. Many hunters over the years have fallen or tripped, sending a shot into their leg or arm. I slowly followed the winding trail back to my Bronco. I found it the way I left it, with the note still under the windshield-wiper blade. My plans were to stop at Gertie's in Long Lake for a good solid breakfast. Before I started the vehicle I looked toward the direction I had come from, to the wooded land that could be hiding a killer. I spoke out loud. "Wherever you are, Norris, you're going to get caught. I may not be there when you do, but I hope you get treated the way you treated Patty. You are definitely going to pay dearly for your deviant acts against your fellow humans," he laughs to himself dispiritedly.

I climbed into the Bronco and sped off for breakfast and, hopefully, a conscious Patty. The parking lot adjacent to Gertie's Diner was about empty. I pulled in close to the building. The Bronco coughed when I turned off the ignition switch. I locked it. The cool air of Long Lake filled my lungs. I stood for a few seconds admiring the water before me. There were two boats far out into the lake. I walked toward the diner. A gray squirrel darted up the leaning maple tree near me.

Gertie was behind the grill working on a set of flapjacks as I walked in.

"Jason, where have you been?" She seemed surprised to see me.

"I've been doing some hiking in the woods up near Newcomb," I responded in a low tired voice.

She flipped the two flapjacks onto a plate and then placed four slices of crisp bacon next to it, with a sunny-side-up egg. Immediately, I knew what I wanted for breakfast.

"Can you repeat that combination? That sure looks good," I asked with a starved look.

"Sure can," she responded with a broad smile.

"Any news this morning regarding the manhunt?" I asked with apprehension.

"A couple of Troopers were in for breakfast. They indicated that the search is still going on. They feel that the killer, Norris, is still in the woods," she replied with a concerned look.

"I think he is, too."

"How is Patty doing? Is she still in a coma?" Gertie asked, looking sad.

"I haven't checked. I'm heading up to Saranac when I'm done here," I replied. I felt the sadness darken my voice. I changed the subject. "Where's your husband? Is he feeling well?" I asked with concern, not seeing him around.

"He's gone to Tupper Lake to pick up some piping. One of our drains has a broken pipe," she replied.

The bacon on the grill sizzled. The flapjacks were a nice shade of golden brown. The coffee tasted extra good after that stale water back in the woods. The peanut butter and jelly sandwich had completely worn off. I was famished.

Gertie placed five pieces of crisp bacon next to the flapjacks and eggs. She gave me a warm smile as she placed the plate before me.

I concentrated on the delicious flapjacks. They were so light, and combined with the warm syrup, they satisfied my taste buds. The bacon crunched as I placed it between my teeth. Gertie returned with a refill for my coffee cup.

The newspaper briefly covered the search for Jewell Norris, escaped killer and abductor of Patty Olson. I flipped to the obits to see who had gone to heaven or that other place. I didn't recognize any of the names. I reached over, picked up my coffee cup, and finished drinking the nectar of breakfast time. *What would we do without coffee?*

Several customers came into the diner as I handed Gertie a twenty-dollar bill. She gave me my change and I returned a two-dollar tip to her. I thanked her and got up. She gave me a warm smile.

"So long, Jason. Come back soon," she said as I rose to leave.

"Take it easy. Say hello to Bob."

I left the diner.

# CHAPTER TWENTY

*In the woods near Newcomb, Jewell Norris is on the move. He is dirty, and the lacerations on his body are showing signs of infection. He has left his hiding place and is on foot creeping carefully in the direction of Newcomb. High in the oak tree, he heard dogs off in a distant section of the forest. This prompted him to change his location. The fully loaded .45 caliber automatic is jammed into the waistband of his filthy trousers. He looks as mean as a junkyard dog seeking a prey. He is following the trail that Jason traveled a few hours before. He stays off the path in heavier brush, but keeps the trail in sight. Suddenly he stops and listens. He has heard someone approaching.*

*Norris strains his eyes and sees the top of a green hat. It is perched on the top of an old man's head. Norris watches with interest. He thinks about grabbing the old man and robbing him, but he hesitates. The old man is bent over and it appears that a fishing pole is on his shoulder. A small pail is in his left hand. Norris crouches low in the bushes and is quiet. He has never passed up an opportunity like this before. He lets the old man pass. Norris doesn't know that he is Bradley Waters, a retired rich banker from New York City, headed to his favorite fishing spot.*

*The old man walks out of sight. The escaped killer begins to move again. He is attentive to his surroundings. Though weakened from lack of proper nourishment, he is still vicious. He creeps along, sticking to the higher bushes and trees. He now can see some of the houses in Newcomb. Traffic is moving toward Long Lake. Norris has made up his mind. He will steal a camper, if he can find one. He needs to get rid of his clothing. He has some money with him, but doesn't know if the town he is approaching has any kind of a store. He knows that going into any business place in this area would be dangerous. He doesn't see any cops around, but what he does see is a clothesline full of blue denim trousers and some shirts. He notices that the clothesline is attached to a garage and house. It doesn't appear that anyone is home at the small one-story wooden house. There are some bushes between the two buildings. It is about 11:00 a.m. He races toward the bushes closest to the brown-painted garage.*

*He checks the yard for a dog, but does not see one. When he reaches the clothesline, he removes a shirt and pair of overalls. He also takes two pairs of white socks. He goes behind the garage and quickly removes his soiled prison clothing, donning the stolen clothes. They smell fresh and clean. He, himself stinks with river water and perspiration. He considers busting into the house, but changes his mind. He stays in the cover of the bushes. The trousers are a little large for him, but his belt takes care of the slack. The denim shirt fits well. It has long sleeves, which cover the tattoos of dragons and the devil. He notices that there is no car in the garage. The side of the garage has a water pipe protruding from a square opening. He can see a cup hanging on a piece of bent coat hanger. He grabs the cup and looks around. No one is in sight. He turns the faucet on. A pump starts and the water gushes out of the faucet. He drinks nine cups of water. He gargles with the tenth cup, and spits it out. He splashes water in his face and wipes it off with the extra pair of white socks, which he then stuffs into a pocket.*

*The escapee is determined to leave this area. He watches the traffic for a long time from behind a clump of small pines. He is paying particular attention to a small rest area. It has no rest rooms, but there is a telephone booth. Norris is poised like a cat waiting to spring at the right moment of time. He is waiting for any type of camper to pull in. He prefers a class C, which is small but with the ability to cook and sleep. He needs sleep. Exhaustion is catching up with him. He tightens up when he sees four Troopers pass by in a police car. They slow down by the rest area, but continue on toward Long Lake.*

*He is persistent. It is late in the afternoon when a small white camper pulls into the rest area. The tiny home on wheels stops. There are no other vehicles in the area or in sight on the highway. Norris calls on all the energy he can muster and runs to the camper. A middle-aged man has exited the vehicle and is wiping his taillights with a cloth.*

# CHAPTER TWENTY-ONE

The breakfast at Gertie's was excellent. I felt stuffed. I filled the Bronco at the gas station just over the bridge in Long Lake, on the way to Tupper. The tank took eleven gallons. My twenty-dollar bill was never the same. The clerk smiled when she gave me back the change. I went to the pay phone to make a call and was advised by the attendant the phone was out of order. I thanked him and climbed into the Bronco.

I tried to call the Saranac Lake Hospital, but couldn't make the connection. My thoughts were constantly wondering how Patty was progressing. I decided that I would stop at the hospital on the way to the Breakshire Lodge. My concern and worry were painfully increasing.

The traffic was light on the way to Tupper Lake. There were no police cars in the yard at the Tupper Lake State Trooper Barracks. I could imagine how tired the Troopers must be from this difficult manhunt. Anxious to learn how the manhunt was progressing, I turned the radio on, but again static interfered with radio reception. Disgusted, I turned the radio off.

Just outside of Tupper Lake on Route 3, I came across a roadblock. Two large burly Troopers stood in the road with shotguns. I slowed down. One of the men signaled me to pull over. I complied.

"Where are you headed, fella?" the taller Trooper asked.

"The Saranac Lake Hospital," I answered with respect. I didn't know either Trooper, and they didn't know me.

"We're looking for an escapee from an Ohio prison. He is a murderer," the taller Trooper said, bluntly.

"Yeah, I heard about that," I responded. I didn't want to go into a long story about being a former member.

"So, be careful, Mister. He could be anyplace. Don't pick up any hitchhikers," the other Trooper said with concern.

"Thanks, fellas. I'll be careful."

The Bronco sputtered a little as I pulled away. The two Troopers were on the job and, knowing about how vicious their hunted prey was, they would stay on their guard. The Trooper was correct. Norris could be anyplace.

I could imagine my work piling up. I thought about my mailbox and how full it would be upon my return to Old Forge. One other time when I was out of town, the box was jammed full of letters, bad check notices, magazines and junk mail. The postmaster had politely warned me that their office was for the delivery of mail, not a storage facility for Jason Black's Private Investigation business. I chuckled to myself. I knew they'd watch my mailbox. They were fine folks.

Jack Flynn in Arizona would be wondering what happened to me. I could well imagine that there would be a call from him on my answering machine when I returned. I wondered when that would be. This was a non-profit time for me in my new career. I was doing this for Patty. I prayed by now that she would be out of her coma. *Damn that Norris to hell,* I thought. *It's his fault.* I couldn't help but think that my trip into the woods was a waste of time. I could have come across him, and that had been what I was hoping for. Instead, I came across a bent over old man by the name of Bradley Waters, a retired banker, wearing a green hat. *Nice man,* I thought.

The parking lot was crowded when I pulled into the hospital area. I located a space at the end of the third line. I was fortunate. I made certain that the Bronco was locked. My shotgun was under a blanket in the back. I was still carrying my 9mm automatic pistol. I hurried to the entrance, anxious to see Patty. The elevator door opened as I was approaching, and a chubby nurse pushing a medicine cart exited the metal cage.

The intensive care unit was humming with activity. I heard a nurse say, "Make room in 206 for a gunshot victim." She was demanding and insistent.

I stopped at the nurses' station. Two nurses looked at me with smiles on their faces.

"Wonderful news for you, Mr. Black. Patty came out of her coma. She is very weak, but she is a very lucky lady," the older nurse said looking directly into my eyes.

"Thank you, nurse. I can't tell you how relieved I am," I replied with joy in my heart struggling to hold back my tears. "May I see her?" I was excited.

"You can look in, but she is sleeping now," the nurse said.

"Thank you."

I looked into her room. Pale, her lids covering her eyes, she was lying on her back. There were tubes in her nostrils, and an IV dripped from the suspended plastic bag. A heart monitor was blipping a line across a screen. Her long blond hair covered part of her pillow. My eyes filled with tears of joy and sadness at the same time. Hopefully, she would recover fully. I was very concerned, but my worry was lessened by the nurse's comments. I just stood and stared at her in the hospital bed. Flowers in vases lined her dresser and some were on a nearby table. I looked at some of the cards. They were from all the folks in Old Forge. One card, with numerous signatures stated, "From the gang at John's Diner, Get well Patty, we miss you." One card surprised me. It was from Dale Rush. The card was beautiful. But the message shocked and upset me. It read, "I love you."

"What the hell?" I spoke aloud, furious and hurt inside.

Could it be possible that Dale was dating Patty? *That can't be,* I thought. *But what of the day that I observed Dale and Patty by the door at John's, and the look on both their faces?* I wondered. *Was he pressing her for a date?* My mind was racing back and forth. *Did I miss something here? Wouldn't Patty have told me? Wouldn't Dale?* I had to gather my senses. This was no time to go off half-cocked. I composed my thoughts. I went around the far side of the bed, leaned over, and gently pressed my lips on her forehead. Yes. I could no longer fool myself. I loved her.

I returned to the nurses' station and thanked the two behind the counter. Both remembered me from my days on the force and all the accidents I had investigated. They smiled.

My heart was resolved and happy as I went down the elevator. I had always thought a great deal of Dale Rush. Dale and I were going to have a heart-to-heart talk in the very near future.

I was leaving the hospital when I spotted the big Dodge of Wilt Chambers. He had just pulled into the parking lot. It took him a while to get out of the truck. A mountain of a man with a kind heart, he was carrying some flowers.

"Wilt! Wilt! How are you?" I was glad to see the big fellow.

"Jason. How are you? We all miss you at the diner and several of the folks around Old Forge are wondering where you disappeared to. Of course I told them you were working on an important case."

"Boy! Am I glad to see you, Wilt. That is so nice of you to drive all the way up here to Saranac Lake."

"How is she, Jason?" The sweat was beading on Wilt's red cheeks.

"I think she's going to be all right. She's sleeping now. The good news is that she has come out of the coma. I'm happy about that."

"Great," Wilt responded, joyfully.

"How would you like to join me for supper? You don't have to rush back, do you?" I asked him sincerely, hoping he'd say yes.

"Sure, I'll be glad to."

"You know where the Breakshire Lodge is located in Lake Placid?" I replied.

"I sure do." He seemed overjoyed with the invitation.

"I'll see you there in about an hour. Is that all right with you?" I asked.

"Fine. I'll be there."

I grabbed the big guy's hand and shook it. His grip and the look on his face reminded me that he was a true friend.

"See you later."

I was hoping that Wilt wouldn't be chewing the tobacco by the time he arrived at the Breakshire. Then I thought, *Oh, what the heck if he is.* I was glad to have a good friend like him. I couldn't help but think about Dale. He was a good friend of mine, too. He knows of my feelings toward Patty.

When I arrived at the Breakshire, I unloaded the Bronco. Tom Huston had a special safe for firearms. He had purchased it to accommodate the many hunters who visited the area. I knew that he wouldn't mind placing my Browning 12 gauge shotgun in the vault for safekeeping. I would keep my 9mm automatic pistol with me.

With everything in order, I proceeded to room #201. It wasn't like my log home, but it offered a bit of solace while I was away. *Ruben must be missing me by now*, I thought. I removed my clothes and boots. As I lay on the bed for a few minutes, I almost fell asleep. I forced myself to get up.

The hot water and the shaving cream felt good on my face. As I gripped the straight razor and removed my fast-growing whiskers, I nicked my chin. The blood dripped and landed on the sink. I held a cold washcloth against the cut for a couple of minutes. It stopped bleeding. *Boy! Does it sting.*

Hot showers are relaxing. I scrubbed religiously. I even whistled a little, remembering as always that my dad sang when bathing. *Must be in the genes.*

I wondered about Norris. I couldn't believe that members of the search party hadn't spotted him in the woods. I couldn't get him out of my mind. I was in hopes that he'd soon be apprehended by the Troopers.

One thing I knew. The Breakshire Lodge had large bath towels. I felt like a million bucks. I threw some powder on my hand and rubbed it all over my chest and arms. I loved the woods, but it was great to feel fresh and clean. And I was famished again.

I had just finished dressing when the telephone sounded a short ring. The desk clerk told me that a Wilt Chambers was waiting for me in the lobby. I thanked her. I combed my hair and patted some of the Lodge aftershave lotion on my face. The nick still stung. I hid my 9mm automatic pistol. I didn't think that it would be necessary to carry it to dinner.

The elevator was on an upper floor, so I chose to take the stairs to the lobby. One of the maids was dusting the stairway with a large mop. I excused myself as I passed her. She gave me a broad grin.

When I opened the door into the lobby I could see the huge man sitting on one of the ten couches in the room. He took up both cushions. He was flipping the pages of a sports magazine.

"Are you hungry, Wilt?" I asked, knowing that he could eat

anytime.

"I could eat a whole Angus." He put the magazine on the end table.

"You're in for a treat, Wilt. That happens to be the special tonight," I answered. I knew Wilt had already read the menu posted by the entrance to the elaborate dining room. We selected a large table in the rear of the dining room and seated ourselves.

"I'm happy that Patty has come around. Sometimes it takes forever to come out of a coma. She is a fortunate gal. The nurses let me peek in at her when I dropped the flowers off. She was lying on her back, sound asleep. What a beauty!"

"I hear you, Wilt. She's a wonderful young woman. I just don't understand how she got tangled up with Kenneth. He's a bad guy." I was firmly convinced of that.

"Yeah, you can say that again," Wilt said, looking at the menu. "I am happy that you and Patty are finally getting together. I look at her as an honorary daughter."

"I know you do, Wilt. If anything ever happens to me, I'd appreciate it if you would look out for her interest."

"You can count on that, Jason." He looked me in the eye.

Our waitress was Sheila, a slender brunette with her hair in a bun. Small earrings clung to her earlobes. She was friendly. She wore her lipstick well. Her fingernails were long and painted black. I knew her since my duty days with the Troopers. I had investigated her father's tragic fatality years ago, when he was struck by a truck hauling potatoes. She had always wanted to be a fashion model.

"Can I take your order, gentlemen?" Her voice was clear and precise.

I looked at Wilt and nodded for him to order. Neither one of us wanted a drink from the bar.

"I'll have the Angus prime rib medium, baked potato, garden salad, some hot rolls and plenty of butter. Oh! And a glass of ice-cold water." Wilt blushed when he looked up at Sheila. He thanked her.

"Sheila, everything looks good. I'll have the salmon steak, home fries, garden salad, hot rolls and a glass of ice-cold water. Thank you," I said. Sheila was a long time waitress at the Breakshire.

Wilt and I discussed the ongoing manhunt. We discussed how

clever Jewell Norris had been in his flight from the police into a land that he had never visited before. He was a smart guy, or else he was just plain lucky. Wilt agreed with my assessment of Norris. I told Wilt that I had spent one night in the woods in the search area without success. I shared with him my thoughts and my belief that Norris wasn't too far away from me at the time, and the fact that maybe it was a good thing that we didn't meet each other in the brush. I truly believed that only one of us would have left the woods. However, I didn't know which one of us would have survived an altercation.

"Jason, you were taking one hell of a chance. I understand according to the news that Norris was a former U.S. Army Ranger before he chose the life of crime. With his training he could have taken you out in the wink of an eye. You were a fool to go into the woods after him. You're not a cop anymore." He spoke in a whisper.

"Yeah, you're probably right, but I'll tell you one thing. We learned a few tricks in the Marine Corps, and don't forget that either, Wilt." I was a little annoyed at Wilt's remark.

"I know, I know, but you're my friend and I want you to be around for a long time. Let the Troopers take care of that bird. They'll get him. It may take awhile, but you wait and see, he'll make a mistake." Wilt was emphatic.

"Yeah, you're right, again." I knew what Wilt meant.

"Listen, Patty is going to want you around until you're an old man, and then some." Wilt laughed.

Sheila had served the garden salads and we were just completing them when she appeared with her tray of steaming prime rib and salmon steak. Wilt and I were ready to take on the solid food. The prime was huge and must have weighed three pounds. And I had never seen such a large salmon steak in my life.

We didn't say much during dinner. I heard Wilt slurp a little, and I knew that he realized what he had done. He blushed again, for the second time. The salmon steak flaked off. It was tender. I was happy that Wilt had gotten rid of his chewing tobacco for our dinner treat. Wilt was a good friend, and I knew that. So was Charlie Perkins. I couldn't help but think of the gang from John's Diner and all the rest of the folks in Old Forge. I didn't give it a second thought, I'd call that town home for the rest of my life. I knew that I'd do some traveling, but I would return to my log home in the end, God willing.

Sheila returned to check on us a couple of times. The third time she found our plates empty. She removed them and left the dessert menu with us for possible consideration. I didn't order dessert. I could understand why Wilt took up two seats at the counter of John's Diner. He ordered two pieces of apple pie with two large cuts of extra strong cheddar cheese. He topped that off with a cup of strong black coffee.

I looked around for Tom Huston, but I was told that he had had to fly to New York City on business. I wanted to introduce him to Wilt, who I had hoped would be interested in carving a large black bear out of a log for the Breakshire. I explained to Wilt how it would make an interesting conversation piece for the Lodge, especially having it displayed in the lobby. I wanted it as a surprise. I had learned that Tom Huston loved the Adirondack black bear.

Wilt agreed with me. He would begin the project in a couple of weeks. I was happy about that. Tom Huston was a good man and was involved in many civic matters in the Lake Placid area. This would be a good way to thank him for his generosity. I told Wilt I'd pay him for his efforts.

We finished our conversation as Wilt indicated that he should leave for Old Forge. Morning comes fast, and Wilt had to be in Lyons Falls the next day to discuss a pulpwood contract with some landowners.

I paid for the meals and Wilt insisted that he leave the gratuity. He left a brand-new crisp ten-dollar bill on the table. Sheila happened to go by and gave us both a hearty thank you and a smile. Wilt blushed for the third time.

"Sheila, thank you for your great service," I said with sincerity.

"Gentlemen, it was my pleasure." She grinned and gave Wilt a wink.

"I'll be back, Sheila," Wilt added. His huge body and triple chins seemed to shake.

I knew Wilt would return. He loved the dinner. Anywhere there was good food, Wilt wouldn't be too far away.

We walked out of the Lodge together. I walked with Wilt to his big Dodge pickup. I shook his hand and thanked him for bringing flowers for Patty. We said good-bye. I waved at him as he headed toward the entrance to the highway. Wilt tooted and the big truck roared off toward Saranac.  I knew that he would probably make a quick stop at the hospital to see Patty before he headed to Old Forge. Wilt Chambers was a gentle giant and my friend.

# CHAPTER TWENTY-TWO

*Jewell Norris shoves his .45 caliber automatic pistol into the ribs of the motor-home owner. The older man turns pale with fright.*

*"Wha—Wha--What do you want?" he asks Norris in a panicky voice.*

*"I'm taking your camper, old man." His snarling voice is demanding and his face is contorted with hate.*

*"Don't hurt me, Mister. I've got a heart condition," he pleads with the gun-toting escaped killer.*

*For an instance, Norris relents his demand, lowering his pistol. Then he raises it to the man's head and continues with his threatening voice: "I want your camper and any money you have. Do ya understand me, old man?"*

*"I'll give you anything. Just take it, but don't hurt me. I don't feel well." The man becomes even paler and he feels weak. His knees shake.*

*Norris knows that the police are getting closer and at any moment a police car can come down the road. He has to move fast.*

*"Open the back door of your camper," he demands of the man, prodding him with his gun.*

*Shaky and frightened, the man fumbles in his pocket for the key to unlock the camper rear door. He places the key in the lock and Norris pushes him through the door. The interior is small but*

153

*contains all the necessary resources for a livable home.*

*"Got any rope?" Norris demands.*

*"In that cabinet drawer, Mister."*

*Holding the pistol against the man's back, Norris opens the drawer and locates some strong twine.*

*"Lay down," Norris viciously commands.*

*Norris proceeds to wrap the twine around the man's hands and ankles. He hurries.*

*"Don't hurt me," the man continues to plead.*

*"Shut up."*

*"You're the fella the cops are looking for! Right?"*

*"I told you to shut up," Norris says with a threatening tone in his voice.*

*"I'll shut up." The old man is fearful of being gagged.*

*The old man is a retired postal worker. His wife passed away about six months ago. It has been his dream to visit the Adirondack Park of New York State. William O'Shea is seventy-five years old and misses his wife. They were married fifty-two years. Both of his sons were killed in the military.*

*Norris looks through the camper. He finds a razor and shaving cream, and turns the faucet on in the tiny bathroom. In a few minutes, the long whiskers have been removed. He takes a pair of scissors and cuts his hair. O'Shea, propped up against a bunk bed, doesn't miss a trick. He watches Norris change his appearance.*

*"Old man, do ya have any sunglasses in this box?" he growls.*

*"In the bottom drawer," O'Shea responds weakly.*

*Norris pulls open the bottom drawer and grabs the largest pair he can find. He wants to cover as much of his face as possible. Norris is thirsty, too, and opens the refrigerator door. The small unit is full of soda pop. Norris opens a can of root beer and guzzles it down. The .45 caliber pistol is jammed in his waistband. The stolen denim jeans hang on him like a sack. O'Shea is afraid of this killer. Norris is a man on the run, who doesn't have anything to lose, but when he looks down at the seventy-five-year-old man he thinks about the father he wishes he could have had. This man is old enough to have been his father. He decides that he won't shoot him at this time in the event he is in need of a hostage. Plenty of time for that later.*

*"Old man, I want you to keep your mouth shut. I'm not going to gag you, but if I hear you hollering, you're going to be gagged. Do you understand me?" Norris is adamant in his order.*

*"Yes, I understand," O'Shea nervously responds.*

*"I'll check in on you later. Is there a road map in the cab?"*

*"Yes, over the passenger side visor. When my wife was alive, she would be in charge of the directions we traveled. I just left the map on her side," O'Shea replies with tears in his eyes.*

*"Quit your blubbering," Norris says in a moderated voice.*

*O'Shea picks up on the killer's change of tone. He thinks that maybe this guy isn't as tough as he appears to be. Nevertheless, O'Shea decides to do what he was told, and keep his mouth shut.*

*Norris takes the keys and opens the rear door of the camper. He goes outside and O'Shea can hear him lock the door. A few seconds go by and he hears the driver's door open. The camper is on a Ford chassis and the engine is the big one, a 460. Norris starts the camper and leaves the small parking area, heading toward Long Lake. Norris feels confident that he is now on the road to freedom. He looks at the fuel gauge. The indicator reflects a full tank. He has a smirky grin on his face that seems to project an aura of confidence.*

*Captain Frank Temple has just hung up the telephone. The Division Superintendent wants an update concerning the manhunt taking place inside the Blue Line of the Adirondack Park. The Captain's forehead is covered with beads of perspiration. No one wants the killer apprehended more than Frank Temple. The Ohio authorities call Troop Headquarters every day to see if prisoner #100021 is in custody.*

*Temple is well aware of Norris's military record. Norris was one of the elite rangers sent in on special missions behind battle lines. He is a survivor and Frank knows it. But the Captain has a lot of confidence in the men and women of Troop "S." Norris will be apprehended. The only part of the equation is, when?*

# CHAPTER TWENTY-THREE

My telephone rang in Room 201 at the Breakshire Lodge. I picked up the receiver. I knew the voice.

"Good morning, Captain," I said.

"Jason, I'm sending a couple of investigators over to the hospital to interview Patty Olson. Maybe she can shed some light on this escaped killer. She is lucky to be alive."

"You'd better check with her doctor first." I cautioned. "Patty doesn't need any setbacks in her recovery," I added.

"We did," he answered quickly.

"What did he say?" I asked with sharp curiosity.

"According to the doctor, Patty is recovering faster than they had anticipated. He indicated that the interview can take place tomorrow."

"I want to be there when they interview her," I flashed back.

"That's why I called." He spoke sharply with a voice of authority.

"Thank you. I really appreciate it. Patty needs me there for support."

"See you at 1:00 p.m. sharp at the hospital."

"I'll be there."

My thoughts were of Patty. Would she be able to handle an interview? I would be there during the questioning. I was pleased that Temple had called me. I knew that Frank was up-front. He didn't believe in those clandestine tactics. I respected him for that. He was a true professional. He would always listen to both sides of a story

157

before he would make a decision, unlike many of his counterparts.

I thought, too, about the members of Troop S. The manhunt was a tiring detail to be assigned to. My memory flashed back to several searches that I had been involved with. It interferes with pending matters and other investigations that are ongoing. People on roadblocks can't help but be on edge, stopping cars and people. It has a way of draining one's strength and endurance, especially looking for a killer, like Norris. I couldn't believe that there were no bona fide sightings.

My work was piling up. I had called the postmaster at Old Forge. I learned that my mailbox was full of mail. There was no doubt in my mind: the flasher on my answering machine had to be working overtime. I operated alone, no secretary or clerk, just me, wearing a half-dozen hats.

I was somewhat relieved. Patty was gaining rapidly. I had no idea when she was to be released. I knew that her neighbor, Harriet Stone, would be more than willing to help Patty until she could return to normal health. In fact, there would be many other people in Old Forge who would lend a hand to Patty.

I called the hospital to check on Patty. The nurse at the hospital gave me even more encouragement. She indicated that Patty was presently asleep. The nursing staff had Patty walking earlier in the day. She didn't feel that it would be necessary for me to make an appearance until tomorrow, at which time the interview was to take place with the investigators. I told the nurse that I would call Patty before I retired for the evening.

I rolled and tossed all night. My mind was busy. I dozed off about 5:00 a.m. and woke with a start, at 7:00 a.m. I turned the radio on and again all I got was static. I was hoping that the news would tell us that Norris had been apprehended. I shut off the radio due to the continual static and I switched on the television. There was no mention of any apprehension. The news commentator did indicate that the manhunt was still operational. There were no sightings of Norris. He was still free.

After a quick shower, I dressed. I was getting homesick for Old Forge and my dog. Patty was on the road to recovery and probably would be released from the Saranac Lake hospital soon. My work was piling up. I hoped that my clients would be patient. I went down to the dining room for breakfast. I could always think better on a full stomach.

The three waitresses on duty were busy. I took a small table in the corner near the window. As always the table was set and a fresh flower with a long stem protruded from a cut-glass vase. I didn't know the waitress who came to my table. According to her nameplate, she was Cynthia. She smiled.

"May I help you?" she inquired.

"Yes, I'd like a cheese omelet, a few hash brown potatoes, a glass of orange juice, and an order of whole wheat toast, and coffee with cream."

"Thank you, sir," she said, and smiled, looking directly into my eyes.

The breakfast was served piping hot. Everything was delicious. The blackberry jelly tasted like fresh berries from the vine. I finished, leaving the two-dollar tip on the table underneath the sugar bowl. I looked for Tom Huston, but he wasn't around. The cashier took my check and currency and gave me back my change. She gave me a smile, which I returned.

When I arrived at the hospital, I was surprised to learn that two investigators had already been there and left. The head nurse gave me all the details. The statement consisted of one handwritten page. The nurse happened to be a notary public and had taken the oath. Patty had signed the statement at the bottom. I was furious that the investigators had not waited for my arrival.

I went to Patty's room. "Good morning, beautiful," I said. She looked weak, and her face was pale. She smiled. I leaned over and kissed her cheek.

"Hello, Sherlock," she said with a weakness in her voice.

"I love you, baby." I spoke in a whisper.

"Me too, Sherlock." She shifted her slender body to her left side.

"How are ya feeling?"

"Much better." She smiled.

I learned from Patty that the doctors wanted her to stay in the hospital one more week until she got her strength back. We talked about Clovis being killed in the accident and how Norris had fled from the scene, and was still on the run and hadn't been seen.

"How will I get back to Old Forge?" she asked with a worried look.

"I'll bring you home; don't worry about that." I could tell that Patty was concerned about the coming weeks. I told her that her neighbor and landlord, Harriet Stone, would watch over her. And that I would become a pest checking on her as often as I could. She was happy about that.

"Why didn't the investigators wait for me, Patty?" I asked.

"They wanted you to know, Jason, that they had to be at another location. They told me to tell you they were sorry and would explain later," she said, looking exhausted.

I told her that I had to return to Old Forge and that I would return to Saranac and bring her home when the hospital released her, and visit her as often as I can throughout the week.

"I'm getting behind on some of my work. I'll stop by Harriet Stone's and let her know that you'll be coming home in about a week. Let's hope that the killer will be apprehended soon. He's got to show up. Somebody's got to catch sight of him."

"Jason, you let the police handle it," she said with a concerned look on her face.

"Don't worry; they'll get him."

I said good-bye to her and left the hospital. The trip to Old Forge was uneventful, except for a car-deer accident between Blue Mountain Lake and Inlet. When I arrived at the Eagle Bay kennel, the sun was low in the bright red sky. Ruben was so glad to see his master that he jumped high in the air, almost knocking a lamp over in the waiting room. The attendant had given the big dog a bath, and a red ribbon was tied around his neck over the collar. I paid the bill.

# CHAPTER TWENTY-FOUR

*The Ford camper drives slowly through Long Lake, heading north on Route 30. The driver, wearing large dark sunglasses, grips the wheel. He sits low in the seat. It is mid-afternoon. Unbeknownst to each other, Jason and Jewell Norris have passed each other. The owner, William O'Shea, is in the rear of the camper. His hands and feet are bound. At the moment, he is helpless.*

*"I'm going to get even with that guy in the grocery store." Norris is speaking out loud to himself with a look of hate and revenge in his heart. The .45 caliber automatic is under an old newspaper on the passenger seat of the camper.*

*In the back, O'Shea has managed to loosen his bonds. He soon frees his hands and unties the cord wrapped around his ankles. He is careful not to make any noise. The camper is accessible only through the rear door. O'Shea gathers his wits, and takes his watch out of the drawer and places it on his right wrist. His mind is racing. He has to get away from the man behind the steering wheel of his camper. He is glad that his wife isn't with him. His eyes tear up when he thinks about her. He knows that she is in heaven looking down on him.*

*Norris keeps his speed well under the limit. He passes a sign that reads, Tupper Lake. He has to stop for a red light. O'Shea, taking advantage of the moment, quietly opens the rear door of the camper, climbs out and walks down the street away from the*

161

*killer. He doesn't look back. His camper continues north on Route 30, without the owner. O'Shea, shaken up and frightened, locates a telephone by a gas station and calls the police. A Tupper Lake based Trooper meets him at the booth in about ten minutes. The retired postal worker tells his story to Trooper K.A. Johnson, who in turn notifies his headquarters. O'Shea is taken to the Tupper Lake's barracks to give a sworn statement on the theft of his Ford camper. Troopers involved in the search detail are alerted to be on the lookout for the Ford Class C camper bearing Rhode Island registration plate number 3Q-2000.*

*Norris, unaware that the older man has fled his captivity, continues north on Route 30. The mind of the escaped killer is seething with one thought: to get even with the owner of the St. Regis Falls grocery store for shooting him.*

# CHAPTER TWENTY-FIVE

I am busy at my typewriter when the telephone rings.

"Hello, Jason," Lieutenant Garrison says, with authority. "Frank Temple asked me to call you to keep you posted on any new details about the manhunt."

"Hi, Roy. What's up?" I inquire curiously.

"We believe that Norris is in a stolen Ford camper heading north on Route 30. We are endeavoring to have roadblocks set up north of Tupper Lake. When Norris robbed the grocery store in St. Regis Falls, he had threatened to get even with the owner, Nate, for shooting him. He may be heading there."

"Thanks for calling, Roy." I hung the phone up.

I checked Ruben's water and food dish. They were full. I strapped on my 9mm automatic, locked the house, and headed to my vehicle. The traffic was light on Route 28. I floored the Bronco, hoping that no one would pull off from a side street. I had to get to St. Regis Falls.

# CHAPTER TWENTY-SIX

*Norris is just south of Meachum Lake when he pulls into a rest area to check on the older man and owner of the camper. He is shocked when he finds the rear door unlocked and swears as he learns that O'Shea has been able to free himself. Surmising that the cops will be alerted, he decides to leave the camper parked in the rest area. He goes to the cab of the camper and takes his .45 automatic from the seat and places it in his waistband. He disappears into the woods heading in the direction of St. Regis Falls on foot. His face is a mask of hate. He is bent on paying Nate back for wounding him.*

*After Norris enters the woods, twenty minutes pass by. He does not see the two Troopers who pull into the rest area to check the Ford Class C camper bearing Rhode Island registration.*

# CHAPTER TWENTY-SEVEN

I appreciated the call from Roy Garrison. As I approached Meachum Lake, I couldn't help but notice the two police cars in the northbound rest area. I surmised the camper was the one Norris had stolen. I pulled in and got out of the Bronco.

"Where is the prisoner?" I shouted loudly.

"Not here," one Trooper replied, bluntly.

"Where in the hell is he?" I retorted.

"We think he's in the woods. He could be anyplace," the Trooper replied, sharply.

"You're Jason Black, aren't you?" the first Trooper asked.

"That's me," I responded.

I didn't feel that my presence would accomplish anything there. I thanked the Troopers. They informed me that the victim was at their Tupper Lake office, and that he was in good shape. I nodded and left the rest area. I hadn't seen Nate in years. Although I had heard about the shootout between him and Norris, I had not talked to Nate. I headed toward St. Regis Falls. I drove slowly. I paid particular attention to the woods on my left. I had a gut feeling that the brazen escaped killer was not far away. I knew that the Troopers were preparing to conduct an intensive search of the area and that some of the Troopers would be sent to St. Regis Falls.

When I reached Santa Clara I pulled alongside of the hotel located on the south side of the highway. I decided I'd sit here for a while and keep my eyes open. Norris could pop out of the woods at any time.

I scanned the edge of the timber with my binoculars. Two large black crows were perched high in a tree, cawing. My mind raced back to the early seventies when I frequented the Santa Clara Hotel. In those days, it had been a great place to visit for a week or two during snowmobile season. The twenty-six rooms were usually full of fun-loving folks. I had known the owner well. She's in heaven now. I could see her bobbing around the large hotel kitchen, checking the pots of boiling vegetables, opening the oven to view the succulent roasts of beef, and at the same time making certain that her customers were taken care of. Mildred and William Collier had operated the hotel for fifty years together, and after William's passing, she had carried on the business. It was a true Adirondack experience. I had often thought about the people who visited the hotel during those fifty years that the Colliers ran it. Sitting in the huge dining room, one could view the many deer heads that line the walls. Many of the deer taken were prize winners for the number of points on their racks. One could almost hear the chatter sitting there in the silence of that huge room. The hunters, the trappers, the loggers, the local people, and the tourists passing through the hamlet had been contributors to those voices of yesterday. Communication was very much alive in that period of time, during the middle 1920's to the 1970's, when people talked to each other in person.

Mildred had worn more than one hat. She had been the postmaster and storekeeper. The post office was located in one corner of their store. Some of my conversations with her revealed that Santa Clara had once been a center of activity. Logging and a large girls' school had once flourished in the community. The railroad had a spur that connected Santa Clara with the outside world. Seven hundred or more young ladies from families of influence attended the boarding school, at the time.

Just in my few encounters, visiting and staying at the hotel as a guest, had been a worthwhile learning experience. From those bits and pieces of information, the listener (me) was able to visualize that period of time and the day-to-day struggle that people like Mildred and William had endured. I also remembered, from when I was assigned to the district, how cooperative the people were. I could attest to the fact that many of them were great cooks and bakers, too.

The pristine beauty of the Adirondack Park had captured not only my imagination, but my heart and soul as well. Where else could one find a land that had so much to offer, from the wildlife inhabitants to the tallest timber and smallest flower of the woods? The streams, rivers, and lakes added to my solace. It provided a sense of complete freedom, but sometimes it was a most difficult place to earn a decent living wage. I wasn't wealthy. I did know that money may bring a person worldly possessions, but it doesn't necessarily bring him or her complete happiness.

I couldn't help but think of Patty, as I sat in the Bronco next to the boarded-up old hotel. I wondered if we, two people from different worlds, could find happiness in marriage. She was once wedded to a man who constantly imbibed alcohol, a man who assaulted her in his drunken state. I, twice divorced (partially caused by my being a workaholic) was now a private investigator. Was it possible for two people with our divergent backgrounds to merge into one workable marital relationship? Time would tell.

Two police cars passed in front of my line of sight. I knew they were heading to St. Regis Falls and Nate's grocery store. I was almost ready to head to Nate's myself, when I spotted a man coming out of the woods. Some distance from me, he was walking slowly and he seemed to be looking around. He stopped walking and ran into some thick brush, crouching down. He was difficult to observe at this point. All of a sudden I saw a three-wheeler coming down a snowmobile trail. The operator was wearing a helmet. He was moving fast and then slowed down to negotiate a right-hand turn onto a side street. He continued down the street and disappeared from my line of sight.

The man who was hiding came out from the thick brush and again was walking in my direction. He moved slowly and kept looking behind him, as though someone or something was following him. He was coming closer. I could see that he was wearing dark sunglasses. He appeared scraggly. Even though his sunglasses covered a portion of his upper face, I knew that he was the killer, Jewell Norris. Keeping my word to Captain Temple, and to cover my butt, I dialed Troop S Headquarters. The Captain's office was buzzed. "Captain Temple speaking." His voice was sharp and authoritative.

"Captain, Jason here. I have to make this quick. I'm in Santa Clara, parked next to the old hotel. Jewell Norris is walking toward me, as I speak. He's getting closer, have to hang up."

"We'll send the Troopers! Be careful!" the Captain said excitedly.

I tightened up. My nerves were on edge. I removed my pistol from my shoulder holster. It was ready to fire. Norris was looking the Bronco over. I could see the bulge under his blue denim shirt. He was approaching the passenger side. I opened the driver's door and exited the Bronco. At least I had the Bronco between us. I couldn't see his eyes, but his face was mean.

I looked at him over the top of the Bronco as I gripped my automatic pistol firmly. I was tense. I knew he had been serving a life sentence for a double homicide in Ohio, before he and Clovis escaped from an underground tunnel. I knew he was dangerous. I spoke first, politely: "Good day for a hike in the woods." I watched him closely.

"Yeah, I was checking my camp. My car won't start, so I had to hoof it out of the woods. Could you give me a ride into St. Regis Falls?" he asked.

I wanted to stall the lying bastard for a few minutes.

"What seems to be the matter with your car?" I asked.

"I--I--I really don't know," he stammered.

"Maybe I could help you get it started, or give you a tow. I've got a chain."

I could tell he was nervous. I was waiting for him to go for the bulge under his shirt.

"I--I don't think you could help me, mister. By the way, what are you doing here by this old building?" he queried.

"I'm doing research on old hotels for an article." I lied and watched him closely.

"What for?" he curtly asked.

"It's a hobby of mine, old buildings," I replied. I was waiting for him to make a wrong move.

All of a sudden four police cars flashed into the parking area by the old hotel. They did not use their sirens. Norris made a move for the bulge under his shirt.

"Hold it!" I shouted, aiming my pistol at his head. He hesitated.

"Don't shoot," he whined.

"Put your hands straight up in the air," I commanded. "I'm making a citizen's arrest and I'm turning you over to these Troopers."

Sergeant James Johnson was at my side when I informed Jewell Norris.

"Sergeant Johnson, I'm turning Mr. Norris over to you." I wanted to tell Norris what I really thought of him, but I chose to curb my remarks. I knew that it would be fruitless to converse with him any further. The Troopers cuffed the killer and took his .45 caliber pistol from him. The pistol was unloaded and placed in an evidence container and marked as such.

The Troopers placed Norris in a police car. The manhunt was officially over. Sergeant Johnson approached me and thanked me for my cooperation.

"Jason, Captain Temple and Lieutenant Roy Garrison will be pleased that Norris has been apprehended, and I'm certain you will be hearing from them. Thanks again, Jason." Sergeant Johnson was sincere. The Troopers involved gave me a wave from their cars and left the parking lot, headed for Troop S Headquarters.

I decided to go into St. Regis Falls and say hello to Nate. He was lucky that we were able to apprehend Jewell Norris. I knew that Patty Olson would be relieved to know that her abductor was headed back to prison. It worked out well. I was glad that I didn't have to harm another person. The justice system would take care of that--at least I hoped it would.

When I pulled into St. Regis Falls, I met several police cars en route to Troop S Headquarters. I parked across the street from Nate's grocery. I thought about Patty and how happy she would probably be that Norris had finally been apprehended. I exited the Bronco and walked across the street. Several customers were leaving the store. As I entered, a loud voice came from behind the meat counter. "Jason Black, where in the hell have you been? I haven't seen you in ages," Nate said, casting a broad smile.

"Nate, you look great! You were a lucky son-of-a-gun. The killer was coming for you, you know."

"I--I know he was. I've had my shotgun ready since he committed the robbery. I work too hard to have some bum come in my store and take my money," Nate said excitedly, throwing his hands up in the air.

"I agree."

Nate poured me a cup of coffee and opened a box of plain fried cakes. We both munched on the fried cakes and sipped the steaming coffee as we chatted about the killers. I told him about my friend Patty, who had been abducted by them. We covered some of the days when I was assigned to the St. Regis Falls district. After an hour had passed, I told him that I had to leave for Saranac and Old Forge. I bid my friend farewell and left.

I drove around town for a few minutes before heading for the Saranac Lake Hospital. There had been some new houses built in the area. Other than that, the town seemed unchanged from my past patrol days in the region. I stopped at the only gas station in St. Regis Falls and gassed the Bronco. I had many fond memories here. I remembered the case of the firebug who had set several fires in the region, and how pleased the community seemed when I apprehended him. He was from a hard-working family, but somewhere along the path of life, the flame from a fire excited him. He was apprehended but the justice system failed to punish the arsonist. He served time in a county jail and was released in two months. I continued to Saranac Lake. The hospital parking lot was full. I found an open space in the last line of vehicles. I locked the Bronco. When I entered the hospital, I went to the gift shop and picked up a "Thinking of You" card and a red rose. I took time to make out the card.

When I reached Patty's room, she was sitting up in a chair next to her bed. I was surprised when she stood up and reached out for me. I embraced her and held her closely. She began to cry; tears slid down her soft pale cheeks. She removed a laced hanky from her nightgown pocket and dried her eyes.

"I'm so glad you're here, Jason. I've missed you. I heard the news about Norris. The news broadcaster interviewed Captain Temple and he mentioned that if it wasn't for you, Norris might still be a hunted killer. He said you were a hero."

"No, I'm not a hero. I did what anyone else would do under the same circumstances. I was able to get the drop on him. I was scared. He was surprised when I pointed my gun at his head. I was just a few feet from him. I think he was exhausted. I was just plain lucky."

"You can say what you want, but you're my hero." She was proud of him. "I have good news: I'm being discharged in the morning. I don't suppose you'd give me a ride home? I'll be ready about 10:00 a.m." Patty blushed and looked into my eyes.

"I'll be here. I have to officially check out of the Breakshire Lodge. I'm glad this situation is over with. And hopefully, we can continue with our lives. I'm glad you're feeling better. You're lucky to be alive, Patty. They were the worst of the worst. As you know, Clovis is dead. I've been worried about you, my dearest."

"Yes, I know you have. What causes people to do these sort of things? I have five brothers who have never been in trouble with the law."

"Patty, it is a combination of all sorts of things. It could have been an alcoholic family, drugs, choosing the wrong people to hang around with, being beat as a child--any number of things. I do know that Norris was a good soldier, up to a point, until he viciously raped an officer's wife and ended up in Leavenworth. From that time on, he went downhill, all the way."

"I know what you mean. I'm getting tired now. I think I'd better get some sleep." She yawned.

"I'll be here in the morning, sweetheart. You can be sure of that."

"Thank you, Sherlock." She hugged and kissed me.

I had hoped that we could have talked longer, but I left the hospital. She seemed very tired. I went to the Bronco in the parking lot. As I unlocked the door I noticed before I got behind the wheel that someone or something had put a dent in the left driver's door. I couldn't remember what type of vehicle was parked next to me. I could feel my blood pressure going up. Why didn't they leave me a note? I cussed all the way to the Breakshire Lodge. I had to stay in Room 201 just one more night. I loved the Lodge, but I had to get on with my life, professionally and socially. My mailbox must be full. I knew that my answering machine had to be loaded with calls. Those check cases, my lifeline to sustaining my home, food and those little extra things in life, were important to me, as well as the business places who accepted them. Brady's Book on checks was my bible. It presented all the information relative to the world of checks, postdated checks, stale-dated checks, forged checks, et al.

Just before I arrived at the Lodge, I pulled into a hamburger joint and grabbed two cheeseburgers and a chocolate-malted milkshake to go. I had enough excitement for one day. I decided to eat in my room.

I parked in the Breakshire parking garage and went directly to my room. I unlocked the door and put the cheeseburgers on the table with the milkshake. I washed up, turned the television on, and enjoyed my fast-food feast. I was hungry. The milkshake was thick and some of the malt had not mixed well with the ice cream and milk. It did have a great flavor. I was going to shower, but decided to wait until morning. I continued to think of Patty. I was afraid to become involved in a serious marital relationship. I pondered over the dilemma of two people becoming one union. I truly loved my life the way it was. I undressed, put my pajamas on, and fell asleep on top of the bed. I woke up at about 2:00 a.m. with a start. I went to the bathroom and drank a glass of water. The water was warm. I looked out the window. The refuse truck was parked near the garbage rack. It was the noise of this vehicle that had awakened me. I had a difficult time getting back to sleep. It must have been 4:00 a.m. when I dozed off again.

*The killer, Norris, opened fire on me. The bullets hit my chest and bounced off. I was still standing and returned fire, but the trigger wouldn't pull back.* The telephone was ringing. I was groggy. My heart was racing and I could hear the pounding in my chest. Apparently, I had been dreaming about my encounter with Norris. My arm reached out and grabbed the receiver.

"Hello, hello, is this you, Jason?" Captain Frank Temple asked with a voice of authority.

"Huh? Yeah, Jason Black here," I answered sleepily.

"Glad I caught you before you left." He sounded happy.

"What can I do for you, Captain?" I inquired, curiously.

"I want you to stop at my office before you head back to Old Forge," he requested.

"Okay, sir, I'll stop," I answered groggily, and hung up.

I lay there, still looking up at the spirals on the ceiling. My mind was racing, thoughts muddled between the dream and the phone call from Temple. I relaxed and took deep breaths. *What's on Temple's mind?* I thought. *He's got his killer locked up. What's he bothering me for?*

After fifteen minutes, I forced myself to get out of bed. I was completely exhausted. I had experienced that feeling as a policeman long before I left the force. The excitement and tension, along with the pressure of being involved in tense situations, such as the Norris apprehension, can sap all the energy out of your body, leaving you feeling like an empty burlap bag. I undressed and climbed into the shower. The hot water on my back brought relaxation to my spine. The water felt good running down my body. I felt refreshed. The scented soap smelled clean and pure. I found difficulty in opening the shampoo packet. It finally gave way and I scrubbed my head vigorously. The lather burned as it entered my right eye. I squirted it with cold water. The stinging stopped. I rinsed myself completely. I got out of the combination tub and shower, feeling like a new man. My mind was clear and calculating. The fog had lifted.

I shaved and was invigorated as the lotion found the pores of my skin. The final step came with the toothbrush in the back and forth and up and down motions. One of the plastic bristles caught between two of my front teeth. For a moment I went back to early childhood and the lessons I had received from my father. He had been a patient instructor when it came to personal hygiene. I had always been thankful to him for that important advice. I missed both mother and father. I loved them.

The dining room was bustling with tourists and a few locals. I sought out my corner table, away from the turmoil. Several familiar faces smiled as I passed.

The fresh flower jutting from the vase greeted me with its freshness. The Syracuse China coffee cup was turned over on the saucer. I flipped it over. Soon, a smiling waitress appeared with a full pot of steaming decaf. She took my order of scrambled eggs, crisp bacon, and whole wheat toast. Her nameplate denoted that her name was Sylvia. She was courteous, thanked me for the order, and hastily departed for the kitchen. I could tell she was busy. I looked around

for Tom Huston. I learned later that he had flown to New York City
to attend a hotel owners convention. *He doesn't seem to be around
much*, I thought. I had missed him several times on my visits to
Breakshire. He was a fine gentleman and I enjoyed our chats.

I retrieved my shotgun from the vault then gathered my property
from Room 201 and took it out to the parked Bronco. I secured the
items in the rear of the vehicle, and returned to the desk. I paid my
hotel bill with my credit card. The cashier was friendly. I told her to
give Mr. Huston my regards. She indicated that she would. The
Breakshire Lodge had become like a second home to me. The price
was fair and the cuisine was excellent.

I hadn't noticed, but when I returned to the Bronco I noted that
it was clean. The garage attendant had washed it. I placed a two-
dollar tip in the metal box attached to the wall located by the water
hose. When I left the garage I spotted him and rolled down the window
and hollered, "Charlie, thank you. I appreciate it!" He smiled and gave
me a big wave.

The Troop S Headquarters was a large building. Rows of new
police cars lined a fenced-in parking area. The cars shone. I couldn't
help but think of all the miles I had driven police cars in my assigned
districts. There were many memories stored in the chambers of my
mind. Some good, some bad, but all learning experiences of the
concept of life. There was no other job like it. I guess you could say
that I had seen it all.

There was just enough room to park between the fence and an
evidence van. I squeezed the Bronco just inside the white lines. When
I exited the driver's door, I was careful not to bump the van. *Close,*
I thought. The long walk to the headquarters entrance was on a slight
upgrade. Several Troopers were coming out of the main door as I
approached the entrance. They all nodded. I didn't know them. I
entered, surprised to see Captain Temple standing by the counter. He
had a fistful of paperwork. He waved as I approached him, then began
the conversation. "Jason, thanks for stopping by. Wait for me in my
office, I'll be right along," he said in a friendly voice.

I turned and headed down the hall to the office. Lieutenant Roy
Garrison had just laid a file on the Captain's desk when I entered the
room.

"Jason, how in the hell are you? Congratulations! That was a great piece of work, holding that killer for us. He could have nailed you. He's a tough guy."

"Yeah, I appreciate your remarks. I could tell that he was exhausted and fortunately he had no idea who I was. When I stuck my 9mm pistol in his face he knew that it was all over. All he would have had to do was reach under that shirt, and it would have been bye-bye. I wasn't going to take a chance with him."

"I heard that!" Captain Temple entered the room, throwing the papers on his desk.

"I was lucky, Captain," I said, looking Temple straight in the eye.

"Well, for your information, Jason, we appreciate what you did for us. If he had gotten into the backcountry, we'd have lost him, especially in that area. I firmly believe he was en route to shoot Nate."

"I believe that," I responded.

"In retrospect, Nate can thank you for saving his life." Temple was sincere in his remarks.

"Excuse me, I have things to do. Good luck, Jason." Garrison left the office.

"Jason, I know how you wanted to become a senior investigator when you were on the job, and I have to admit I could have been instrumental in helping you with your goal, but I didn't. I'll never forget that night in Nedrow, south of Syracuse."

"Me neither. I was just doing my job, and if I had it to do all over again I would do the same thing." I looked Temple in the eye. He didn't flinch. I didn't flinch.

"I'm sorry that it worked out the way it did," he said, his face flushed.

"Is this what you wanted to tell me, sir?"

"No, I wanted to let you know that you'll probably be getting a letter of appreciation from the Governor and the Superintendent." Temple smiled.

"What for?" I asked, knowing.

"For your apprehension of the killer, Norris," he said with pride for Jason.

"Thank you, Captain, I have to be at the hospital. Patty is being discharged and I'm taking her back to Old Forge."

"Thank her for her cooperation. She's a fine young lady. According to her statement, Norris and Clovis didn't violate her sexually. Patty was very lucky. Norris will be returned to prison. He's not standing trial in New York State."

"What? You've got to be kidding!" I was furious.

"He'll be in prison for the rest of his life, with no chance of parole," Captain Temple replied.

"Thanks for the great news! I can't believe it. I thought they'd arrest him for kidnapping and unlawful imprisonment, at least."

"He is dangerous. The Ohio authorities are en route here to return him to Ohio." He spoke with authority.

"Take it easy, Captain." I left the office. I could feel my blood pressure rising.

# CHAPTER TWENTY-EIGHT

When I arrived at the Saranac Lake Hospital, Patty was already in the lobby, sitting in a wheelchair. She looked a lot better than she had a few days before. I walked toward her. "Hi honey, you're looking great. Are you ready to head for home?"

"I'm so glad to see you, Sherlock. Yes, I'm ready." She looked up at me smiling.

The nurse pushed the wheelchair out the door and we proceeded to the Bronco. All the necessary paperwork was completed. I helped Patty into the passenger front seat. She looked at me with a tear in her eye. I thanked the nurse. I got into the driver's side, leaned over, and gave Patty a kiss on her forehead. We were Old Forge bound.

I explained to Patty that I was a little late getting to the hospital because Captain Temple wanted to see me. I noticed that she was quiet. She looked tired. The ordeal of being the victim of an abduction is frightening. She had every reason and right to be a little withdrawn.

"I want to thank you, Jason, for driving me home. Wilt stopped to see me again and he told me if you couldn't make it, that he'd be glad to drive me back to Old Forge." She spoke softly. I could feel her studying my face.

"That was decent of Wilt. He is a person you can count on. Charlie Perkins is just like him. Even though Charlie's got a raft of kids, he'd take time to help out anyone. Both Wilt and Charlie are people you can trust and depend on," I assured her.

"Yes, you're right. Everyone is good to me. They all know what

179

Kenneth was like during my marriage to him. In the beginning, there was love and tenderness, but the more he drank, his personality changed. He became a mean guy. I'm so glad that I didn't have children by him. Do you understand what I mean?" She looked sad.

"I know exactly what you mean, Patty. So many people today have similar dilemmas. My marriages were failures. I was so wrapped up in a profession that tore me away from the home, sometimes for days and weeks. That isn't fair to your mate. It truly takes a very special woman to be married to a law officer. There is so much push and pull. You're dealing with every type of person, good and bad. Many times the investigations you're working on fail to be solved or brought to an appropriate ending, or to the satisfaction of your superiors and the person doing the investigation. You live and breathe the twists and turns, and many times you reach  a dead end." It felt good to share my feelings with her.

"It must have been very hard for you to cope with those problems."

"Yes, it was. The relationships faded away. Not that I didn't care for and love my wives--I did--but I devoted all my time to my police profession. You can't do that, and have your marriage survive. You have to draw the line. Sometimes that is the most difficult thing to do."

"I understand," she said, still looking sad.

"I could be in Arizona doing the same type of work in private investigation and earn much more than I can make here in the Adirondacks, but I chose the mountains over the desert, where it is ungodly hot in the summer. I've told you how much I love this region. I never want to leave it, permanently. Maybe to visit other locations, but always to return here, where I belong," I said, looking over at Patty.

"I like it here, too, Jason. This is where I want to spend the rest of my life, God willing."

"I agree. Patty, what arrangements have you made about work and your care?" I asked, curiously.

"Just before you picked me up at the hospital, I called my landlord, Harriet Stone. She's going to look in on me and cook my meals for a week. The doctor wants me to rest for seven days, and then I can return to work. I have already arranged that with Lila at John's Diner."

"Are you certain? Do you feel strong enough?" I asked with concern.

"I'll be fine, honey." She looked up at me.

The drive to Old Forge was very scenic. I watched Patty as she looked out the window. She asked me to stop at Tupper Lake for a moment. She wanted to look at the lake. I pulled off at a rest area, near the Tupper Lake Troopers' station. She looked out over the water and watched a couple of seagulls dipping and diving toward it. Finally she told me to continue on. I obeyed.

I knew that the ordeal she experienced was difficult. Never knowing if she were going to get sexually assaulted or beaten or even killed. The pressure on her had to be intense. She told me there had been scary moments, when Clovis lusted over her. She explained that God and the Angels protected her. I didn't dispute her comments.

Autumn was here. The colors were not at their peak stage, but the yellows and golds were displayed radiantly with touches of red, nature's artistry on stage. Shades of other colors appeared less predominantly. We came across tourists standing off the roadway, snapping pictures, while others had their camcorders catching this moment in time on film.

Hunting season was in progress, and occasionally a hunter dressed in red and black checkered clothes would be seen entering the woods. In this section of the state, hunting with high-powered rifles and large caliber revolvers was permitted.

Patty wasn't saying very much. I looked over at her and she was looking out her passenger side window taking in the splendor of the scenery. I was getting hungry.

"Would you like to stop for some lunch?" I asked.

"Yes, I wouldn't mind," she replied, looking up into my eyes.

"Do you feel strong enough to go inside a restaurant?"

"That will be fine, yes. I feel much better since I've gotten out of the hospital."

I didn't stop at Gertie's. It was packed. I continued on to the Adirondack Hotel. Their parking area was less crowded. I parked in the shade, near the steps to the entrance.

I assisted Patty getting out of the Bronco. She walked slowly.
I put my arm around her waist to give her support, moving slowly up
the wooden steps. The hotel was a large structure. I didn't know the
year that it was built. I did know that it had been many years ago.
Since then a few modifications had been added to it. The hotel had
a large front porch. Comfortable chairs lined the porch where guests
could relax and take in the aura of Long Lake's pristine beauty.

We were greeted by the hostess. She led us to a comfortable
booth with padded seats. The table was neatly arranged with
silverware and linen napkins. A vase contained an autumn array of
assorted ferns and thistles, accompanied by a light- orange tablecloth.
The menus were ready for our viewing.

The offerings for lunch were listed just inside the folded cover.
There were many selections. I looked across the table at Patty. Her
blond hair flowed on the top of her shoulders. She appeared slightly
pale, which was understandable, after her ordeal with the two escaped
killers. She was looking at the bill of fare with intensity. Patty looked
happy. She looked over the table into my eyes, and asked,

"Jason, what looks good to you?" She smiled.

"I think I will have the roast beef sandwich with horseradish and
a cup of hot tea."

"That sounds good," she replied, reaching for my hand.

Our waitress appeared at the table. She was friendly. Her name
tag told us that she was Gwen. Her auburn-colored hair was pulled
back into a tight bun. Her fingernails were long and painted red. Patty
decided on a tuna-fish sandwich on whole wheat toast with a glass of
milk. Gwen wrote our orders down. We learned that she was going
to enter the Paul Smith's College in about a week. She was interested
in entering the food service industry.

Our lunch was delicious. Patty ordered another glass of milk. I
had my tea warmed using the same tea bag. The tangy horseradish
went well with the thinly sliced roast beef. We both were a couple of
happy campers. We decided that dessert was out of the question for
the moment. We continued to chat for a while. I looked into Patty's
eyes. I knew that I loved her very much, but I was afraid to pursue
a matrimonial path. Having experienced the pains of divorce and the
humiliation that it caused me, I didn't think that I wanted to marry again

at this juncture of my life. I didn't want to hurt Patty. She was a good person who had experienced a rocky road in her marriage. I enjoyed being with her, but to unite as husband and wife, would have to be put on the shelf. My love for her was deep, but my commitment for marriage was lacking. At least, that was the way I felt at this minute.

Gwen brought our check. I gave her my credit card. I added her gratuity to the slip. She ran it through the machine. "Thank you, Mr. Black. Have a pleasant afternoon." I nodded. Before we left, both of us drank a glass of ice cold water. It was refreshing and quenched our thirst.

Patty wanted to see the main dining room. I slowly walked Patty into it. She was amazed at the many tables that were prepared for the evening meal. The aroma of roast beef reached our nostrils, as well as pork and roast turkey. The chef and his staff in the kitchen were like artists preparing for an art show. Each presentation would be judged by their critics. Patty remarked about the Adirondack décor. She was impressed. "Can we come back sometime, Jason?" I looked at her and smiled.

"We'll be back."

We left the hotel and crossed the highway to the edge of Long Lake. I told her that Long Lake is situated in the center of the Adirondack Park. She had never been to this community to stop and browse before, but had only passed through. She liked what she saw. The mountains reached toward the heavens. On just the right day, when the weather conditions changed, the white mist would rise and linger. Like other parts of the park, the woods were filled with all sorts of wild animals. There were plenty of mountains to climb. The surrounding ponds and lakes were a fisherman's delight. And like every community throughout the park, there were numerous activities, such as antiques, photo shows, craft shows, and places to dance. There was no shortage of things to do, for every age group. To me, it was in itself a wonderland, where the pulse of interaction never stopped in any of the four seasons. I could tell she was enjoying herself. I told her that we'd better leave now, before she became overtired. She turned and looked up into my eyes. She reached out for an embrace. I did the same. We held each other closely and kissed.

We walked to the Bronco, entered the vehicle and continued south. Patty noticed Hoss's Country Corner, and asked if we could stop.

"Jason, I've always heard so much about Hoss's and while we're here, could we take a moment to browse."

"Certainly, I just don't want you to become overtired." I pulled into the parking space next to the store.

We went into the store, took a few minutes viewing their book section, and purchased Patty a pair of earrings. We decided to continue our trip to Old Forge, promising to return another day. Patty was impressed with the selection of books and the quality of the clothing line. She wanted to return when she was feeling stronger and had more time to spend there.

The highway, curvy with mountains on each side of us, was crowded with cars and some log trucks. When we reached Blue Mountain, Patty asked me to stop. Blue Mountain Lake sits at the base of the 3700 foot Blue Mountain, where from the top can be viewed over 160 mountains and over a dozen lakes. It is known for the Adirondack Museum and a center for the arts. I told Patty that Blue Mountain Lake was on my list of great places to visit and linger. She agreed.

"Are you getting tired?" I asked her. She had gone through the worst kind of an ordeal.

"Yes, I am getting a little bushed," she replied.

The remainder of the trip was without stops. We drove through Old Forge to Patty's rented home. When we pulled into the yard, we were amazed to see Wilt standing on Harriet Stone's porch. He and Harriet looked up and waved, giving us big smiles. Wilt rushed over to the passenger side of the Bronco, opened the door for Patty, and helped her out. The big man gave her a hug. Harriet came over and kissed Patty on the cheek. I got out of the driver's side and greeted our friends.

Harriet spoke. "Patty and Jason, would you like a nice cup of coffee and something sweet?"

We were both still full from the Long Lake stop, but we couldn't hurt Harriet's feelings. "Yes, we will have coffee and sweets," As I spoke up I noticed that Harriet had a card table set up on her porch.

It was filled with cookies, pies and cakes.

Harriet said, "You should have gotten here fifteen minutes ago. Cars were parked along Route 28. Everyone wanted to welcome you home, Patty."

"That's right," Wilt chimed in with a big smile and laugh.

All four of us crowded around the table. There were numerous things to partake of. Patty chose a brownie. Harriet cut herself a piece of spice cake. Wilt cut two large pieces of apple pie. I chose a sweet roll with raisins. We sat along the porch railing and sipped our coffee and nibbled on our sweets, all except Wilt, who made short work of the delicious apple pie, along with a quarter pound of extra sharp cheese. We talked about Patty and her ordeal with the killers. Harriet told her that she was not going to let her be alone for a week or two, and that she had her spare room all fixed for her to stay in. Patty objected, but Harriet won the debate. Patty was the official queen and houseguest of Harriet.

Wilt and I discussed the local happenings. "Jason, I've finished carving out that black bear for Mr. Huston," he said proudly.

"That's great, Wilt," I remarked. I was anxious to see it.

"I painted it black and made two eyes out of some old buttons. I know he'll like it. The old log looks like a real bear. I busted one of my saw chains, which happened when it got stuck under the leg, but the old bear is ready to be delivered. Maybe we can get together in a week or so, when you get caught up, and decide on the day to deliver it."

"We certainly will. That was nice of you to do that for Mr. Huston. He'll really appreciate it, Wilt," I commented.

I walked across the porch to where Patty and Harriet were talking. "Sorry to interrupt, ladies, but I have to be going. I have to pick up Ruben and it is getting late."

Wilt had already bid farewell and was backing out of the driveway. The ladies understood. I told them that I would be in contact later. I looked at Patty's face. She was smiling. They waved as I pulled away.

The urge to stop at John's Diner was dispelled by the late hour. There were very few cars in the parking lot when I went by. The trip to the Eagle Bay Kennel didn't take long. Because of the late hour, the attendant advised me that they would send me a bill in the mail. Ruben barked loudly as the attendant removed him from their runway. The dog jumped all over me and whined. It was his way of letting me know how much he missed his master. I gave the attendant a substantial tip. When I left the kennel and headed for the Bronco, Ruben took advantage of his moment of freedom and ran around in wide circles. He had been penned up too long. I opened the rear door and he leaped into the back. He drooled all over. I was happy to see my partner. Ruben was getting older. His K-9 experiences with the Troopers had been interesting. I was aware of his four years of dedicated service. He had been recognized on several occasions, along with his handler. Now he was retired, and I had been lucky in gaining possession of him.

Darkness had come and when I pulled into my drive, two large bucks and a doe were nibbling on some flowers at my flower-box. Ruben's ears perked up and he barked. The deer looked us over one more time, then made a beeline for the woods. My security light had just come on. Finally, we were home. I was still thinking of Patty and how generous Harriet had been to bring Patty into her home and take care of her for a couple weeks. I knew Harriet was a religious woman and had been known for helping friends and neighbors. It gave me a good feeling to know that people like her were still on board in this complex, sometimes confusing society.

I let Ruben run around the yard for a few minutes while I unloaded the Bronco. The log home seemed musty to me. I opened several of the windows and turned on a couple of fans. As I expected, the red light on the answering machine was pulsating. Ruben was at the screen door. I let him in. I turned the gas on under a teakettle of water. *A cup of coffee would taste good,* I thought. I noted that the instant coffee and decaf were getting low. Normally, I keep a running grocery list each week, but with the interruption of the manhunt I hadn't kept up the list.

After capturing the fresh air, I closed the windows and shut the fans off. I readied for bed, checked Ruben, went to the bathroom, brushed my teeth and climbed into the covers. The strain of the pressure and tension for the past few days had drained me. I fell to sleep as soon as my head hit the pillow.

I awoke with a start. Ruben was sitting beside the bed looking at me. One ear was sticking straight up in the air and one was flopped over. I rubbed the sleepiness from my eyes and reached out to him. He slobbered all over my hand. I threw the covers back, got out of bed and put Ruben into his runway. Then I went to the bathroom and showered. The hot water was refreshing on my tired back. I dried off, shaved, brushed my teeth, and dressed. I could see the red light blinking on the answering machine. I had been so tired when I arrived home, I had had to put off checking the calls. I decided that I would have breakfast at home and then listen to the answering machine.

I didn't have any milk for the pancakes, so I used water with some canned condensed milk. I had some precut Canadian bacon, and soon the heavy black iron frying pan was emitting the aroma of sizzling slices, reaching every room in my log home. The pancakes came out golden brown. I was going to medium fry a couple of eggs, but the egg box was empty. I knew that grocery shopping had to be one of my main priorities.

I washed the dishes and swept and dusted throughout the house. To my surprise there was little dust and dirt. I mopped the kitchen floor. When I finished the cleaning, I decided to make up a grocery list: eggs, milk, bread, canned peaches, pancake mix, dog food, and numerous other items of necessity.

The next task took me most of the day. There were over one hundred calls on the answering machine. Some were from businesses telling me that their bad checks--insufficient funds--had been taken care of by the person(s) issuing the checks.

Private investigator Jack Flynn called from Phoenix, Arizona. He indicated that he was going to be working on a custody case in California and would be away from his office for about two weeks.

I returned a call to Tom Huston at the Breakshire Lodge in Lake Placid. He was not in, but had left a message for me to stop at the Lodge when I was in town again. The message reflected that it was not an urgent matter.

I typed ten letters to bad check passers, advising them to contact their respective banks relative to problems with stale dated checks that had been issued to several businesses.

Patty was sleeping when I called Harriet to see how she was

feeling. Harriet assured me that she was getting the best of care. She had prepared several eggnogs for Patty. I told her that I would call later in the day and to give Patty my best. Harriet wanted to chat longer, but I informed her that I was trying to catch up on pending matters. She understood.

About noon I checked on Ruben and let him out of the runway. He bounded off to the woods. When he returned, he jumped up on me by the side door and knocked me down. He wanted to play, so we wrestled for a few minutes. I had to stop when the telephone rang. I returned Ruben to his runway and hurried inside. The call was from Todd Wilson, Chief of Police. We talked for about fifteen minutes. He was interested in the apprehension of Norris. I brought him up to date on all the information that I was privy to. Todd advised me that everyone I knew in town was asking about me. There was even a rumor, according to Todd, that a group of people wanted to have a dinner for me. I told Todd that I didn't want to attend any social function for that reason. Norris was apprehended and the justice system would take care of him. Todd asked me if I'd be interested in a part-time job with his department. I thanked him for the offer, but declined. I had had enough exposure to the police world and I had all I could take care of in the private investigation business. I thanked Todd for calling and hung up the phone.

I was relieved to clear my answering machine. I made calls to several businesses. Two of the calls were from civic organizations seeking funds. One dealt with the elderly and the other was for a children's fund. I told each that I would send my donations to them via the U.S. Post Office.

With the household duties under control, letters written to clients, and bills paid, I took time to head to the supermarket. The parking lot was full. The usual line of grocery carts was depleted for the moment. I spotted a middle-aged lady unloading a cart. I rushed out of the store. "Excuse me ma'am, I'll take your cart back for you," I said, lucky, to retrieve one.

"Oh! thank you, sir," she replied with a warm smile. I headed for the door, which opened automatically, as it always does.

I heard a scraping noise as though the door were binding up. I entered the busy store to find people rushing here and there, grabbing at the fresh fruit and vegetables. There was a line in front of the meat counter. I soon learned that the store had a sale on sirloin steaks. The two butchers looked flushed. I thought that the pressure must be unbearable, with all the meat-seekers talking at once. The deli girls were moving at a fast clip. Swiss cheese with the large holes fell to the waxed paper as the slicing machine went back and forth. The girl not slicing was removing fresh hot rolls from the ovens. People were standing around waiting patiently for their turn.

I went down each aisle selecting the items that were marked on sale. I had a few coupons that I had cut from the local paper. Some of the items on sale, with the appropriate coupon, saved me money. I saw Harriet Stone pass by the end of the cereal aisle. She spotted me and said, "Patty's doing great." I waved at her and asked her to give Patty my regards and to tell her that I would call her later in the evening.

I liked this store. It had a good selection of products, and the owners and staff were friendly people. They also worked very hard to give the public the best of service. I enjoyed our grocery relationship. I ran into Jay, checking inventory with his calculator. I told him about the door. He informed me that a car had backed too close and slightly touched it, and that the door company was coming to correct it. He had two pencils behind his ear. He was one busy store-owner, and did his job well. He smiled and thanked me for my concern. When I reached the deli counter, the line had thinned out. Jay's wife, Millie, was giving the girls a helping hand. She saw me and came over to take my order. I asked for a pound of Virginia baked ham and a half-a-pound of American cheese. I requested she slice both extra thin. I picked six of the fresh rolls, thanked Millie, and moved down the aisle to the meat counter. I spotted a small top sirloin roast and put it into the cart. The pork chops looked lean and they ended up in the cart, too.

The butcher stuck his head out of the sliding window! "Congratulations on apprehending that killer, Jason," he said with a big grin. "You were lucky he didn't shoot you," he added, looking concerned.

"Yeah, guess I was lucky," I replied.

I asked him if he had a large bone for my dog. He told me to wait a minute. He returned with a huge bone with some meat on it. He had placed it in a large plastic bag. I thanked him and moved on to the checkout area. I appreciated the bone. He had marked "no charge" on it with a marker. *Ruben will like this*, I thought.

"Plastic or paper, Jason," the bagger said, smiling.

"Plastic," I replied, quietly.

I watched the cashier scan all the items. She was quick. The bagger placed the filled plastic bags in the cart. I paid my bill of $45.12 with my credit card.

The post office parking lot was full of cars. My box was crammed full of assorted mail. I hastily thumbed through the letters. Two of the customers nodded at me when I left the office.

There wasn't very much traffic on the way home. Ruben jumped up on the runway fence and welcomed me with a series of loud barks. I parked the Bronco close to the rear side door. "Settle down, Ruben," I shouted. He went to the side of the fence and lay down, putting his big head between his front paws. It took me only a few minutes to unload the Bronco. I checked my grocery list as I put the items in their respective locations. I looked at the listing of the scanned purchases. There didn't appear to be any mistakes.

Harriet's telephone was not busy. She answered, "Hello." I asked for Patty. "Just a minute," she said. I talked to Patty for fifteen minutes. She said,

"I'm feeling much better, Jason. How are you?" She seemed joyous.

"I'm fine, did my grocery shopping and have it all put away. Just thought I'd check to see how you are doing." We chatted about generalities and she informed me that she had been in touch with John's Diner. She would be returning to work in about a week. I told her that maybe we could have dinner at my place some night during the forthcoming week. She seemed overjoyed by the invitation. I told her to take care of herself. She thanked me over and over for the ride home from the hospital. I assured her that it was an honor to be able to assist her in a time of need. We finished talking, and hung up. I was pleased that she was feeling better. She sounded so bubbly, and that was a good sign.

I went to my desk and looked over my mail. I noticed an electric bill, a bill for propane, a telephone bill and a bill from the Eagle Bay Kennel. The only bill that was of a significant amount was the kennel bill, $322.16. I thought, *Ruben, are you worth that money?* I chuckled to myself. I was wondering where my credit card bill was from Mountain Bank. Sometimes the bills are a day late.

I glanced at the clock. I decided I'd take Ruben for a walk in the woods. It would be dark shortly. I filled his water and food dishes. I snapped the leash on him. He rubbed his nose against my pant leg. "Settle down, boy," I said. We walked to the end of my property and cut into the woods along a narrow path. The big dog sniffed the trail and pulled hard, at times, on the leash. The K-9 was still in good physical shape despite his rigorous career with the State. I loved the big guy, and when I was with him I felt very secure. His ears were very sensitive to any sound. He loved to chase the chipmunks. They were fast and darted in and out of the brush and up the trees. Many times, Ruben would stand at the bottom of the tree and wait for the chippy. *Just like a cop,* I thought.

When we returned from our walk I put Ruben into his run. I went inside and noticed the red light on the answering machine was blinking. I pressed the replay button. "Jason, this is Dale. Give me a call tomorrow morning, early. Glad you're home safe and sound, hero." I laughed at his remark. I certainly didn't feel like a hero. Anyone under the same circumstances would have done the same thing--that is, if he had a gun. If he didn't have one, probably that person, whoever he might be, wouldn't be with us anymore. Norris would have seen to that. I was just plain lucky. I wondered what Norris's childhood could have been like, especially after his mother had been gunned down in front of him, in a bar. What events had occurred during those formative years that created this deviant individual? What chance did he have to become a contributing citizen? He was a hardened criminal, but he didn't molest or rape Patty, and even in a way protected her from Clovis, according to my conversations with Patty. Those answers will never be known to me. I realized that I had been most fortunate not to have had to use deadly physical force against the killer. It was the luck of the draw.

I looked at the clock and noticed the hour was late. I turned on the floodlights and two does ran across the yard. Ruben didn't bark.

I let him out of the run and he ran into the house. I had left the door open. I looked around the yard and went inside, locking the rear side door. I always kept the front door locked. Ruben was lying in his favorite location. Once in a while he would bark during the night, especially if the raccoon was up on the roof.

I undressed, put on my pajamas, brushed my teeth, shut the lights out, and set the alarm clock. I climbed into bed and turned on my reading lamp. I read one paragraph of a new mystery and dozed off.

The alarm went off at 7:00 a.m. I pushed the covers back and got out of bed. Ruben was sitting in the doorway. His ears were pointed straight up and his tail was swishing against the floor tile. "Good morning," I said. Ruben answered with a faint bark. I let him out. He ran off into the woods. I went into the bathroom and splashed some cool Adirondack water into my sleepy eyes. The cold water woke me up. I dressed. Ruben was back at the side door and announced his presence with a quick, sharp bark. I went outside and put him in his runway.

I called Dale, wondering why he wanted me to call him so early. I dialed his number and he answered on the second ring.

"Hello, Jason. How's the hero this morning?" he quipped.

"Knock the hero stuff off," I kidded him back. Actually it sounded good, but unnecessary. "What can I do for you at this early hour?"

"I'm taking you to breakfast. Be ready in ten minutes." He hung up in my ear.

I hadn't seen Dale in some time and I figured he wanted an update on the events of the recent manhunt. After all, Dale had spent considerable time with me in the air searching for Patty and the two killers. He deserved to know what happened, other than what he had read in the paper. Curiosity still haunted me about my observations at John's Diner, but I felt hesitant to confront him.

Ruben barked at the vehicle coming into the yard. It was Dale. I locked the house and joined him. I looked over at the dog and he appeared depressed, sitting with his back to us. Dale asked me how Ruben had been doing after his kennel visit. I told him that he was happy that I had returned.

"What's up?" I asked.

"Well, nothing much. I thought maybe you'd like breakfast on me, for once. "You're always picking up the tab," he said jovially.

"Thank you, Dale. By the way, I want to thank you, too, for taking me up with you during the search for Patty and those two killers."

"I was glad to help in any way. How is Patty?"

"She's feeling a lot better," I replied.

I couldn't believe that John's Diner's parking lot was full of cars and pickups. I surmised that something was up, but I kept my mouth shut. Dale found a parking space at the end of the lot. He let me out first, because it was a tight squeeze next to the wooden fence on the passenger side. I noticed that Dale was careful when he exited his vehicle. He didn't want to scratch Wilt Chamber's big Dodge truck. He knew that Wilt wouldn't appreciate a dent in his highly polished vehicle.

Dale held the door open for me and we entered. To my surprise, Gracie Mulligan was the only person in the dining area. It was quiet--in fact, damned quiet. Gracie seated Dale and me near the front window. My mind was spinning. The parking lot was full, but no one was in here. The mystery was short-lived. I suddenly heard a lot of voices and giggles. I looked at Dale. He looked sheepish. I heard the loud voice of Wilt. "Welcome home, hero!" he hollered. Dale and I turned around. People were streaming through the rear door into the dining room. There was gigantic Wilt, Charlie Perkins, the Chief of Police, Todd Wilson, Harriet Stone, Patty Olson, and two dozen more. Wilt apparently was the spokesman for the group. After everyone was seated, he stood up in front of us. He had a sheet of paper in his hand. He was wearing a white shirt and brown trousers.

"Welcome, friends and neighbors. Thank you for coming. All of you here are acquainted with Jason Black," he said. Everybody applauded. I was feeling very uncomfortable. *Why did Wilt do this to me?*

Wilt continued, "Jason, I'll make this short. We--all of us here, and from the folks that couldn't make it here this morning--we just want to thank you for apprehending that killer up in Santa Clara. We appreciate it as citizens of this community. Some of us here were hoping that Norris would have gone for his gun, but he didn't, and because he didn't, you were able to make a citizen's arrest without injury to anyone. Again, I said I'll make it short. Thank you, Jason, for a job well done. I understand the Troopers were glad to get their hands on that bird." Wilt came over to shake my hand and presented me with a computerized document, which was brief. In large letters it read, WELCOME HOME HERO.

I was moved by Wilt and everyone in the room. I stood up and thanked everybody and assured them that I was doing what anyone else would have done under the same circumstances. "Thank you very much, folks," I said.

Harriet and Patty joined Dale and me at our table. Gracie Mulligan was working all alone in the dining room. John and Lila were in the kitchen readily awaiting our orders. Everyone was talking. Patty did stand up and thanked everyone for their prayers and assistance in the search for her. Chief Todd Wilson stood up and thanked everyone in the room for the support they had given his department during the search in the Old Forge area. He did mention to Patty that she would soon have her Jeep. Everyone applauded Chief Wilson for his remarks.

Our table ordered pancakes, sausage, eggs and orange juice. Patty asked Gracie Mulligan if she wanted her to help. Gracie told Patty she appreciated the offer, but she would take care of all of us. Both Lila and John went to work at the grill, and it wasn't very long before the orders started coming out to the tables. Dale told a couple of aviator jokes. We all laughed. I looked at Patty and sensed that she was enjoying the moment.

I was surprised when Wilt Chambers stood up at his table. He tapped the water glass with his spoon. Everyone became silent. You could hear a pin drop.

"Ladies and gents, could I have a moment of your time? When Jason was out-of-town looking for Patty, we started a collection. Since Patty, by the grace of God, has returned to us, I think it is a good time to present her with our collection. Patty, if you could step over here, I have something for you." Wilt handed Patty an envelope containing $275.00 in U.S. currency, and then Charlie Perkins and Wilt presented her with a portable radio. Everyone applauded and Patty's face flushed from the surprise. Patty stood up facing her friends. A few were sipping their coffee. She stood in silence for a moment. A tear rolled down her left cheek and she dried her eyes with her handkerchief. I could tell that she was overcome with a sense of gratitude. She would, I know, file a claim as a victim of a crime. This would assist her in paying her hospital bills, but she had lost much wage-earning time.

She spoke softly. "Friends, your generosity is appreciated more than you may realize. Again, I thank you for your kindness and the support you have extended to me. I will always hold that dear to my heart." The tears returned in both eyes and rippled down her pale cheeks. Some of the people in the room were moved by her remarks. This young woman of thirty-six years had been through enough grief for a lifetime. She looked at me and added, "Sherlock, thanks for being there for me."

My knees went weak. I smiled and replied, "You'd have done the same for any one of us in this room." I got up from the table and she came to me and we embraced before our friends and God. Wilt was drying his eyes, and so was Charlie Perkins--*two tough loggers,* I thought. There was another round of coffee and further chatter. I could tell that Gracie Mulligan was getting tired from lugging the filled coffee pots to all the tables. John and Lila were standing in the doorway to the kitchen getting ready to help clear the tables as soon as all of us left the dining room. I could see that everyone left substantial gratuities on their respective tables. I was moved by the gathering. It was a sincere display of humanism.

I said good-bye to everyone as they passed by Patty and me. Some of the women embraced Patty with firmness. Wilt and Charlie were standing together and didn't leave. After everyone cleared the room, the two warm-hearted loggers came over to us. They gave Patty a big hug.

Charlie said, "Take care of yourselves. Wilt and I have to go to work now. We've got a big contract to fill and the paper company wants everything done yesterday, if you know what I mean."

Wilt added, " Jason, you let me know when you want to deliver the bear to Mr. Huston. We'll use my big Dodge pickup."

I turned and replied, "I'll call you, Wilt. We should probably deliver it on a weekend, when you're not logging."

"Sure enough," replied the big man. The two woodsmen left the diner.

I talked with Patty and Harriet Stone for a few minutes. Even though it was mid-morning, the two of them appeared to be tired. "Take care, ladies," I said. They both smiled and in unison replied, "See you later, Jason." I thought, *Harriet is old enough to be her mother.* I wondered what Patty's mother was like, and her father, too. Cupid, the Roman god of erotic love, certainly had my attention, but the scars from my previous marital journeys were deeply ingrained in my heart. I just felt that even though we were close, the chances for matrimonial bliss seemed like a faraway island in the South Pacific.

Before I left John's, I gave Gracie Mulligan a five-dollar bill. She didn't want to take it, but I insisted. When I went out the door, Harriet and Patty were just turning out of the driveway. The black shiny 1962 Plymouth looked like a collector's item. Harriet kept the car in her garage and religiously waxed it twice a month. I knew that she had been offered four times the amount that the car was worth, but in respect for her late husband, Rockwell Mulligan, she held her ground like the "Rock of Gibraltar."

The aroma of roast chicken escaped from the fan vents of John's kitchen. I had looked at the noon specials on the way out of the diner. The top listing was meticulously printed; Chicken & Biscuits ------- --$3.75. *My taste buds could react to that item,* I was thinking.

I was just opening the door to the Bronco, when I heard my name being called. I turned around and saw Paul Hart approaching: Paul, one of our local attorneys in town, was 42 years of age, single, slender, with premature gray hair. He was active with the town fire department. Paul was well liked for his honesty and he worked long hours for his clients.

"Yes, Paul, can I be of service?" I was curious, for he seemed anxious to talk.

"Congratulations! I hear you're some kind of a hero. That was a good job. One of my lawyer friends in Saranac called me and told me about it. He also mentioned that he was appointed to represent Norris on the extradition proceedings. During the court process, Norris's handcuffs were removed, and he threw a punch at the judge, breaking the judge's glasses. It took six people to subdue Norris and handcuff him again. You were lucky to get the drop on him."

"They should have never taken the cuffs off. He's a tough guy," I replied.

"You bet he is, according to my friend." Paul smiled. "Jason, I've got some work for you."

"What's up?" I asked.

"It's all here in these two folders. I've not included everything about the cases, just the necessary information. Both cases deal with a divorce action. I want to show association on both of them. One action is a wife claiming her husband is committing adultery every Saturday night at a Utica motel. The second case is a husband claiming that his wife is involved in an adulterous activity on Saturday night at the same motel. It is going to require photographs."

"Which Saturday night do you want me to begin?" I asked. I really didn't like this type of case.

"This coming Saturday. Try to get more than one photo. The cars and the two of them entering the room is all I need," Paul indicated.

Attorney Hart explained that the affair had been ongoing for almost a year and the complaining parties had been hopeful that it would cease without pursuing a divorce action in supreme court. The four people had been good friends and had traveled together in the States and abroad. Neither couple had children. Paul had been their attorney for several years. It was both sad and tragic. Nevertheless, their close relationship as four friends was ended and bitterness prevailed. I was able to relate to the dilemma, but my own ordeals were attributed to my being a workaholic.

Since my divorces, I had had plenty of time to reflect. I didn't want either to happen, but because of high stress jobs, such partings do occur all over America. Divorce affects the elite, the middle class, and the poor. It strikes all professions in all walks of endeavor.

Anyone who experiences the loneliness can compare it to a family death experience. Remembering that you were once connected to a person you adored, and then for reasons that cannot be fully explained, a change of heart or mind takes over your inner self and the relationship wilts like a rose without water.

I thanked Paul Hart for the work. We shook hands and departed. I got into the Bronco and placed the two folders in my briefcase. I took a quick look at the frayed briefcase and noted that I should purchase a new one. This one had seen its best days.

Before I went home I stopped at the post office. My box contained several letters. A post card from California caught my eye. All it said was "Congratulations, Hero." It was signed J. Flynn. I thought, *how in the hell did he hear about the Norris case in northern California?* I looked through the rest of the mail. There was a letter from Tom Huston, a few magazines, and two newspapers. I nodded at Lila from John's Diner. I imagined that she was glad to get a short break from that hot kitchen. Right away I remembered the first item on the noon specials, Chicken & Biscuits. I knew that they would be serving it for the dinnertime meal. I continued on to my log home and, of course, Ruben.

My dog barked when I got out of the Bronco. I went over to the runway and checked his water and food dishes. I added water. He wanted to be petted, and I obliged him. I set a large bone by his food dish. I took a broom from the kitchen and swept some cobwebs from around the floodlights. The spiders and bugs were attracted by the nighttime lights.

I went inside and went directly to my combination office and den. Living alone isn't easy, especially if one has enjoyed a marital arrangement. To combat the loneliness, I found it comforting to have pictures hanging on the walls. The den was the place that became my picture gallery. In one old picture that dates back to World War I is my handsome father and his 4th Infantry Company of young men like himself. The trees in the background are stripped of leaves and there is an aura of a battlefield in the distance, where many soldiers would die, and did. My father missed the roll call of death, but was gassed later on in the war. From 1918 to 1960 he suffered a slow death and then he died. To the rest of the world he may have been a tiny grain of sand, but to me he was the hero, not me. The hanging pictures kept my memories alive.

I called Patty. She told me that she and Harriet were in the process of baking some sugar cookies for a church sale. They had already finished one half of them. Twenty dozen was their goal. I asked her if she would like to come for dinner on Sunday. "Yes, I'd love to," she responded.

"Great. Turkey and dressing okay?"

"Sure," I could tell she was happy to be asked. "You're so thoughtful, Jason," she added.

We talked for a few minutes about the gathering at John's Diner and various events going on in town. She told me that she had received a letter from one of her brothers who is now living in Kentucky. He asked her to come and live with him and his wife. My stomach did a flip when she told me this. I pretended that it didn't faze me, although it did. I told her, "Patty, that is nice of your brother." The conversation drifted to Harriet. Patty told me how wonderful Harriet had been to her during her stay, then concluded, "I've got to run, Jason. You know, cookies can burn."

"Go ahead, see you on Sunday, about 3:00 p.m." We hung up.

I made a few telephone calls and attempted to contact Tom Huston. Tom was not in. *I'll call him later*, I thought. I checked my files concerning some pending check cases. I wrote ten letters to the check passers.

The next few days went by rapidly. I had the Bronco serviced. The garage where I take it replaced the rear brakes. They adjusted the emergency brake and aligned the head lamps. The right rear tire was worn to a point where it no longer met the required tread depth, so I had them replace it with a brand new one.

After leaving the garage I stopped at the library and did some research. Our local library was an active one and its director worked diligently to maintain interesting programs for the public. The resources were excellent. After about two hours of reviewing business law and several sections pertaining to family court, I was famished. I stopped at the supermarket and ordered a ham and cheese sub. I don't usually consume my lunch in the Bronco, but today I did, along with sipping a cold soft drink. The ham and cheese was delicious. I was parked in the rear lot and noticed a couple of locals who were married, but not to each other, having a casual conversation. At least, I thought it was casual until he French-kissed her. I put my head down. I didn't want to see it. It was none of my business, unless I was working on a case for pecuniary gain.

# CHAPTER TWENTY-NINE

It was Saturday evening. I glanced at my watch: 9:15. At the motel, situated just outside of Utica, the parking lot was nearly filled up. Two cars came into the lot. One contained a middle-aged man and the other a woman of the same vintage. They parked side by side. The man exited his car first, then the woman. I noted the makes and plate numbers and entered them into my book. The couple embraced in the parking lot. The attractive woman had an overnight bag hanging from her right shoulder. After the display of tenderness, arm in arm they walked slowly toward the motel. They stood in front of the door looking in my direction. The moment was just right. My 35 mm camera with the telescopic lens recorded my two targets, three times. The lens made it possible to bring their handsome faces to me, front and center. The floodlights provided enough light. They casually embraced again and entered the room. The light in the room was turned on. The man closed the drapes. Five minutes later the light was turned off. I took photos of the two cars and the plate numbers. My only purpose for being there was as an information gatherer. It was a civil matter. Paul Hart had informed me that the damaged parties did not want to pursue a criminal action against their mates for adultery. The butterflies were doing a dance in my stomach. I didn't like this part of my profession as a private investigator, but if I didn't do it, someone else would.

I left the parking lot. I couldn't help but think that all over our great country, this activity was occurring in all sorts of places. At least this couple was enjoying a comfortable room. Maybe some day they would have to answer to a higher authority... *oh! that sweet mystery of life*, I thought.

The trip back to Old Forge was uneventful. I couldn't help but think about the youth of our nation. The most important product of our survival, the children, who will grow, become educated, and take over the jobs of the elderly. I didn't want to think of the kids who would be side-tracked along the way. The runaways who end up in the large cities, entrenched in the drug culture, prostitution, and other illegal activity. All the fellows I had served with during those different years had used their energies to keep the youth on the correct path. They took their positions very seriously for starvation wages. How many of our finest scholars and contributors to our country have destroyed their own chances to excel? Hopefully the drug-users will wake up and shed the curse of gradual destruction to themselves and their families. Every cop in America in the front seat of their patrol cars observes these deplorable conditions on a day-to-day basis. The days of yesterday when the beat cop walked his assigned district have been set aside, and consequently that once great rapport with the citizens has weakened somewhat, except in rare cases. All the high-tech equipment will never replace the walking patrols of police agencies. Those officers knew their people and the people knew their police officers.

I arrived at home at about 11:00 p.m. Ruben was on guard. He knew who his master was. I locked the Bronco. I then let Ruben out of his runway. He took off for the woods, and after five minutes he was back sitting by the rear side door. I let him in. I removed the film from my camera and placed it in a brown envelope. I went directly to my office and typed my observation report for the attorney. I planned to hand-carry the film and report to Paul Hart in the morning. You do not let a sensitive report and film lie around. For the night, I placed it in a secure location.

Before I retired for the evening, I removed the small turkey from the freezer. I should have removed it earlier, I realized, but hoped it would thaw in time for our dinner guest on Sunday. I petted Ruben and he wanted to wrestle. "Lay down, Ruben, not tonight," I said. I brushed my teeth and undressed. I put on a pair of pajamas that were warmer. Our mountain air was changing. I had no sooner hit the pillow, than I fell asleep.

The alarm went off at 7:30 a.m. I lay in bed staring at the ceiling, still fuzzy in the head. I rubbed my eyes and yawned so loudly that Ruben came bounding into the room. His ears were straight up in the air. "It's okay, boy," I said. He replied with a short gruff bark. I pushed the covers back and headed for the bathroom. The water felt cold as I splashed it into my face. I looked in the mirror. My whiskers needed to come off. I decided to shave and bathe before breakfast. The hot shower felt soothing to my aching back. I finished, took my favorite towel from the rack, and dried off. I put on my bathrobe and let Ruben outside. He darted off for the woods. When I went to light the gas burner under the teakettle, the match flickered out before it lit. The second try was successful. In five minutes, the water was boiling, and in another two minutes, I was sipping the coffee. I scrambled two eggs and a slice of ham. The toast came out of the toaster with a jolt. I was due for a new toaster, but I was waiting for a sale. Breakfast was fast and tasty. Ruben was whining at the side door. I went out and put him into his runway.

I turned the oven on to 350 degrees. After it heated I put it back to 300 degrees. I braised some onions, garlic, celery, and green peppers. I made an unsweetened corn bread. I took some dried bread and broke it up. I combined all the ingredients, adding some of the corn bread and some turkey stock I had in the freezer. I mixed it thoroughly, adding two eggs and seasoning. I stuffed the turkey and placed the rest of the unused dressing in a pan, covered it, and put it in the refrigerator. I peeled the potatoes and squash. The cabbage was fresh. I sliced it finely with my new French knife, then I placed it in the refrigerator.

I called Paul Hart. He told me to drop off the film and report at his house. I checked the stove. Everything was all right. I washed my hands and slipped on a shirt. I took the items from the secure storage area and went out to the Bronco. While the vehicle was warming up, I locked the door and checked Ruben. I added water and food to his dishes.

I turned the Bronco, headed toward Route 28--and hit the brakes hard when a six-hundred-pound black bear strolled out of the woods directly in front of me. His eyes were looking at me. I looked away. I didn't believe in having eye contact with this big guy at the moment. Ruben started to bark. The big bear ambled on. I wished I had a camera in the vehicle, but I didn't. I continued onto Route 28, turning toward Old Forge. There wasn't very much traffic. When I pulled into Paul's driveway, he was waiting on his porch for me. I got out of the vehicle.

"Good morning, Jason. I appreciate you bringing me your report and the film." Paul appeared to look tired.

"No problem," I replied. I handed the envelope to Attorney Hart. He handed me an envelope. It contained a check for three hundred dollars.

"That should take care of all your expenses," he added.

"Thank you, Paul. Call me anytime." I got into my Bronco and backed out of his driveway. We waved.

I had to drive past John's Diner. Church had let out and people were rushing to get a table. It was always crowded on Sunday morning. I tooted at Wilt as he pulled his big Dodge pickup onto Route 28. He tooted back.

When I saw Wilt, I was reminded that we had to take the bear up to Tom Huston, soon. *I'll call him sometime Monday*, I thought.

I pulled into my yard and saw that large bear for the second time. The aroma of roast turkey reached my nostrils. I was famished.

It was 3:30 p.m. when Harriet dropped off Patty. I asked Harriet if she would like to join us for a turkey dinner. She declined, giving the reason that she had to meet her friends for a bridge game. I told her she was more than welcome.

"Thank you, Jason, but the girls are short a player and I promised them that I'd sit in for Gracie Mulligan." I knew she really wanted to stay, but she was committed. Patty and I watched her drive out of the driveway heading toward Old Forge and her bridge game.

I turned toward Patty, put my arms around her frail body, and drew her close to me. I could feel her warm breath on my neck. Ruben was watching from his runway and started to whine. We didn't pay attention to him. The kiss was warm and of a long duration. Patty's chest pressed against mine. Her mouth was pushing hard on my lips. I could feel her long fingernails as she held me firmly. Both of us knew that the passion was building. This wasn't the time or the place. She pulled away from me gently and looked into my eyes. With our arms entwined we walked toward the runway where Ruben was sitting. His ears reached to the heavens. His jealous whine was barely audible.

"Can I make you a drink, sweetheart?" I asked.

"No, Jason, I'm on medication for my nerves, and the doctor indicated no drinking except water or tea," she said, curling her lips with a smile.

We went inside the house. She clung to me. The aroma of roast turkey permeated the air throughout the log-home. I had the table set. The candles were in place. I possessed only two linen napkins and they were displayed by the best china plates I owned. I noticed that she had something on her mind. I didn't know what it was. We both washed our hands for dinner.

The two candles were lit. They flickered. I seated her at the table. It took me a couple of minutes to cut several succulent slices of turkey from the brown turkey breast. Next to it, I placed a generous helping of my corn bread dressing, then mashed potatoes, a medium sweet potato covered with brown sugar, six long tender carrots with orange glaze, and finally the light brown giblet gravy. Separate dishes contained cabbage salad and cranberry sauce. The cuisine was ready for consumption. I said grace before we began our dinner.

Patty's eyes were like shining diamonds in the glow of the candlelight. She smiled and thanked me for inviting her. We said very little during dinner. She seemed relaxed and appeared to be enjoying the moment. She took a sip of her iced tea with lemon. Not to brag, but the dinner was excellent. Patty was interested in the preparation of the corn bread dressing. I explained it to her. I told her it was necessary to make certain the onions, garlic, celery and green pepper, were finely chopped prior to braising with a spoon of melted butter added. I told her that the unsweetened corn bread adds a mealy effect to the mixture and that she could garnish the top of the dressing with chunked apple or pineapple if she so desired. I added another slice of turkey with dressing to her plate. I noticed she loosened her belt on her tiny waist. Her multi-colored dress matched the turning foliage of the start of the autumn season.

We sat at the table for some time. She held my right hand in her left. Her eyes met mine and she whispered, "Your dinner was wonderful, Jason." By looking at her, you'd never suspect that she had gone through a stressful experience with two killers. How grateful I was she survived the ordeal! She looked up at me and said, "I have something to tell you. My brother, Caleb, contacted me and wants me to come to Kentucky and live with his family. Out of my five brothers, he is the oldest, and watched over us after our parents died." There was a look of sadness on her face.

"Do you think that you will be going?" I asked, hoping she wouldn't. I was surprised.

"He didn't set a specific time, and told me to think it over. In a way, I'd like to, but Jason, I wouldn't be able to see you very much. Kentucky is quite a distance from Old Forge," she replied. Tears formed in the corners of her eyes.

I removed my handkerchief and blotted her tears, then leaned over, gently kissing her lips. She told me that she would wash the dishes. We worked together I covered everything for the refrigerator. She stacked the dirty dishes on the sink cabinet. An hour passed and the kitchen was spotless. I thanked her for helping me. I reminded her that she was my guest. She smiled and said, "Hush!"

I was pleased by the way the dinner came out. I asked Patty if she felt good enough to go for a walk in the woods and possibly climb part-way up Bald Mountain. She agreed, providing that we let Ruben go with us. I noticed that she was wearing sneakers that had good ankle support. Before we left, I went into the office and picked up my small camera. I put my small .25 caliber pistol in my pocket, just in case we came across a rabid coon. I didn't tell Patty, because I didn't want to upset her. However, I didn't want her to sustain a bite from a coon. I didn't want one either. Recently, there had been reports of coons chasing tourists in different locations in the park.

Ruben was ready for our jaunt. His tail was in motion. He pushed against his runway gate as I lifted the latch. He went directly to Patty. She petted his handsome head. She asked me how long Ruben had been a K-9 in the Troopers. I told her that he served with distinction for four years.

"You take such good care of him, Jason," she remarked.

"I try to. He is a wonderful companion and very protective, especially after dark," I responded, looking at Ruben.

The trail up Bald Mountain was well worn. It was a popular spot for tourists who sought a medium level of exercise. On top of the mountain was a fire tower that wasn't active. We walked along the trail slowly. Ruben was ahead of us checking out the underbrush. The trees were turning to the bright yellows, golds, and reds. The smell of fall was in the air. We met some hikers coming off the mountain. They nodded as we waved. Two of the men were carrying camcorders. The younger women with them giggled as they passed us. I wondered if they were their daughters, but that notion was dispelled when I looked back down the trail and saw one couple in an embracing position. It appeared that they were kissing. The big guy placed his camcorder on a stump. The other couple had continued on. Then I remembered that Patty and I had an age difference of twelve years. Patty asked me what I was looking at. I replied, "Oh! Nothing, really. Just a couple enjoying the aura of autumn." I didn't want to go into detail.

I asked Patty if she was getting tired. She looked up at me and indicated that she shouldn't walk too much further. I noticed that she had slowed her pace. I was breathing hard. I could hear the pounding of my heart in my ears. It sounded like the drums of a marching band. Ruben was out of sight. He seldom left my side, and I wondered if he was trying to make me worry. I gave him a shrill whistle, and soon he came running toward us at full speed. Today, Ruben was moving around the woods like a pup. He seemed to have adjusted to Patty's presence.

We met several sightseers moving toward us up the trail. Some of them had canteens draped across their shoulders. Some had cameras hanging from their belts. The season for picture-taking was here and I knew the shutters would be clicking away. The Adirondacks' vastness offers millions of scenes for the photographer. This beauty isn't only captured on film; hundreds of artists visit the park in all seasons to interpret the essence of their favorite seasons. It could be a watercolor of a bog, or a stand of oak trees, or an oil painting of an Adirondack camp dating back to the turn of the century. All genres are present. The concept of art covers a multitude of variations. The artist who sketches with charcoal, or pencil and pen, is often observed sitting on the end of a decaying log drawing a doe and her fawn. Bears are another interest of the artist, but caution must be used to avoid close encounters, especially with the landfills closed. The landfill, when in operation in the Old Forge area, drew many tourists during the evening hours to view the bears in the dump. Sometimes a dozen black bears could be seen following the smells of discarded rubbish or food.

Ruben raced to the gate of his runway. Patty and I walked slowly toward the log home. She had been telling me about her parents and how hard they had to struggle to make enough money to feed six children. It was a sad tale.

Patty filled Ruben's water and food dishes. Ruben sniffed one of her sneakers. She petted his big head. He loved the attention. She shut the gate and walked toward me. I could understand why she was so popular with the townspeople. She told me that Lila had called her to find out when she'd be able to return to work at John's Diner. She told Lila that she would report for work this coming Friday. I could tell that Patty was ready to return to her customers and, of course, her gratuities. She had bills to pay.

We sat at the kitchen table. I made some tea. I filled the two cups. We talked about some of our mutual friends. Patty had received dozens of cards and flowers from her customers. She told me how kind Wilt and Charlie, the two loggers, had been to her. Wilt had enclosed a large bill in his card. The giant of a man was just a big sentimental guy, who loved people. He worked hard and saved his money. He loved his big Dodge pickup and his log truck. Wilt had two huge skidders to haul logs out of the woods. He had cut a lot of timber in the region and possessed excellent reforestation ethics. He loved the park. He was good to the park and the park was good to Wilt. He had a larger logging operation than Charlie Perkins. For years Wilt had begged Charlie to go into partnership, but Charlie opted to maintain a smaller business. Charlie was heavily insured. He had many mouths to feed, and if a tree ever fell on him he wanted to ensure that the feeding would carry on. Wilt and Charlie were diamonds in the rough, and I could count on both of them.

I embraced Patty, and we kissed in the kitchen. She was full of passion, but I hesitated to become involved at this time. We were close friends, and having been through the stress of divorce and sadness, I just couldn't bring myself to partake of the moment. I looked into her eyes. My heart was pounding with the excitement. I asked her if she wanted to go home. "Yes, I'd better leave now," she responded, breathlessly.

She got her pocketbook from the table. I locked the house. We walked over to Ruben's runway and she patted his ears and head. He looked up at her and whined, his way of saying goodbye. We entered the Bronco and I drove her home. When we pulled into the yard, Harriet was standing in the doorway. I tooted. Harriet waved at us. I kissed Patty on her forehead gently. She embraced me and got out of the vehicle and went inside. I watched her until the door closed. I backed out of the driveway and drove back home.

I pulled into my drive and parked close to the house. My security light illuminated the yard. In the past I had experienced some gasoline theft from the Bronco. The bright light kept the thieves away. Ruben was waiting for me. I let him out of the runway and he ran into the woods. Shortly, he returned and we went inside.

The flashing light was pulsating on the answering machine. I walked over to it and pressed the button. The message was from Wilt Chambers. "Jason, call me before you go to bed." I dialed his number and the telephone rang twice.

"Hello," Wilt said.

"What's up, Wilt?" I asked, yawning.

"Jason, I was wondering if we could deliver the black bear to your friend in Lake Placid in the morning. I have to go to Vermont next week for a load of two-by-fours and I wanted to get the bear out of my shop. I don't have a lot of extra room. I'm in the process of carving three more bears for a lodge in Canada."

"Let me check my calendar, just a second…Wilt, I have nothing to do tomorrow. Do you want to pick me up? I don't think the bear will fit in the Bronco." I knew it wouldn't.

"It won't fit in your vehicle. We'll take the Dodge. I'll pick you up at 6:30 a.m. sharp, and we can grab breakfast at Long Lake. Is that all right with you?"

"Fine. I'll see you in the morning," I replied. We hung up.

I thought about Wilt and his kindness in carving the huge black bear for Tom Huston's lodge. Wilt was a very generous, hard-working man. He loved people and always could find that speck of goodness even in the hardhearted members of our society.

The alarm clock was already set for 5:30 a.m., so I didn't have to change it. I went into the bathroom, brushed my teeth, and cut a long hair protruding from my left nostril. I had a pair of sharp scissors, and when doing that procedure you have to be careful. One time I snipped my nose and it bled for an hour. I donned my pajamas and said my prayers. My memory flashed back to the time I was a child and how my loving mother would tuck me in and we'd say our prayers together. I was five years old. Dad would be standing in the doorway with a big smile. Sometimes when mother was busy sewing or playing the piano, dad would take over the saying of the prayers. I missed them very much. I knew that if there were a heaven, they were there.

I woke up with a start! Ruben was growling. I climbed out of bed. I told Ruben to settle down. He didn't. I looked outside. The large bear was back. He was standing up with his front paws on top of the Bronco. I went to the door and opened it. I hollered at him. "Get the hell out of here!" The bear's head slowly turned. I repeated the order. He put his front feet on the ground and slowly moved toward the woods. Ruben was trying to push me aside so he could chase the big guy, but I wouldn't let him outside. It was sort of ironic, especially with Wilt and me headed to Lake Placid in the morning with a *carved* large black bear. I told Ruben to go lie down. "Good boy, Ruben. You're a great watchman!" I returned to bed, wondering if the big bear had scratched the top of the Bronco.

It seemed like a second had passed when the alarm clock released the irritating *ring, ring, ring.* I had been dreaming of a pie-eating contest and Wilt wasn't the contestant, I was. The pies kept coming and I was passing them out to the audience. Then the bell sounded.

Ruben was sitting at the foot of the bed. His tail was thumping on the floor. I rubbed my eyes and kicked the bed covers back. *Damn that bear!* I thought. I went into the bathroom and turned the shower on. The hot water and soap bubbles felt good. I could hear the teakettle whistling. I rinsed in ice-cold water and shut the shower off. The warmth from my robe felt good. I went into the kitchen and turned the burner off.

Ruben was at the side door begging to go out. I unlocked the door and opened it. He didn't waste any time, but made a beeline to his favorite location. I took a sip of my coffee and returned to the bedroom. I made the bed, which is a ritual every morning. I took a pair of slacks and a shirt from the closet and dressed hurriedly, as Wilt would be arriving shortly.

I checked my desk and sealed several letters that were going out to people who had issued bad checks. I decided to take the letters with me and drop them into the Inlet Post Office, which was on the way. My letters to the check passers were always casual and never demanding, which can cause some of them to become irritated. My recovery of funds for the businesses was eighty-five percent successful. The checks that couldn't be collected were turned over to the criminal justice system.

# CHAPTER THIRTY

The big Dodge pulled into the yard on time. Wilt tooted the horn. I made a quick check of the house and made certain the gas jets were turned off. I left my front drapes open. I went outside and locked the door. Ruben was in his runway darting back and forth. Wilt had gotten out of his truck and gone to the fence to give Ruben a couple of dog biscuits. He was the only person I permitted to do this. Ruben loved Wilt.

"Good morning, Jason."

"Good morning, Wilt." We both went to the rear of the truck and lifted the tarp. Wilt's masterpiece lay on its back. It looked real.

"This one came out very good," Wilt said, proudly.

"It looks great, Wilt," I added. I knew Wilt appreciated my comment.

"Jason, I'm buying breakfast," he said.

"I'll let you." I was famished, and it would take an hour to get to Long Lake.

Wilt pulled over in front of the Inlet post office and I got out and put the letters through the mail slot. I climbed back into the big pickup. Wilt shoved it into gear and we headed for Long Lake and a big breakfast on Wilt.

We chatted all the way. There was little traffic on the road at this time of the morning. When we climbed the hill in front of the Adirondack Museum, two log trucks were moving slowly. Wilt tooted when he passed them. The logs hadn't been cut too long, according to Wilt.

The parking lot of Gertie's wasn't filled up. Wilt backed in. Both of us could stand a good breakfast. I let Wilt go through the door first. He had to turn sideways to make it through. Gertie was where she always was, by the  hot grill.

"Good morning, Jason, and good morning to you, Wilt." She turned and smiled. "Wilt, you haven't been here in ages," she added.

"I know, Gert, I'm sorry, but I don't get up this way too much. I'm working mostly around Old Forge and Boonville." Wilt's face reddened.

"We'll forgive you Wilt, but when you're up this way, stop in and see us." Gertie considered Wilt a good friend.

"Sure will," Wilt said, looking at the menu.

We sat at a big table. There were only a few customers eating their breakfast. Wilt ordered six hotcakes, four eggs, two slices of ham, and coffee. I selected scrambled eggs with crisp bacon, whole-wheat toast, and a cup of hot tea. Wilt was sitting on two chairs. They creaked when he reached for the sugar bowl. It took a few minutes for Gertie to prepare the order. Wilt and I chatted about how pleased Tom Huston would be to have one of Wilt Chambers' chainsaw-carved black bears standing in the lobby of the Breakshire Lodge. Wilt told me that this particular bear was a special one. He indicated that it measured six-foot-eight-inches tall in the standing position. I was looking forward to seeing it placed in Tom's lobby. Wilt told me that he had taken pictures of it and had one in his file for me.

I asked Gertie where her husband was. She said that he had driven to Tupper Lake for grocery supplies. I could tell that Gertie was happy to see us. She personally served us. The tray was loaded. She took care of Wilt first and then placed my heaping plate of scrambled eggs in front of me. Everything was nice and hot. I couldn't wait till I picked up one of the four pieces of crisp bacon. It was crunchy, and the taste was more than satisfying to my taste buds. I looked over at Wilt. He was adding some soft sweet butter to his golden brown hotcakes. He sliced his two pieces of sizzling ham and ingested some. My good friend loved food. The gentle giant looked over at me. I could see his gold tooth clamped on a piece of the ham.

Gertie came over to the table to fill Wilt's cup and asked me if

I wanted another tea bag. I told her that I had plenty of tea, and that everything was delicious. We finished our coffee and tea and Wilt paid the check. We waved at Gertie as we departed.

"See you later, come back," she said, smiling.

"We will." We promised, as we left.

Wilt and I walked across the street to where the seaplanes were moored. No one was on the beach. I told Wilt about the time I had stayed in Long Lake for a full week of fishing. "It's a beautiful lake, Wilt," I said, breathing the fresh air deep into my lungs.

"The lake looks like a mirror lying on the water. It's so still. I agree, she's a beauty." Wilt stared across the lake toward the mountains. He didn't say anything else for a moment. He reached into his pocket and took out a plug of chewing tobacco, and with his right hand placed it in his mouth. We both turned and walked to the truck.

Wilt asked me if I wanted to drive. I told him that I'd rather be the passenger. I thanked him for the offer. The truth is that I don't like to drive anyone else's vehicle. We headed toward Tupper Lake. The traffic was light. We conversed about the region. Wilt told me about the logging in the 1920's, long before he was born, when his father, Clayton, owned a small logging company. He mentioned the fact that the men used two-man saws, during that era of time, and how his mother cooked for the logging camp, near Santa Clara. The senior Chambers wanted his son, Wilt, to become a logger. When Wilt mentioned his father, his eyes watered. I asked him about his family. Wilt told me that his family was close-knit. He told me how his two brothers had died in a car accident during the Korean War. The highway was covered with black ice, at the time, and his brothers' car skidded across the highway and went down a steep embankment, striking a grove of trees. Both Hayden and Luther died at the scene. I looked over at Wilt. Tears continued to slide down his huge cheeks.

We passed the Red Fox Restaurant coming into Saranac Lake. I remembered that during the 1980 Olympics several of us, off-duty, had visited the restaurant several times. The food was excellent at the time. The owner played the piano for the customers. Just below the restaurant, Wilt swerved to miss a yellow cat that darted onto the roadway.

"Holy Cow!" I shouted loudly.

"Damn those cats!" Wilt snarled, gripping the wheel of the Dodge. "Whew! That was close," he gasped.

The American flag was furling on top of the tall flagpole at the state police headquarters. Autumn was in the air. Colored leaves blew across the highway in front of us. Traffic was light and had been all the way from Old Forge. Wilt was fully composed from talking about his family. I knew he was a big teddy bear and very sentimental when it came to his family. However, I had seen the other side of Wilt. One night at a restaurant between Old Forge and Boonville, I saw him take two wise guys into the parking lot. I remembered one of them called Wilt a fat tub of lard. He settled the matter in a hurry. Several of us looked out the window. The fellows were being shaken by Wilt. We could hear both of them pleading with him. "We were only kidding, mister," they said in unison, with their feet dangling a foot off the ground. I could tell that Wilt was thoroughly angry.

The parking lot of the Breakshire was half full of cars and vans. I could see that the parking garage was filled up. I told Wilt to pull up near the delivery door.

"Jason, before we go in I want to ask you something," Wilt said with a serious expression on his face.

"Go ahead, Wilt." I was curious.

"I know it isn't any of my business, but what's happening with Patty? I saw her at John's the other day and she looks very sad. She told me about her brother in Kentucky. He wants her to come and live with them."

"We had dinner at my place recently, and everything seemed okay."

"I was just wondering. I had hoped that you two would get together."

"We'll talk about it sometime."

"Okay."

I went inside and Wilt stayed with the truck. Tom Huston was just inside the front door. He smiled when he saw me. I asked him if he could spare a moment. He came over, shook my hand, and patted me on the right shoulder. "How have you been, Jason?"

"Fine! You indicated in your letter that you wanted me to stop and see you."

"Yes, I did. Remember the case of the wanted killer from Arizona? Well, you told me to keep an eye open for a woman that might make an inquiry about him. She appeared. I didn't get her name. I told her that the state police had taken him away. She didn't say a word. She turned around and went out the door in a hurry. I looked out to see if she had a car, but didn't see any."

"Thank you for telling me about it." I said, stroking my chin. "By the way, Tom, could you step outside with me a moment?"

We went out the front door and walked around to the service entrance. I introduced Tom to Wilt. They shook hands. Wilt told Tom that he had a beautiful lodge. Tom thanked him. I let Wilt do the talking at this point.

"Mr. Huston, I'd like to show you something in the rear of my truck," Wilt said. His face beamed with pride.

The three of us moved to the rear of the truck.

"Mr. Huston, I have something for you. You might say it is from Jason and me," Wilt continued, beaming.

Wilt lifted the tarp, and Tom Huston's eyes got big. He jumped back, surprised. Before he could say a word, Wilt told him that he had carved this particular black bear for him and his lodge.

"Wilt, thank you so very, very, much. The bear is beautiful. It must have taken you a long time to carve and paint it. It's going to look great in the lobby! Thank you both for this generous gift," Tom said, thoroughly surprised.

The three of us lifted it carefully out of the pickup truck and carried it around to the front door. Guests of the Breakshire Lodge flocked around us as we carried it through the front entrance. Mr. Huston guided us to a specific location and we set it down in an upright position. I could hear the guests making favorable comments about the huge black bear. The eyes looked real. The claws looked sharp. I waited for the growl.

Tom informed his staff about the newcomer to the lodge.

I could tell that he was happy to have the bear. I didn't tell him that I had paid for part of the bear's creation. I didn't think it was necessary or appropriate. I did know that Wilt and I had a close friend in Tom Huston.

He insisted that Wilt and I go into the dining room for coffee and lunch.

Wilt went into the restroom to wash up. Tom came over to me and advised me that a business friend of his, Cleo Lawrence, owner and operator of the Hearth Hotel in Lake Placid, had a problem. Tom went on to tell me that if Wilt and I had a few minutes to spare after lunch, he would like me to talk with Mr. Lawrence. I agreed. Tom would arrange for Mr. Lawrence to come to his office.

I led the way into the dining room. Wilt followed me closely. The noon hostess smiled. She was carrying two menus. "This way, gentlemen," she said distinctly. We followed her. She selected a large table. "Will this table be all right, gentlemen?" she asked. I detected an English accent. She appeared to be in her forties, tall and slender, with black hair pulled over her ears into a tight bun. She had hazel-colored eyes. I had not seen her on my previous visits.

Some of the guests looked over at us when Wilt placed two chairs together. They watched him sit down and quickly turned away when Wilt looked at them. The menus were new. On the front was a picture of the Breakshire Lodge. Wilt and I opened them up and looked at the entrees. Our waitress appeared with two glasses of iced water. I could hear the cubes in the glasses make a crackling sound. I looked over at my friend. Wilt drank down the full glass of water.

"Are you ready to order, gentlemen?" our waitress asked politely, giving us a broad smile.

Wilt spoke first. "I'll have the grilled salmon with the O'Brien potatoes and cabbage salad. Wilt loved salmon.

I ordered next. "The broiled sirloin with baked potato, please."

"Thank you, gentlemen,"

Sonya--I noticed by her name tag—spoke cordially.

I told Wilt that Tom wanted me to speak to a friend of his before we started back to Old Forge. I didn't go into detail. All I knew was that his friend had a problem.

I knew, also, that the private investigation business wasn't a lucrative enterprise all the time. The line is thin between private detective work and the regular police organization. I attempted to honor that difference between the two concepts. My broad base of contacts throughout the law enforcement community, including town, county, city, state, federal agencies, and Interpol, was intact. Without these sources, you might as well go out of business.

Sonya arrived at our table. Wilt's salmon looked delicious. I was a bit envious until she set my platter before me. The broiled sirloin was sprinkled with bits of parsley and melting sweet butter. The baked potato, split in the middle, was oozing with butter. Sour cream and chives waited in a separate dish. Wilt and I shared a generous serving of candied carrots. The homemade bread was warm. Wilt had coffee and I ordered hot tea. I gave a piece of sirloin to Wilt. He was still hungry.

"Delicious," he said, licking his lips.

"Great food, Wilt," I replied. Wilt not only knew his logs, but was attuned to the best in cuisine. The lunch was perfect.

Wilt ordered hot apple pie with vanilla ice cream. I didn't order dessert, but had my tea warmed with hot water. The green tea tasted good with a dash of lemon. I looked over and the big man was ready. His fork was poised. Sonya set the steaming pie, piled high with vanilla ice cream, directly in front of him. He made short work of the dessert.

The waitress stopped by the table. We thanked her for the fine service. Wilt and I left a five-dollar gratuity in the center of the table. We got up and left the table. I asked Wilt to wait in the lobby for me, then proceeded to Tom Huston's office.

A man was in conversation with Tom when I entered the office.

"Come in, Jason. I'd like you to meet a good friend of mine, Cleo Lawrence, owner and operator of the Hearth Hotel."

"Pleased to meet you, Mr. Lawrence." I extended my hand; we shook. Lawrence appeared to be in his mid-fifties. He had red hair and his face was sprinkled with tiny freckles. His eyes were pale blue. He was about six foot tall with a slender build. His clothes were expensive looking. He spoke excellent English.

Tom said, "I'll leave you gentlemen for now," then excused himself and left the office. I sat down in the other stuffed chair. Both of the chairs were covered with leather, and when you sat in one, it was comfortable.

I looked Lawrence directly in the eye and asked him, "How can I be of assistance to you, sir?"

"I would like you to look into something for me." He spoke

eloquently and I could tell that he was cultured. "I hired a French chef about six months ago. He interviewed for the position with excellent credentials. The references on his application were all restaurant owners from the Montreal area. He is an excellent chef with a vast knowledge of the culinary art. He is masterful in European cuisine and that includes the French cooking of Paris as well as of Canada. I find no fault with his craft."

"What seems to be the problem with him? What is his name?" I asked, taking a small notebook from my shirt pocket.

"His name is Jean LeBeau. He is forty years of age. He is five foot eight inches in height. He has black hair and blue eyes. Not married. He drives a black Lincoln town car, bearing Quebec plates. He resides at my hotel, and on his days off he goes to Montreal or Burlington, Vermont. His parents are both deceased and there are no other siblings, to my knowledge. He is fluent in English, Danish, and French." I wrote as fast as I could. He continued, "Mr. Black, I have confidential information that my chef is involved in a large-scale cocaine ring that involves the movement of this drug from Tucson and Phoenix, Arizona, to Montreal. I cannot reveal my source of information." He spoke softly and in a low whisper.

"Why haven't you notified the police about this?"

He went on to tell me, "Mr. Black, I run a legitimate business. I don't want to get the local authorities rushing to my hotel with sirens and red lights flashing. Tom informed me that you might be able to assist me in contacting the proper authorities, without causing me or my business a great deal of embarrassment."

I told him that I would see what I could do. I explained to him what my daily fees would be, plus expenses. I could tell that Lawrence was serious and understood his dilemma. Having visited the southwest region of our country, I was well aware of the illegal drug activity that takes place. Phoenix is considered the hub of cocaine trafficking. Mr. Lawrence told me that he wanted to employ me to discreetly investigate his chef. I agreed. Mr. Lawrence told me that LeBeau would be going on a week's vacation in seven days. Until then, he would be working steadily in the hotel's kitchen. He told me that a room would be available at his hotel for my use. He also said that he had interest in a car rental company and would have a vehicle

I could use.

My mind was racing as Mr. Lawrence made his wishes known to me. I immediately mapped out a plan in my mind, which included the move I would make to the Hearth Hotel. I assured the redheaded hotel owner that we would find out what his chef was involved in. Mr. Lawrence would not disclose his source of information, but I calculated that the source had to have a connection with LeBeau.

I thanked the hotel owner, and promised him that our engagement concerning LeBeau was strictly private. Mr. Lawrence reached inside his suede jacket and took out an envelope. "Here, this will start you off. You will find the keys to a Pontiac Le Mans and two thousand dollars for expense money. There will be more, if you need it." I gave him my card and told him that I would come to his hotel in a few days to begin my probe.

I left the office. I met Tom returning to his office and thanked him for the contact with Lawrence.

"See you later, Jason." He patted me on the shoulder.

"Take care, Tom."

I went into the lobby. Wilt was sitting on the large couch reading a copy of *Adirondack Life*.

He looked up at me, smiled, and asked, "All set to travel?"

"Yes, thank you for your patience, Wilt." I knew he would wait for however long it took. He was a loyal friend.

The trip back to Old Forge was a good one. Wilt told me stories that his dad had passed down to him about the excitement of being a rough and tumble logger. He told me about the fights between the French and the Poles in the logging camps, dating back to the 1920's. His father had described how kind these men were when they went to town after a month in the woods. They would spend their money and always made certain to give something to the local kids in the neighborhood. They were strong men with big hearts. The loggers would have a good time for a few days and then again return to the deep woods to their axes and saws and logging camp life. I loved to listen to Wilt. The images were so clear about the characters he told me about. It was just like being in a room full of woodsmen. You could almost feel the punch in the nose or hear the men singing after they downed their whiskey and beer.

We talked so much that we passed Gertie's Diner in Long Lake and didn't even look over at their parking lot. The rest of the trip into Old Forge was beautiful. Colored leaves fluttered across the highway and the smell of autumn was definitely in the air and in our hearts. Numerous photographers were taking pictures along Route 28. Some were using tripods, and others were steadying cameras on the tops of their automobiles. I wondered, as we passed, what type of film they were using. Mother Nature was being good to the photographers on this day.

Wilt asked me again about Patty. I told him how fond I was of her, but having experienced two failed marriages, I wasn't ready to go down that path. I told him that I had to be certain before I gave up my freedom again. He agreed with me. We changed the subject.

We were approaching Eighth Lake when we saw it. Wilt applied the brakes and the Dodge came to an abrupt stop. Standing in the middle of Route 28 was a cow moose. She appeared to be well over seven hundred pounds. Wilt reached over and opened up his glove box. He removed his camera and opened the door on his side, being careful not to spook the cow. A northbound car had also stopped to view her. I was amazed at her stately appearance. It was the second moose I had seen in the Adirondacks, although my game protector friend, Bud Martin, had informed me that approximately sixty-five moose are presently in New York State. The animal just stood there looking at us. Wilt snapped the button on his camera six times. She finally moved off into the bushes. The bull moose probably was in the vicinity; however, he didn't show himself.

Just outside of Inlet, the Inlet Police had a car pulled over. Wilt looked at the car and told me that the left rear tire appeared to be flat. We assumed that the officer had come across the car and stopped to render assistance to the elderly lady behind the wheel. We slowed down to a crawl until we passed them.

I had Wilt drop me off at the entrance to my place. I thanked him again for the kind gesture he had made in presenting Tom with the carved bear. We stopped and I got out of the truck. Wilt told me that he'd see me later and drove off. I walked down the narrow lane toward home. I could hear Ruben. He knew I was home. The barking didn't stop until I opened his runway. He jumped up on me and almost knocked me over. "I'm not fair to you, Ruben, leaving you all the time." Ruben whined and pushed his big head against my right leg. I patted him and rubbed his back. He finally settled down. I let him run for awhile. I swept the walkway, as Ruben raced back and forth to the woods. Several chipmunks were screeching in the trees nearby.

My mind was racing. I knew that Ruben would have to be boarded at the Eagle Bay Kennel while I was in Lake Placid. I loved the big shepherd. Our bond was strong. It wasn't long before the big dog came bouncing out of the woods. He went directly to his runway gate. I met him there and opened it for him. I filled his water and food dishes. I petted him and closed the gate. The autumn leaves in their brilliant colors were lazily falling to the ground.

I entered the house and could tell immediately that it had to be aired out. It seemed musty. I opened several windows and turned two fans on. I checked the freezer to see what I was having for supper. I took out some liver and placed it on the counter.

The red light was flashing on the answering machine. I ran the messages. The first one was from Todd Wilson and the second one was Patty. I immediately called the Chief. Todd answered the telephone. He informed me that my friend, Charlie Perkins, had been forced off the highway by a drunken driver. Charlie had received some minor injuries, but his big rig was totaled. I thanked the Chief and hung up the phone. I felt bad for Charlie. He had a big family. He had to work continually to stay on top of things. I called his home, but there was no answer.

Patty answered the telephone on the first ring. "Hello, sweetheart. This is Jason."

"Hi, Sherlock. Where have you been?" she asked. She apparently missed me.

"At Lake Placid. Wilt and I delivered the carved bear to the Breakshire Lodge," I said, proudly.

"Honey, I have some news for you. My brother, Caleb, has wired me an airline ticket. He wants me to fly to Kentucky for a couple of weeks. I asked Lila if she could get someone to work in my place and, luckily, Maggie is going to work for me."

I was shocked to hear this. "Do you feel good enough to travel?"

"Yes, I have recovered from my ordeal. I haven't seen my

brother in years. He even mentioned that he might be able to get a hold of my other brothers and have a small reunion with them and their families while I'm there." She sounded excited.

"I'm going to miss you, but I think that is nice of Caleb. He must think a lot of you."

"He does, honey. Do you mind?"

"No, not at all. I'll miss you, but I have a case in Lake Placid that I will be tied up on for a while. I have to put Ruben back in the kennel for a week or so."

"Oh! That will work out just right, then," she said.

"How are you getting to the airport? Do you need a ride?" I asked.

"Harriet is taking me. She has to see a doctor in Fayetteville, so it will work out just right," she said, sounding sad. "I'll miss you, Jason. We're leaving early in the morning, about 4:00 a.m."

"I'll miss you, too, sweetheart. Tell Harriet to be careful driving." I felt lonely and sad that she was going away, but I couldn't be selfish. It wasn't fair to her.

"Patty, did you hear about Charlie Perkins' accident?"

"Yes, honey, I did. He is lucky that he wasn't killed." We discussed Charlie for a few minutes. We both agreed that it would be difficult for him and his family until he purchased another log truck.

I told Patty to have an enjoyable time with her family in Kentucky. We hung up after saying that we loved each other. After I placed the phone on the receiver, an emptiness took over my whole being. I thought about our last words spoken to each other. I knew that I would miss her. Would she miss me as much?

Ruben was anxious to run into the woods. I opened his gate. He nuzzled his big head against my knee, then ran off into the woods. I cleaned up his runway and checked the food and water dishes. Shortly he returned. I closed the gate. Ruben and I entered the house.

I checked the windows and locked the doors. Ruben went to his favorite place and lay down. I went into the bathroom. I had just started brushing my teeth when the telephone rang. I quickly gargled with some cold water, wiped my mouth off, and rushed to answer the phone on the fourth ring. "Hello," I said.

"Honey, I'm going to miss you." It was Patty.

"I'm going to miss you too, sweetheart. Maybe this will be good for us, to be apart for awhile." We talked, and after saying goodbye, we hung up at the same time.

I finished brushing my teeth and went to bed. Ruben was all set for the night, lying in his favorite spot. I set the alarm for 7:00 a.m. I went to bed and fell off to sleep.

My deep slumber was disturbed when a loud roar reached my ears. I soon learned that Dale Rush had flown low over the house. I couldn't mistake the red Stinson. I just reached the window as it skirted over the treetops. *What the hell?* I thought. *He must be on some kind of a mission. Maybe he is taking some hunters into the hard-to-reach hunting areas.*

I decided that I'd visit the Laundromat this morning. The soiled laundry was piling up. I stripped the bed and made it with fresh sheets and pillowcases. I shook out the two blankets and bedspread. I couldn't help but think about Patty. She must be in Kentucky by now. It had been years since she had seen Caleb.

Ruben whined to go outside. I opened the door and the big dog ran off to the woods. I finished dressing. Ruben returned shortly and I put him in his runway. I double checked his food and water dishes. I added some food. The water was okay. I locked the house and put the laundry bags into the rear of the Bronco.

The vehicle started on the first engagement of the ignition switch. Nothing was coming down Route 28 going south. An out-of-town log truck was slowly creeping up the long grade headed north. I reached the Laundromat and was pleased to find a parking spot close to the door. No one was using any of the machines. I had my pick. The first three machines near the dryers were my choice. I placed the white clothes in one and the colored in the remaining two. I used their soap and bleach. The owners of the establishment were hard workers and had been in Old Forge for years.

With the machines in operation and running smoothly, I walked over to John's Diner for a quick breakfast. Most of the early customers had already had their breakfast and were off to their jobs. I entered the diner and immediately observed Lila flipping three hotcakes over on the grill. She flashed a smile at me. I chose to sit at the counter.

"What will you have this morning?" she asked.

"Two eggs scrambled, whole wheat toast, and a cup of tea," I said. I was hungry. I glanced at the Utica paper. It seemed to be getting thinner every day. Not much news this morning.

Lila served my eggs steaming hot. I put some ketchup on them and some blackberry jelly on the toast. I sipped some tea. Everything was delicious. Lila hurried back to the kitchen to work on her lunch menu. She and her husband worked hard. They had a good business.

I thanked Lila and put the paper back on the counter. I left a dollar for a tip.

"Have a good day, Jason!" she hollered from the kitchen.

"You, too!" I left the diner and returned to the Laundromat. The machines had clicked off. I opened the dryer doors and removed the fresh washing from the machines. I inserted fifty cents into each dryer. The big dryers went into motion as the clothes bounced against the glass in the door.

The week went by rapidly. I was able to write letters and catch up on pending check cases. My fee checks began to arrive from various businesses, and I banked them all. I had met some great people during the collection process. Many of them commented on the way I handled the delinquent checks. The ones that had a hint of criminality were turned over to the police department. I had nothing to do with that type of action.

Today's private sleuth is much different than the unshaven, trench coat-wearing detective of fictional stories. I have met many private eyes who pursue a different brand of ethics. In the real world of investigators, they work in the area of civil law, interviewing witnesses of accidents, looking into insurance claims with a suspicious twist, and assisting lawyers in difficult custody cases, as well as undertaking numerous investigations into the business and commercial havens of our society. Actually one could say that it is a profession of many hats. It is a service of gathering bits and pieces of fact in a logical manner to illustrate a given situation or dilemma. I have found that in the private investigative business, like in that of the my former career of being a Trooper, common sense and hard work still prevail. I opt to do the best job possible for my clients.

As the week progressed I made arrangements at the Eagle Bay

Kennel for Ruben's visit. I informed the attendant that I didn't know my return date but would stay in touch with them concerning Ruben's stay.

I had toyed with the idea of a motor home, which could be moved to an area where I would be working, but I had decided to own my own home in the Old Forge area. The entire park is a beautiful place, but I chose to reside in my personal favorite location, in a community of interesting people who work diligently to meet their goals. That's not saying that the many towns, villages and hamlets throughout the region lack people of such qualities. If I could afford it, I'd have a home in every town of the Adirondacks. There is no place on earth that can compete with our park.

# CHAPTER THIRTY-ONE

The day had come for me to go to Lake Placid and the Hearth Hotel. Ruben was dropped off at the kennel. The house was checked over and secured. I had called Wilt, Dale, and Charlie Perkins. Charlie had his new rig and was back in his logging operation. The three of them told me they would keep an eye on my place. Before I left town, I dropped a note off to Patty in Kentucky. My pending cases were in good order. I was now off on a new adventure. This time I had my 9mm automatic pistol with me. I selected warmer clothing, as the temperatures were dipping a little lower, especially in the evening time.

I couldn't leave the area without stopping at the kennel. Ruben was in the runway, lying down with his back to me. I approached the fence. "Ruben, come here." The two ears stiffened. He got up and ran toward me. "Come on, baby, come here." I reached in and petted his back. He looked at me. I wished that I didn't have to leave him, but I had to. "Take it easy, Ruben." I turned and walked to the Bronco. The trees were shedding their colored leaves. I entered the Bronco and drove north on Route 28. Traffic had picked up. The leaf peepers were poking along about 35 m.p.h. One guy ahead of me was zigzagging from one side of the lane to the next. I soon learned he had one hand on the steering wheel and the other on his camera, attempting to snap a photo of a tree displaying bright red leaves. I was able to pull alongside of him and pass him without connecting with the left side of his car. I wished that a police officer could have caught that little act, but there was none in sight. When I got by him, I looked into my rearview mirror. The joker finally pulled off the road. I continued on toward Blue Mountain.

As I climbed the hill in front of the Adirondack Museum, traffic was moving slow. More leaf worshippers. A Trooper's car with flashing lights and siren came toward me headed south on Route 30. I pulled over to the right as far as I could. I was wondering if the guy with the camera a few miles behind me had been involved in some kind of a mishap. I shook my head and continued on. The museum was packed.

The cars and pickups were bumper to bumper going into Long Lake. I made the left turn at Hoss's Country Corner and headed for Gertie's Diner. I found a space and pulled in near the front door. I made certain that the doors were locked before I got out. I had my camera and binoculars lying on the floor in back of the driver's seat. I covered them up before I went inside.

Gertie was behind the counter. Luscious cheeseburgers were on the hot grill. She had just placed the American cheese on each burger. The milkshake mixer was purring. She spotted me.

"Hi, Jason, good to see you," she said.

She had just turned some bacon over. It sizzled and the aroma seduced my taste buds and sense of smell. I looked around for Gertie's husband. He wasn't around. The diner was crowded. I found a small table in the corner. The waitress came over with a menu and a tall glass of iced water. I told her that I'd like a hamburger with onion and a cup of green tea. She smiled while writing the order on a pad. I didn't recognize her. Her name plate read "Lottie." The customers ranged in all ages. I thought, what a gold mine Gertie and her husband have. I sipped my iced water. It was cold, and tasted good.

Lottie soon returned with the burger. The teapot was steaming. I had a moment of frustration when I attempted to put ketchup on the burger. It finally flowed. The sandwich was delicious. The tea was hot. It didn't take long to consume my late lunch.

Lottie returned with the check. She looked me in the eye. "Are you Jason?" she asked. Her lipstick was bright red.

"Yes, I'm Jason. Why do you ask?" I was inquisitive. She was about thirty-five years old, about five foot five, with jet black hair, cut short. She had a mole on her neck and I spotted a hickey just below her ear.

"Oh! I just wondered. They speak highly of you here, and I wondered what you looked like." She giggled.

"I'm just an ordinary guy," I said, rather annoyed.

I couldn't believe what I had just heard. She giggled some more and was gone. I looked at my check. She had overcharged me by one dollar. I got up from the table and went over to the cash register. Gertie met me there.

"Everything okay, Jason?"

"Fine, Gertie. Good burger."

"Wish I could talk, but you can see I'm busy," Gertie said. She smiled.

"Thanks. Hello to your husband." I left the diner. Too crowded.

I enjoyed the rest of the trip to Lake Placid. Traffic had thinned out and I kept the speedometer around the double-nickel. Two Trooper cars were parked in the yard of the Tupper Lake barracks when I went by. I pulled into the parking lot of the Hearth Hotel late in the afternoon. I happened to see the big black Lincoln of Jean LeBeau, the head chef. I left everything in the Bronco for the moment. I entered the hotel and asked for Mr. Lawrence. He came out of his office and motioned me to come in.

"You're a day early, Jason. Good to see you," he said, smiling.

"Yes, I am. I have to interview a client on another matter. I hope I'm not causing any difficulty for you by arriving ahead of time."

"No, not at all. The Pontiac is ready for your use. It is a part of my car collection, which I house in a storage barn. It is full of gas. I have it parked across the street in the parking lot. It is beige in color." He opened up the top drawer of his desk. "Here are the keys for the car and the key to your room that I have arranged for you. You can put your things in the room anytime. I think that is about all for the moment. Jean LeBeau advised me that he has to go to Burlington, Vermont, day after tomorrow."

"I'll be ready. Do you have any idea about the time he'll depart?"

"He usually leaves here around 8:00 a.m. By the way, he has never seen the car you will be using. If there is anything you need, just contact me."

"Good, we don't want to spook him. And thank you, sir. I believe I have everything that I need."

I finished my conversation with Lawrence, then proceeded to the Bronco and removed my suitcase and the case containing my binoculars and notebook. I proceeded to room 212. I unlocked the door and entered. It had a large double bed, television set, and comfortable chairs. A cherry-wood desk was near the window, which overlooked the parking area. The large black Lincoln was in plain view. There was a telephone on the desk. The room was beautiful. I felt at home, except that I missed Ruben. The walls were papered with mountains scenes. The temperature in the room was sixty-seven. The air conditioner was turned off. In the corner was a small refrigerator full of soft drinks. It was ice cold.

The bed looked comfortable. I removed my shoes and stretched out for a few minutes. I almost dozed off. I looked at my watch. It was late afternoon. I turned over, reached for the telephone, and dialed Troop S Headquarters. After two rings a familiar voice answered.

"May I speak to Lieutenant Roy Garrison, please?" I asked.

"Lieutenant Garrison, speaking."

"Roy, Jason Black here. Could you join me for dinner this evening at the Breakshire?"

"Hello, Jason. Just a minute. I'll check my calendar.......I'm free, Jason. What time?"

"I'll be in the dining room at 5:30 p.m., sharp." I was glad that Roy could join me. We talked for a few minutes and hung up.

I wanted to roll over and snooze, but I forced myself to get up. I thought about Patty, way down in Kentucky. What was she doing? I missed her. And I missed Ruben, too. I finished hanging up my clothes and put a few things into the drawers. I didn't know exactly how long I'd be here. I wondered why a successful chef would get involved in a drug ring, if it were true. According to Lawrence he had the best of references and was being paid $750.00 each week, plus a 401K for investment purposes. Is it greed that motivates the pursuit of illegal activity? Time would tell.

I decided that I would take a fast shower before I went to the

Breakshire to meet Roy.  I undressed and went into the bathroom.
The tub was large.  The shower curtain also was covered with images
of snow-capped mountains and pine trees.  Lawrence was true to the
Adirondack concept of the high peak region, as illustrated in the decor
of his hotel.  The water was soft as it pelted my back.  The large green
bar of scented soap broke into bubbles as I applied it to my arms and
legs.  It refreshed me.  I turned the shower to cold and the water
erased the tiny bubbles.  I felt like a new man.

I arrived at the Breakshire at 5:30 p.m.  Roy was just getting out
of his unmarked black Dodge, four-door, with three whip antennae
sticking up in the air.  I parked the Bronco about five spaces from him.
I went directly into the lodge.  I didn't think it would be smart to
approach Roy in the parking lot.

I approached the hostess by the dining room entrance.  I didn't
recognize her.  She smiled.

"There will be two of us," I said.  Roy joined me at that moment
and the hostess led us to a table in the far corner of the dining room.

"Good to see you, Jason," Roy said.

The hostess laid two menus on the table.

"Glad you could make it, Roy."  There were very few people in
the dining room.

"What can I do for you, Jason?"

"I have been engaged to conduct a check on an employee of a
local establishment, here in Lake Placid.  I do not want to reveal the
name of the person at this time.  In the event my investigation reveals
that criminal activity is about to take place or is occurring, I will contact
you with all the details."

Roy was listening intently.  "I understand, Jason.  I would rather
not know who it is at this juncture."

"I didn't think you would."

We looked the menu over and we both decided to have grilled
salmon, baked potato and a garden salad.  Our waitress was Libby.
She took our order.  We ordered iced tea with our meals.  Roy asked
me how Patty was doing since her ordeal.  I informed him that she was
back to work, but was presently visiting her brother in Kentucky.  We
continued to chat about general subjects and the recent retirees from
the Troopers.  Roy shared with me his future plans after retirement.

He told me that he didn't know exactly when he would retire, but when the time came, he was looking forward to Alaska and some salmon fishing.

Libby had a big smile when she approached our table with her large tray. She served our meal. The salmon looked delicious.

"Is there anything I can do for you, gentlemen?" she asked.

Roy replied, "Everything looks fine," as he reached for a warm roll.

"Looks great," I added. The sour cream and butter had been added to the potato by the chef. There was enough for three potatoes.

Roy and I reminisced about the 1980 Olympics. Both of us had been assigned to the detail at the time. We decided that it was one of the highlights of our careers. Roy told me that he was on a diet and that he ate fish three times each week. We finished our dinners and, so as not to tempt Roy, I decided not to order my favorite dessert.

I learned that Nate, in St. Regis Falls, now had a German shepherd in his grocery store, twenty-four hours a day. Roy indicated that he had stopped in to see Nate and the dog had cornered him. Both of us agreed that it wasn't good for business.

I picked up the check and looked for Tom Huston. He wasn't in sight. I thanked Roy for meeting me and we said goodbye. Roy left through the lobby. The cashier thanked me. I told her that the salmon was excellent. The mint candies by the register were tempting; however, I passed them by.

Before I left the lodge, I stopped at the telephone and called Harriet in Old Forge. I asked her if she had heard from Patty. She told me that Patty had called her twice and that she was enjoying herself at her brother's home in Kentucky. I told Harriet to give her my regards when she called again. I missed Patty.

When I went down the steps, I looked at the flowers in the two large beds. They appeared to be the victims of a cold frost the night before. The multicolored leaves were falling from the large trees in the front of the lodge. I looked out over the lake. Two ducks flew low in front of me. I unlocked the Bronco and climbed in. I sat there for a minute taking in Mother Nature's beautiful day. It was breathtaking.

I had the evening free. I turned right out of the parking lot and headed toward Saranac Lake. I drove through the village. When I came to the Red Fox Restaurant I looked over. It was closed. I continued west on Route 3 and turned north on Route 30 toward Malone. When I reached the road to Santa Clara, I turned left. The highway was generally straight and level, with a few slight grades. I pulled over when I reached the old hotel that Fannie Collins and her husband had operated for over fifty years. This was where I had met Norris and taken him into custody, making a citizen's arrest. I drove around the hamlet for a while and then headed back to the Hearth Hotel. I was going to stop in to see Nate, but decided against it.

Three unloaded log trucks were parked near the entrance of Paul Smith's College. I slowed down. The loggers were standing near the pavement. The hood was up on one of the trucks. I tooted when I passed, and all three waved. One truck looked like Charlie Perkins' new rig, but I couldn't be certain. I knew that Charlie would understand if I didn't stop.

The parking lot at the hotel was half full of leaf peepers. I parked and went up to my room, which smelled fresh and clean. I went to the window and looked out. The big black Lincoln owned by Chef LeBeau was still in the same location.

I had just lay down when the telephone rang. I answered it.

"Jason, this is Lawrence. I've learned that the party we discussed yesterday will be leaving the parking lot about 8:30 tomorrow morning."

"Thanks," I said. I heard the click in my ear. I lay back down and soon fell off to sleep.

I slept longer than I wanted to. It was dark when I awoke. I went into the bathroom and splashed some cool water in my face. I went downstairs and looked into the dining room. It was full. I went out of the hotel and crossed the street to the parking lot. The Pontiac was parked at the far end. Mr. Lawrence had advised me that the tank was full and ready to go. I decided to go to the coffee shop and get a sandwich. The Pontiac started immediately. The car was clean and in excellent shape. I drove out of the parking area and, instead of going to a coffee shop, I proceeded to the Red Fox Restaurant. During the 1980 Olympics, I had visited the restaurant and the cuisine was excellent. The traffic was light.

When I arrived I located a parking spot at the end of the parking area. I got out, and locked the car, and walked up the steps into the barroom. The bar had two patrons. The dining room was partially full. I sat at the bar. The bartender approached me. I asked him if the owner were in. He told me that he was in New York City attending a conference. I hadn't seen Paul Sylvester since the Olympics.

"What can I do for you?" The bartender asked.

I asked him if I could order a ham and cheese sandwich at the bar.

"Certainly," he replied, writing the order on a pad.

I asked for a cup of coffee as well.

Music was playing in the background. The bartender brought my sandwich. I asked him for some cream for the coffee. The ham was shaved thin and the Swiss cheese had been sliced a little thicker. My first bite told me that the ham was fresh. I had lucked out. I had a refill on my coffee. I knew that two cups at this hour would assure me of a wakeful night. I tipped the bartender, paid the check, left the restaurant, and went back to the Hearth Hotel.

The wake up call was on time. I heard bells in the distance. Finally, reality brought me to lift the receiver on the phone.

"Mr. Black, this is the night clerk. You wanted to be wakened at 7:00 a.m., sir." The night clerk sounded sleepy.

"Thank--thank you." I hung up the receiver.

The water at the Hearth Hotel was soft and gentle. The soap bubbled up, and I managed to feel refreshed. I picked out a pair of slacks and a light turtleneck. It was cool outside, according to Channel 9 on the television. I dressed, then called room service and ordered two peanut butter and jelly sandwiches. I asked the person on the other end of the phone to wrap them up. In a matter of fifteen minutes, the sandwiches arrived. I gave the kitchen worker a dollar tip.

I peered out into the parking lot. The black Lincoln was parked in the same location. At 8:00 a.m. I left my room. I was carrying my pistol and binoculars. I respected firearms. My father had taught me early on about rules concerning guns. I had put my two sandwiches in my carrying case, which also contained a plastic bottle of water. I met no one in the hotel hallway as I made my way to the front entrance. I left the hotel and crossed the street to the Pontiac. I opened the door and entered. I started the car and backed around into another parking space where I could view the entrance to the hotel's main parking lot. I sat back and relaxed—and watched.

The black Lincoln drove slowly out of the driveway and turned in the direction of Route 87. The two lanes were curvy and hilly as I followed the Lincoln. I stayed a considerable distance behind Jean LeBeau. There was other eastbound traffic. The Lincoln continued to be in my view. I was surprised when we reached the Route 87 ramps for north and south traffic. He didn't take the northern direction. Instead, he got on the highway and headed south in the direction of Warrensburg, Saratoga, and Albany. The southbound lanes of Route 87 were full of workers and tourists. The Pontiac performed remarkably well. LeBeau was keeping his speedometer between 60 m.p.h. and 65 m.p.h. I couldn't help but wonder why he chose the southerly direction. We passed several exits. Near Albany, he pulled into a southbound rest area. He proceeded to the southern end of it. I pulled behind a parked truck loaded with baled hay. I could still observe the Lincoln. I watched LeBeau get out of the car. He was looking in all directions. He walked around the Lincoln twice, then walked toward the restroom. He went to the telephone and made a call. The call didn't seem to last long. He hung up the receiver and ducked into the restroom. There were several cars and trucks parked along the curbs. I was pleased, as they afforded me good cover. In about five minutes, LeBeau, who was wearing black slacks and a white shirt, came out of the restroom and walked toward the Lincoln. He kept looking around. I looked at him through my powerful binoculars. As he stood by his car, he seemed very nervous. He was rubbing his right eye.

I was glad that the hay truck didn't move. I thought this was the best spot to watch the French chef. He scratched his nose and sneezed. I continued to observe. He then opened the driver's door and reached inside. He put up the hood on the Lincoln and tied a white handkerchief to the outside mirror. *This guy acts very nervous*, I thought. I watched his actions closely.

I happened to glance in my rearview mirror and saw a green tow truck coming into the rest area. It was moving slowly. I put my binoculars down and laid my head against the door, pretending to be asleep. The tow truck moved past me. He went directly to the

Lincoln.  A scruffy-looking man got out of the tow truck and approached LeBeau. They shook hands. I noticed the truck didn't pull in behind the Lincoln, but stayed in the lane next to it.  The driver opened up a compartment on the right side of the truck and took out two boxes. LeBeau moved toward his trunk and opened it.  The driver hurriedly placed the two taped boxes into the trunk.  I could see that the boxes had printing on them in large letters.  Both of them read AUTO PARTS. LeBeau shut the trunk, hurriedly.  He gave the truck driver a brown manila envelope.  The driver then got back into his truck and drove away.  I had made a note of the New York plate on the rear of the tow truck.  *Thank God for these powerful binoculars!* LeBeau looked around and closed his hood.

The Lincoln drove out of the rest area.  I followed at a distance behind him.  When he came to the first exit, he got off Route 87, crossed over to the northbound entrance ramp, and got back on Route 87. So did I, at a safe distance. LeBeau didn't hurry.  He kept the Lincoln between 60 and 65 m.p.h. I stayed about a half a mile behind him.

I took my cell phone out of my carrying case and called Roy Garrison at Troop S Headquarters. Roy got on the phone.  I spoke. "Uncle Roy, the blackbird didn't go to the cornfield by the north pasture.  He stopped to pick up some seed and is now heading back home along the footpath."

"Okay, Farmer Jones, I got it." I heard the click.  Roy and I had discussed the possible moves of LeBeau during our dinner at the Breakshire Lodge.  The Lieutenant now was aware of the direction the chef was taking. LeBeau was about one half mile ahead of me, driving at approximately 60 m.p.h.  What we didn't know was the chef's destination.  He could be heading for Montreal or Burlington, Vermont. No one could be positive the two boxes contained an illegal drug.  But from my observations and the body language of Jean LeBeau, I believed that his conduct was not conducive to legitimacy. He was up to something!  I was now about fifteen miles south of Plattsburgh when my cell phone rang. "Hello," I said.

"Farmer Jones, the fence is in position."....click.

I knew it was Roy's voice.  I knew that a roadblock was about to be established about five miles south of the Plattsburgh exit. Cars traveling south on Route 87 started blinking their lights. This indicated to me that the northbound lanes were blocked. Ahead of me, I saw the Lincoln's taillights go on. A large cattle truck was pulled across the two northbound lanes of Route 87. One would think that an accident had taken place. The Lincoln came to an abrupt stop. I saw two Troopers standing near the truck loaded with cattle.

I pulled off on the shoulder and continued to observe the blocked highway and the frustrated chef. He was out of the Lincoln waving his arms in the air. All of a sudden he ran in my direction diagonally across the northbound lanes. I got out of the car. The two Troopers were in foot pursuit of LeBeau. The well-built chef was running now like a football player. I couldn't believe what I was seeing. He was just about to jump over a fence when I tackled him. He started to strike at me with his fists. We wrestled on the ground and, luckily, I ended up on top. I cooled him down a little when I connected with his nose. The left cross punch worked for me. His nose seemed broken. The two Troopers ran up breathing hard. They rolled him over on his stomach and cuffed him. One Trooper said, "You must be Jason."

"Yeah, that's me." I was out of breath, too.

"Good job, Jason. Thanks for your assistance." I had never met these Troopers before.

As I was walking toward the cattle truck, with the two Troopers bringing up the rear with LeBeau, an unmarked police car pulled up. I could tell that it was Roy when he got out of the car. There was another plainclothesman with him. I didn't recognize who he was. Roy hollered, "You fellas okay? How about you, Jason?"

"Yeah, everybody's all right," I replied.

"Hey, officer," LeBeau hollered. "The big guy there broke my nose." LeBeau was groaning.

Roy replied, "You're lucky that he only broke your nose." The chef shut his mouth.

Roy walked over to me. "Good job, Jason. Wish we had you back in our unit."

"You had me once, but my efforts were never really appreciated by the upper management."

"Yeah, I know what you mean."

I respected Roy. He was a good man, and the north country BCI members were lucky to have a hard-working Lieutenant who backed up his unit. I couldn't leave Captain Temple out of the equation. He, too, was a dedicated member and had represented the Division in the highest tradition of police service.

The Troopers read the rights to LeBeau after I made the citizen's arrest. Defeated, LeBeau gave written permission to Lieutenant Garrison to search the Lincoln and the contents of the two boxes. The subsequent search revealed thirty kilos of high-grade cocaine, and a .380 caliber semi-automatic pistol, which was loaded, hidden under the front driver's seat. In addition, there surfaced a black address book containing a list of illicit drug dealers and people associated with a drug cartel in Mexico and Arizona, with connections in several major cities. The names were in French and Spanish.

I gave Roy a handwritten statement relative to breaking LeBeau's nose in self-defense. In the meantime, LeBeau made oral admissions to Lieutenant Garrison regarding his participation in the widespread drug operation. Roy thanked me again and I left the scene. This case was now in the hands of law enforcement and was just a drop in the bucket of illegal drug activity in our country.

The drive back to Lake Placid took about two hours. I returned the Pontiac to the parking lot across the street from the Hearth Hotel, and locked it. When I walked through the entrance, Mr. Lawrence was sitting in the lounge reading the *Wall Street Journal*. He looked up and seemed surprised. "You're back early, Mr. Black."

"Yes, could we talk in your office, sir?"

"Certainly." I followed him to the office. We went in and he closed the door.

"Have a seat, Jason," he said.

I related to Mr. Lawrence the series of events that took place from 8:30 a.m. on. I suggested that he probably should make arrangements to hire a new head chef. I told him that it was unfortunate that a professional of LeBeau's capabilities should be associated with that type of activity. He agreed. I thanked Mr. Lawrence for contacting me through Tom Huston.

He said, "Jason, if we have anything in the future that requires a private sleuth, we'll certainly call you." I was flattered by his remark. "I've written a check to you for an amount that should adequately cover your fee." This is on top of the $2,000.00 in expenses. If this doesn't meet with your approval, please tell me." He spoke candidly, handing me a white envelope. I thanked Mr. Lawrence for his generosity. "Jason, in the event you should ever need a job, I'll create a security position for you at the Hearth."

"Thank you kindly. I'll keep that in mind. I will be returning a portion of the expense money by check when I get back to my office. Thank you again, sir."

I returned to my room to pick up my belongings. I was glad that this case was closed. I felt bad about the young chef. He seemed frightened. I didn't know what the street value of the cocaine was, but I did know that the cartel bosses wouldn't be pleased with Chef LeBeau.

I proceeded to place my clothes and equipment in the rear of the Bronco. I left the parking lot and headed to the Breakshire Lodge to say hello to Tom Huston. I learned that Tom was still in New York, and had not returned from the convention. I thanked the desk clerk and left for Old Forge.

# CHAPTER THIRTY-TWO

On the way home I remembered that the New York State Woodsmen Field Days was taking place in Boonville. I wondered if Wilt Chambers had gone to the event. I knew that Charlie Perkins would be entering his new rig in their annual parade. When I reached Long Lake I stopped for a minute at Gertie's Diner. She was sitting at the counter working on her menu for the following week. We chatted for awhile, and then I told her that I had to rush off. She asked me how Patty was and told me that I should take Ruben with me on my trips. Just before I opened the door, she jumped up and put two bran muffins into a paper sack. I offered to pay for them.

She said, "No, they'll be stale in an hour."

I put a dollar bill on the counter.

"Jason, come on, give in." Gertie retorted.

"Nope, gotta pay, Gertie." I told her to say hello to her husband. "I'll see you later, Gertie."

I arrived in Eagle Bay just before the kennel closed. Ruben went wild when he saw me. I had missed him. I missed Patty, too, and all my contacts in the area. To me, there isn't another place on earth like Old Forge and the Adirondack Park, inside the Blue Line. Of course, that's my personal opinion.

I pulled into the driveway. I had not anticipated that the LeBeau matter would end so quickly. In a way, I was glad that the case was concluded. The Troopers had the case now as it became a criminal matter. I knew that Lieutenant Roy Garrison would pursue the case to the end. The war on drugs seemed like an endless battle. The profiteers didn't care about the users and addicts.

Ruben jumped out of the Bronco and headed for the woods. I unloaded my things and unlocked the side door. It felt good to be home. I liked sleeping in my own bed.

As usual, the red light on the answering machine was pulsating. I put my clothes in the closet.

Ruben was sitting just outside the screen door. His ears were at attention. I went outside and put him in his runway. I filled his water and food dishes, then gave him a big hug and rubbed his back. He liked that. I saw that some branches had been blown down by the wind, so I pulled them into the woods.

The majority of my incoming calls were concerning bad check cases. The last call was from Patty. I'd call her in the morning. I turned the burner on under the teakettle and heated some water for a cup of green tea. I noticed that I had to purchase some more cups. I had only six in the cupboard. I poured the water over the tea bag. It was nice to sit at the table and sip tea. Through the windows I could see the leaves fall from the oak trees. It was starting to get dark. I was very tired. I went out to the runway, brought Ruben inside, and decided to go to bed. Ruben went to his favorite spot and lay down.

Sleep came rapidly. My last thoughts were of Patty. I would call her tomorrow.

I awoke to the telephone ringing. I had a difficult time opening my eyes. I reached over and lifted the receiver. "Hello," I said sleepily.

"Jason, I just called the Hearth Hotel in Lake Placid and they said you checked out," Wilt said, excitedly.

"The case moved rapidly, that's why I checked out and came home."

"Would you like me to pick you up in the morning? Thought we could go to the Woodsmen Field Day. Charlie told me they've got some new skidders on display?"

"Yeah, that sounds great."

"I'll pick you up at 9:00 a.m. and we can have some breakfast in Boonville, okay?"

"Sounds, great!" I said goodbye and hung up the phone. I fell into a deep sleep.

The alarm clock went off at 8:00 a.m. I threw the covers back. Ruben was standing by the door to go out. I let him out. I went into the bathroom and took a shower. The large towel warmed me up. It was chilly. Autumn had arrived.

Wilt pulled into the yard at 9:00 a.m. sharp. Ruben let out a bark. Wilt got out of the truck and went over to see Ruben. I checked the windows and doors and locked up.

"Hi, Jason."

"Wilt, how have you been? Thanks for picking me up."

I was looking forward to the Woodsmen Field Days. We both petted Ruben. Wilt was wearing a red shirt with a large chainsaw displayed on the back.

"Sharp looking shirt," I said.

"I've got one for you, right here," Wilt blurted out.

Wilt handed me the shirt and I changed by the truck. The material was medium weight and comfortable.

"Are you hungry, Jason?"

"Yeah, I'm hungry, Wilt." I could tell that Wilt was famished.

We got into the truck. Wilt tooted the horn at Ruben. We drove through Old Forge to the Moose River Road and turned right along the river toward Boonville. The color of the foliage was an artist's dream. It was going to be a beautiful day. Wilt had the truck radio tuned into 101.3 FM and we listened to the music. The Moose River road is narrow and curvy. Anyone driving the highway has to be careful. Sometimes rounding curves finds you face to face with other vehicles.

"Jason, have you heard from Patty?"

"She left a message on my answering machine. We'll call her today, Wilt. I miss her very much."

"Everybody that comes into John's Diner misses her, too. I know I do," Wilt said, seriously.

"You're right, everybody does. She's an excellent waitress and makes everyone feel at home."

The radio was playing fiddle music when we pulled into Boonville. Traffic was heavy. People were walking all over town. Log trucks, pickups, and other vehicles were parked in every available space. Wilt pulled into the yard of a friend of his and parked the truck. We were now in walking distance of the fairgrounds.

There was a long line of people from all over the United States waiting to enter the grounds. Unbeknownst to me, Wilt had purchased the tickets earlier. He smiled when he handed me my ticket. We walked past the booth to the ticket takers. You could hear chainsaws being run at different locations. Some woodsmen were climbing big poles, while others were chopping big blocks of wood with double-bladed axes. We stopped at one site to watch two men carving out wooden animals with different-size chainsaws. Sawdust was falling to the ground. The fairgrounds were a hub of activity. One exhibition was that of the building of a log cabin. Wilt told me that he had attended the large parade on the first day of the affair. The parade lasted for two hours and displayed log trucks, skidders, and various floats pertaining to the wood industry. We continued to walk to the many booths. The displays of clothing, logger shoes, belts, buckles, axes, saws and tools were eye-catching. Wilt picked up some literature on two different portable sawmills.

We spotted Penney Younger where he was looking at a generator. He waved at us. Pen could be found hosting a western jamboree show on 101.3 FM. from 1:05 p.m. till 3:00 p.m., Monday to Friday. He was a popular fellow and knew everybody for miles around. Everybody liked Penney. Wilt and I waved back.

I thought about my father, how in the late 1920's and early 1930's he had entered the pulpwood business. The family photo albums reflected the old trucks and buzz saws, along with antiquated axes and other equipment he used. He would be surprised to see all the modern equipment on the market today.

Wilt and I stopped at the axe-throwing contest. The participants were accurate in their throwing. Every time an axe hit the target, Wilt would flinch. He knew some of the contestants. They hollered over to him. Wilt waved, and we continued on. I was surprised to see a group of loggers gathered around a bench. All of them were standing up except two. It appeared to me that they were preparing to arm wrestle. Wilt and I watched. The two men were flexing their wrists. They got into place with their elbows set in position. The two men were muscular. Their wrists were thick and large. They were gripping. One of the men became flushed in the face. They were groaning and grunting in an attempt to do each other in. They both gritted their teeth. Both were powerful. All of a sudden, one of the men's arms gave way to the power of the victor. The match was over. All the people who had gathered to watch burst out laughing and slapped each other on the back. It had been all in fun.

"Wilt, do you realize we haven't had our breakfast?" This was not like Wilt to skip a meal. I had a hunch that he may have had something to eat before he picked me up.

"Oh my God, I forgot all about it."

"So did I," I replied. "We got so involved with the displays."

Wilt glanced at his watch. It was 11:20 a.m. We decided to wait till noon and then we'd locate a tent where they sold sausage sandwiches with the works. We continued to visit the numerous booths and sites. Someone said that the crowd had reached about 26,000 in attendance.

Wilt told me that Charlie Perkins had been in the opening-day parade with his new log truck, but had had to leave the field day celebration to pick up a special load of hardwood logs near Burlington, Vermont. I had been looking forward to seeing Charlie. I was disappointed.

It was five minutes after noon when we went into Ted's tent. You could smell the aroma of onions and green peppers on the hot grill. The sausages were sizzling. We ordered three of them. Two for Wilt and one for me.

After lunch I tried to call Patty in Kentucky. There was no answer. I decided to wait until I got home. We continued touring the grounds and visiting the different displays. Wilt and I laughed, and he sang a song about loggers. He had a strong baritone voice. It sounded good. People gathered around to hear him. After he finished, the people applauded. "Wilt, I didn't know you could sing like that," I told him. He blushed.

Wilt and I have attended several Woodsmen Field Days, but the crowd that day seemed the largest ever. We saw many people we knew. Everybody was having a fun time.

Wilt stopped to talk to a fellow logger, and I continued on. I went to a booth that represented the early operations of the logging industry. As the son of an early logger and pulper, I have a keen interest in the subject. Compared with modern logging, the earlier operations were crude. A lumberjack's life was difficult. Some of the early logging camps were big, square log buildings, where the men slept on bunks.

I learned that in the mid-1800s, the logging industry was in full operation. The forests of the country were full of hard-working lumberjacks. They were a strong, tough group of woodsmen who were proud of their job efforts, and each claimed to be the best at what he did.

Wilt caught up with me at the booth. We both looked over the collection of old photographs reflecting early log drives that took place years before modern equipment was developed. The collection was extensive and interesting. There were pictures of yesterday's loggers in the process of chopping, sawing, ax-throwing, log-rolling and tree-climbing. Wilt and I continued on past several displays. I noted that a great deal of effort and hard work had been put into this year's field days.

We left the fairgrounds at about 5:15 p.m. Wilt stopped to gas the truck, then headed toward the Moose River Road. We were rounding a left-hand curve on the narrow two-lane macadam highway, when a large black car came toward us on our side of the road. Wilt pulled the pickup sharply to the right. It was a near miss. The car didn't slow down. We continued on to Route 28. I noticed that Wilt's forehead was sweating.

"Whew, that was close," he remarked.

"You're not kidding there," I agreed.

We were passing John's Diner when Dale Rush pulled out of the driveway. Wilt tooted the horn. Dale waved at us. Wilt wanted to stop at the diner for dessert.

"Drop me off at my place first." I couldn't eat another morsel of food, after spending a day at the field days.

"Well, maybe next time," Wilt said, disappointedly.

I worried about Wilt's weight. He seemed to be getting heavier.

Wilt dropped me off at the entrance to my driveway. He turned the big pickup around and headed back to John's Diner. We had had a good time at the Field Days. Ruben heard me. He barked loudly. When I came into sight, he jumped up on the runway gate. "Good boy, Ruben."

I filled his water dish. He had plenty of food. I let him out of his runway. He raced around the yard. He didn't go into the woods like he usually does. I was glad to get home. Ruben came to me and I petted his big head. I opened the gate and he went into the runway.

When I entered the house it seemed musty. I opened the windows. I had forgotten to turn on the dehumidifier.

I checked the answering machine, no new messages. I thought about Patty and wondered what she was doing in Kentucky. I missed her so much. I heated some water for tea. I decided not to eat anything. I was stuffed. I had overeaten at the field days. I always tried to watch my weight.

I called Dale Rush. I hadn't talked with him in a long time. He answered on the third ring.

"Hello, Dale," I said.

"Jason, where in the hell have you been? You're a hard man to catch up with."

"I've been busy."

I told him about our day in Boonville. He told me that he had attended the first day of the event and had purchased a new generator.

"I'm taking some hunters up to Catlin Lake in the morning. Would you like to ride along?"

"I'd love to. I don't have anything special to do tomorrow."

We talked for a few minutes and then hung up. Dale would pick me up at 7:30 a.m. I had no sooner placed the receiver on the phone, than it rang. I picked up the receiver.

"Hi, Sherlock. I love you," she said softly.

"Honey, is that you?" I was overjoyed. "How's everything in Kentucky? Are you okay? How's your brother?"

"Yes, I'm all right, and my brother is, too. I've missed you so much, Jason." She sounded sincere. "Caleb wants me to stay in Kentucky with him and his family. I'm so lonesome for you. I'm torn. I want to be with you, honey."

"I've missed you, too," I told her.

"I miss my job at John's and all my friends. I consider Old Forge my home and that's where I want to be. And most important, to be with you, if you'll have me. I'm serious, Jason."

"Are you certain that's what you want? Could you put up with this hard-nosed guy?" My knees felt weak and the palms of my hands became moist.

"I know you're independent, but I also know under that crust, you are the most considerate person I know. I'm coming home, Jason. I've already checked on the flights. Will you pick me up at the Oneida County Airport on Thursday around noon-time?" Her voice was soft and gentle.

"Thursday, around noon. I'll be there, sweetheart." I felt the sting of "Cupid's arrow."

"I love you, Jason." Her voice was gentle.

"I love you, too, baby," my heart was pounding in my chest.

When I hung up the phone, the pit of my stomach churned and churned. I turned on the yard lights. The security light was already lit. I went out to the runway and let Ruben out. He ran to the woods. In a few minutes he returned and we went inside. I checked the windows and doors. The house was cool. I had left the windows open too long.

I thought about Jack Flynn. I hadn't heard from him in a long time. I'd have to call him in a couple of days.

The toothpaste tube was almost empty. I undressed and put on my heavier pajamas. I took a book off the shelf and climbed into bed. "Good night, Ruben." He was already asleep.

# CHAPTER THIRTY-THREE

Morning came rapidly. The shower felt good. The bar of my favorite soap was getting thin. My whiskers came off, but not without a slight cut under my chin. I had let Ruben out before I showered and he was already sitting by the side door. He's a good dog. I dressed, made the bed, and started breakfast.

The coffee water was boiling on the stove. I scrambled two medium eggs and some Canadian bacon. The toast popped out of the toaster, golden brown. After I finished eating, I hurriedly washed the dishes and swept the floor. I had very little dust to contend with in the log home. I wondered if Patty would like my home on a full-time basis. Cupid's arrow was accurate.

Ruben started barking. Dale had pulled into the driveway. I checked to make certain that the burner was shut off. I grabbed a jacket and went outside. I locked the door. I made a quick check of Ruben's food and water dishes. They were full. I patted Ruben on the head and shut the gate.

"Good morning, Dale," I said sleepily.

"Morning," he replied with a big smile.

We talked all the way to the marina. When we arrived, two hunters were standing by the Stinson. The lake was like a mirror. Dale parked down by the water's edge.

The taller of the two hunters walked over to us. He greeted us with a hearty handshake.

"Beautiful day to fly," he remarked.

After the introductions, the hunters' gear was stowed away. I noticed that they had a pup tent for the two of them. I helped them with their rifles. The guns were in cases. I could see Dale giving a last-minute check of the Stinson. I looked around for the grumpy owner of the marina. He was not in sight.

"I guess we are all ready to take off," Dale said with a grin. We assisted the hunters into the plane. Then we climbed aboard. The engine started. I watched Dale put on his sunglasses. I was glad that I had mine with me this morning. The sun was bright and reflected off the water. Dale slowly taxied into deeper water. I hadn't been in the Stinson since the search for Patty and the two killers. The lake was clear of fishing boats and the pesky wave runners. Dale continued to taxi in a southerly direction on Fourth Lake, then turned and headed north. He looked at his gauges. He revved the engine.

"Everybody got their seatbelts on?" he asked.

I looked out at the water. The Stinson was gaining momentum and soon lifted off. I could see the Inlet church steeple just below us. Dale circled Inlet twice. The hunters had asked Dale earlier to fly over Inlet a couple times. One of the hunters took a photo and thanked Dale. Catlin Lake is located between Long Lake and Newcomb. It is close to Rich Lake. I learned from their conversation that both of the hunters were bus drivers and had hunted that region for several years.

Dale climbed to three thousand feet. The Stinson performed well. The hunters and their gear had considerable weight. It didn't seem to affect the plane. When we passed over Blue Mountain the hunters remarked, "What a beautiful sight!"

Dale and I looked at each other and smiled. We were pleased that the hunters were attuned to the Adirondack Park and the natural beauty that Mother Nature has bestowed on us. I could hear the hunters chatting. One of them mentioned to the other an idea about building a camp in the region. We crossed over Long Lake. Many of the leaves had fallen from the trees. Dale circled Catlin Lake. He brought the plane in from the south end of the lake. The landing was smooth. He taxied to a small dock on the north shore and, at about thirty feet from shore, cut the engine. Both of us were standing on the floats and I was able to climb onto the dock to secure the Stinson. One of the hunters wanted to take a photo of us standing by the plane. He took two.

I assisted Dale with removing the hunters' gear. We helped them carry the items to an area about two hundred feet from the dock. Dale assured the hunters that he would return for them in a week. We bid them farewell and walked back to the plane.

We were just about ready to board, when a large fish jumped out of the water. A splash ensued and the fish disappeared.

"Should have brought your fish-pole, Jason,"

"Guess I should have," I replied.

We climbed aboard and soon we were winging our way south toward Fourth Lake.

Dale asked me how Patty was doing in Kentucky. I assured him that she was doing fine and enjoying her vacation with her brother Caleb.

"Jason, I've wanted to tell you this for a long time. I asked Patty for a date several months ago. She turned me down," he said sheepishly.

"Why are you telling me about this?" I asked, curiously.

"Well, I pushed her pretty hard on the subject, but she wouldn't budge," he added. "I just wanted you to know. When I heard the rumor that you and Patty were dating, I backed off."

"I appreciate your honesty. I observed you talking to Patty once in the diner and you looked a little upset."

"Yeah, I was. That was when she refused to go out with me."

"Oh! I see."

We didn't continue the conversation. I knew what Dale was trying to tell me. I didn't hold anything against him. I felt relieved. Dale was a good man. He wanted me to know that he was no longer pursuing Patty. We talked about other things all the way back to Fourth Lake.

Dale circled the marina twice before he set down on the blue water of the lake. I noticed that there were two boats in his landing pattern. The boats left the area and Dale made a perfect landing. He taxied toward the dock and cut the engine about thirty feet from it. We were both out of the cabin standing on the floats as the plane closed in on the dock. Dale fastened the line. I noticed that the marina workers were busy storing their customers' boats for the forthcoming winter.

The plane was secured. Dale gave it a final cursory inspection.

"Jason, I've got to pick those hunters up in a week. If you're not tied up, maybe you'd like to take another ride," he said.

"Sure, I'd love to."

Dale dropped me off at the entrance to my home. I walked slowly, looking at the breathtaking colors that Mother Nature had presented for another autumn. The air was cool and I took some deep breaths. Ruben spotted me, but didn't bark until I was within a hundred feet of the runway. His ears were straight up and his tail was in motion. "Good boy, Ruben." He barked twice and then settled down. I opened the gate and he ran off to the woods. I proceeded to clean his runway and fill his food and water dishes. I had just finished the cleaning, when I spotted him running toward me at a fast clip.

We wrestled on the ground for a few minutes. Ruben placed his big mouth on my right ankle and clamped down firmly. "Hey, Ruben, loosen up! You're retired." He applied a lot of pressure, but it didn't break the skin. The next thing I realized, Ruben was licking my face with his tongue. "Settle down." I was firm with Ruben. I brought him into the house with me. It was getting near suppertime.

I had just started peeling three potatoes when the telephone rang. I picked up the receiver.

"Hello, Jason."

"Jack Flynn, how have you been and where have you been? I haven't heard from you in ages." I was happy to hear from him.

"I've been busier than ten hens on a tin roof. I've got more irons in the fire than you could shake a stick at. I could use you here in Arizona. You won't change your mind about coming out, will you?"

"Jack, as we have discussed before, the Arizona heat and I do not get along together. I'm sorry, but my niche is here in the Adirondacks. It isn't very busy for my work, but I'm making a living and I'm happy here. I wouldn't be able to take the heat and the added pressure of a heavy caseload."

"I know, but you can't hate a guy for trying."

"How's Ruby?"

"She's great. I let her go home early today."

"Give her my regards, Jack."

Jack and I talked for an hour on the phone. He told me about a missing persons case that he had been working on. He informed me that he could hire ten operatives and still would have to hire more because of the work coming into his office. I wished him well and told him to contact me if any of his cases brought him into New York State.

The call from Jack threw my schedule off. I put the potatoes on to boil. I took the chopped beef out of the refrigerator and shaped it into large hamburger steak. I then boiled some carrots. The onion sliced well. I braised the pieces off with a little garlic and green pepper. I added some seasoning. The aroma permeated the log home.

The meat was sizzling when I removed it from the iron skillet. I placed it on the plate next to the boiled potatoes and carrots. The mixture of onions and peppers covered the steak. I sliced the bread and poured my cup of green tea. Ruben was sitting in the corner of the dining area staring at me. "Lay down, Ruben," I commanded. He lay down and placed his big head between his paws. "Good dog."

The horseradish gave the hamburger steak a little more zest. The carrots were tender. The potatoes from Idaho were excellent. I wished that Patty were here to enjoy this humble dinner and keep me company. I missed her. I knew that I was in love.

I finished supper and picked up the table. Ruben watched me while I washed the dishes and put things away. Again I was thankful that there was a strong bond between Ruben and me. I took good care of the retired K-9 and he watched over our little domain. After all the kitchen work was completed, Ruben and I went for a walk. The night air was cooling, as autumn swept in. The leaves were still lazily floating, in spiraling flight, landing on the floor of the forest. With the exception of a chirping chipmunk, the forest was quiet and an inner peace took over. Ruben's big head pushed against my right knee. Again, I wished that Patty were here to join us in this moment of peaceful tranquility.

We were just about ready to turn around and head back to the house, when Ruben became alert. His ears went up and his tail stiffened. We heard movement in the brush. Fortunately I had a leash on Ruben. The six-hundred-or-more pound black bear came out of the bushes. The hulking beast filled the path. His huge head turned toward us. Ruben barked loudly. The black bear was in no hurry to vacate the path. He stood his ground. We stood our ground. It was a staring match for about five minutes. The bear's big head shook from side to side, and he growled loudly, throwing his head up in the air. I could see the huge white teeth in his large mouth. My knees felt weak. Ruben continued to bark. The bear whirled around and slowly retreated away from us. We watched him. He turned his big head once more to appraise the situation. I watched him go out of sight. Ruben and I turned around and walked toward home. "That was close, Ruben." Ruben walked close to me, pushing his big head against my right knee.

The bear was not new to our area. He was the same one I first saw a few weeks before. I was careful not to leave any refuse around that would attract his sense of smell. I knew that the landfills were closed and, by this action, the bears were on the move. There had been several bear complaints in the region, where the animals would pull down bird feeders and break into refuse bins. I loved the bears, but they had their place, and it wasn't on my porch. I took my bird-feeder down after the landfills closed.

Ruben and I entered the house for the evening. He immediately went to his favorite spot. I went into my office and did some paperwork.

I wrote a check out to Mr. Lawrence of the Hearth Hotel in Lake Placid. The check was for $1900.00. We had agreed I would return any unused expense money on the LeBeau case. The check he'd issued to me for $400.00 was more than enough for the work I did on that matter. I would mail my refund in the morning.

I checked the records relative to bad check cases and opened up several envelopes that contained my fees for collecting the checks. Those that needed further action in a court proceeding would be sent to the local police department.

The mail to be sent was kept in a special large envelope. I was not the best bookkeeper, but I tried to maintain good records.

Ten o'clock p.m. came rapidly. My eyelids were heavy. I let Ruben out for his quick run to the woods and prepared for bed. I was tired. I let Ruben back into the house. I secured the door and went to the bathroom, brushed my teeth, and donned my warm pajamas. The night air was becoming cooler. I said good-night to Ruben. I intended to start reading a new book, but fell off to sleep when my head hit the pillow.

# CHAPTER THIRTY-FOUR

I woke up at 6:30 a.m. Ruben was sitting by the door waiting to make his daily morning run to the woods. I pushed the covers back and went to the door. He looked up at me. I opened the door and Ruben took off for the forest. He moved fast. Two does were grazing in the backyard. Ruben didn't even pay attention to them. He came back in a few minutes. I slipped on my bathrobe and went out to let him into his runway. I put some food in his dish. His water dish was full.

I turned the burner on under the teakettle and went to the cupboard. I decided to make a cup of decaf. This morning it was time to have French toast with Canadian bacon. I planned on giving the house a good cleaning. It was Wednesday. Tomorrow I had to be at the Oneida County Airport to pick up Patty.

The French toast was delicious. I cooked the bacon until it was crisp. After breakfast, I did the dishes. I then swept and mopped the kitchen floor, ran the cleaner, and dusted throughout the house. The next job I tackled was washing the windows. I used a warm water and vinegar mixture. The windows sparkled.

I had completed the housecleaning by noon. I took all the soiled laundry to the Laundromat. I was lucky. No one was using the machines. The place was empty. I filled four machines. I decided not to have lunch until I got home. There were some hunting magazines on the shelf. I thumbed through them. The wash cycle was about ten minutes and another five for the rinse cycle. When the

259

machines clicked off I transferred the wet laundry to the dryers. This was about a forty-minute cycle. The two dryers clicked off. I removed the dried items and folded them, placing them in the clothesbasket in an orderly fashion.

I drove home. It was quiet in town. The majority of the tourists had left the region. Ruben was pacing back and forth in his runway. The large black bear was standing near the gate. When I pulled in, the bear lumbered off into the woods. I took Ruben inside with me.

I put the laundry away. I decided to iron some shirts and slacks. It was getting near the time to wear warmer clothing, especially in the evening. Ruben was nervous. I assumed the bear shook him up. "Lay down, Ruben. Everything is okay." I petted his back and neck. He finally lay down in his favorite spot.

I completed the ironing before the news came on. On one of the shirts, I sprayed too much starch. The rest of them turned out okay. I hung them in the closet. I couldn't help but wonder if Patty liked to iron.

Bedtime came rapidly. I let Ruben out for a quick run to the woods. I hoped the big bear had moved to another area. Ruben returned and I let him in. I put the ironing board into the closet off the kitchen and after the usual ceremony went to bed. I rolled and tossed all night. I must have fallen off to sleep around 4:00 a.m.

# CHAPTER THIRTY-FIVE

I woke up at 7:30 a.m. The dog was sitting near the foot of the bed pawing at the covers. I pushed them back and got out of bed. Ruben went over and stood by the door. "Just a minute, I'll be right with you." I let him outside. I was still sleepy.

While Ruben was in the woods, I shaved and showered. I thought about Patty. This was the big day. I had to be at the Oneida County Airport by noon. I dressed in casual clothes.

I made some coffee and scrambled an egg. The bread was depleted, so I replaced it with an English muffin. I opened up a new jar of grape jelly. The crunchy muffin was good, especially with the jelly. I finished eating and did the dishes.

As I was putting Ruben into his runway, I heard an airplane. It seemed to be coming closer. The roar was loud as the red Stinson appeared over the treetops. Dale circled the house twice. He appeared to be about two hundred feet from the top of my house. He then turned north and was gone. Ruben was alert in his runway. "Settle down, Ruben. It was Dale, it's all right, big boy." I knew that the dog's ears were sensitive and the drone of the plane's engine annoyed him.

I went inside to my office and prepared some mail for the post office. My case-load was heavy with check collections. My contacts throughout the park had given me plenty of advertising by word of mouth. Another function I performed was the serving of civil process. These jobs came from various attorneys, from whom I would receive a serving fee.

I noticed that my stamp supply was getting low. I added that to the list of things to do. It was difficult to concentrate on work and think about Patty at the same time. I placed some papers and the mail in my briefcase and left the house after locking the door. I went over to Ruben in the runway and petted him. "Be a good dog." Ruben barked.

I gave my old canoe a cursory examination. It was behind the house on two sawhorses. I hadn't used it in a while. It looked in good shape.

The door on the Bronco was unlocked. I got in and started the engine. I tooted at Ruben as I turned around and headed toward Route 28. Traffic was light. I stopped at the post office, mailed my letters, and picked up some postage stamps. The staff in the post office was busy as usual. They all smiled. One of them said, "Hi, Jason, where have you been?" I waved and left the office. On the way out, I opened my box and took out the mail. I thumbed through the letters. It appeared that I had thirty more check collections to work on. I was pleased about that.

I stopped at the jewelry store and made a purchase. Cupid's arrow had really done a job on me.

I arrived at the airport at about 11:00 a.m. I parked, got out of the Bronco, and walked into the airport building. I checked the flight schedule. Patty's plane was on time, according to the monitor. I located a telephone and called Harriet. I told her that Patty was arriving around noon and that I was taking her to my house. I didn't go into any detail, but I knew Harriet was very perceptive. She told me that she understood and thanked me for calling.

My hands were perspiring. I felt nervous. I paced back and forth near the waiting area. I recognized a couple who were waiting for a flight. I continued to pace and my hands continued to perspire. It was warm in the airport. I had promised myself that I would never marry again. I was twelve years older than Patty. I endeavored to keep my mind clear and think straight. I looked out at the tarmac. All I could see was the large wing approaching the terminal. I quit pacing and positioned myself by the arrival door. I glanced at my watch. My stomach was doing butterflies. My knees felt weak.

It seemed like an eternity before the attendant opened the arrival door. I watched a heavyset man with a carry-on case waddle through the door. He had a big black mustache. Then came a frail elderly lady walking slowly, gripping her pocketbook. It appeared to be made out of alligator skin. The next person who came through the door was a sharp U.S. Marine Sergeant. He removed his hat as a beautiful auburn-haired woman came out of the crowd and embraced him. The marine had a short crew-cut. He smiled at the woman and kissed her.

Finally Patty emerged into view. I rushed to embrace her tiny body. The petite blond in my arms started to cry. Patty squeezed me tightly. She was crying and smiling at the same time. I wiped the teardrops from her cheeks. We were oblivious to the others around us.

"Patty, I've missed you more than you'll ever know. I love you, sweetheart." My heart thumped loudly.

"Dearest, I never want to be away from you again. Never, never," she said, holding me tightly.

Our kisses were warm and lasted much longer than they should have. Patty and I walked to the baggage area and retrieved her two bags. She was wearing gray slacks and a purple blouse. Her blond hair was beautiful. She wore little makeup. The jacket that matched her apparel was over her arm. A porter offered to carry the bags. I told him politely that I had them. He smiled.

I told Patty that I had called Harriet to tell her Patty would be spending the day with me. I asked Patty if she would like to stop for a sandwich. She agreed.

We drove over to Hale's Restaurant in Utica. The parking lot was full. Noon-time brought many white-collared workers into the restaurant. We parked and walked inside. A smiling hostess led us to a booth. I let Patty seat herself and then I sat down. We looked the menus over. The choice was easy. Both of us ordered the grilled chicken sandwich with curly fries and two glasses of iced tea.

"Well, sweetheart, tell me, how's your brother and his family?" I wanted to know.

"They were wonderful. I hadn't seen them in so many years. They wanted me to stay with them. I told them that I couldn't. I want to be in the Adirondacks and I want to be near you, Jason," she said, looking directly into my eyes.

"I want the same thing, Patty. I love you and I need you."

The waitress served the chicken sandwiches and curly fries. The glasses of tea were ice cold and a slice of lemon complemented each glass. The food was delicious. The mushrooms and dressing over the tender chicken was a treat. We both enjoyed the lunch. Patty and I continued to talk, then decided we should let someone else have the booth. Customers were lined up, waiting.

The drive to Old Forge was enjoyable. Patty sat close to me. Her hand rested on my knee. We didn't talk very much on the way to my house. She was smiling each time I glanced over at her.

"Honey, would you like to go for a canoe ride when we get home?"

"I'd love to, Jason. I've never been in a canoe," she answered.

When we pulled into the driveway, Patty squeezed my hand. Ruben was darting back and forth in his runway. I pulled close to the house. We got out. Patty went over to Ruben and embraced him. Ruben's ears were straight up. I unloaded the Bronco. I went over and petted the big dog and checked his water and food dishes. I had to fill both.

I unlocked the house and took Patty inside. I went back out and put the canoe on top of the Bronco and secured it. I put the two paddles into the rear of the vehicle. Patty freshened up. I told her again how wonderful it was to have her home. She told me that she was happy to be back and anxious to return to work.

"Are you ready for the canoe ride, sweetheart? There are no special rules. This canoe is a wide bottom canoe. When we get to the lake, I'll help you into it and give you some suggestions."

"All set," she said, excitedly.

We drove to Inlet and down the South Shore Road to the area where we could put the canoe into Fourth Lake. Patty assisted me in taking it off the top of the Bronco. She took the two paddles out of the Bronco. In a few minutes, we were both in the canoe. I was paddling from the rear and Patty was paddling from the front. She adapted well. My only suggestion was not to make any drastic or sudden moves. She agreed. The leaves were still falling from the trees. The banks along the lake were covered with beautiful colored leaves. The air was clean and fresh. We appeared to be the only people on the lake. The tourist season was winding down.

We had been on the lake for an hour taking in the beauty of Mother Nature's offerings. I pulled into a shallow cove. I helped Patty around so she could face me. The canoe rocked slightly, but soon settled. We could hear the lapping of the water against the flat rocks on shore. This was the moment I had waited for.

"Patty, I'm going to make this short. I have something to say." I was nervous.

"What did you want to say, dearest?" She was eager for my response.

"Patty, I'm a little older than you and have seen and experienced life with ups and downs." I stopped, wordless. "Oh, shucks!! Will you marry me?" My hands were moist.

The silence was torture. She turned her head and looked out over the lake. It seemed like ages before she turned to look into my eyes.

"Yes, Sherlock, I will marry you."

I reached into my jacket pocket and brought out the small box. I opened it. Patty's eyes danced as I removed the ring. The diamond was small. I took her left hand and placed it on her finger. She looked at it and then looked into my eyes. We leaned toward each other and embraced.

"I love you, Jason," she said.

"I love you, too." I held her close. The canoe moved slightly.

I was about to begin the third marital journey of my life. I had lived alone for a long time and, in doing so, had become independent in thought and in my life's pursuits. My hopes were, that in joining with Patty in marriage, it would only bring us future happiness and tranquility as husband and wife with our faithful companion Ruben, our beloved German shepherd. Only time would record the future events of our life as a private investigator and a popular waitress, in a place called the Adirondack Park, inside the Blue Line.

End

*(continued from back cover)*

He served three years and three months with the 27th Infantry Division until 1950 when he entered the U.S. Air Force during the Korean War, serving in Keflavik, Iceland. In 1953 he became a member of the New York State Police where he served in Troop "D" and Troop "B" until 1982 first in uniform and then as a member of the Bureau of Criminal Investigation. After retiring he served in the banking sector for seven years. A life long learner, he received his B.S. Degree from the State University of New York. He resides in the Adirondack Park of New York State. He is a published poet and writer of short stories.